Constellation
Blood Empire Trilogy
Book One

ROBERT SCANLON

For all the wonderful Readers in the world.

You make it a better place.

Copyright © 2016 Robert Scanlon

Illustration © 2016 Tom Edwards

TomEdwardsDesign.com

All rights reserved.

ISBN: 0-9944092-1-4
ISBN-13: 978-0-9944092-1-8

CHAPTER ONE

I LAND MY STOLEN LIGHTCRUISER—which I've frivolously named 'Slingshot'—with precision in the designated zone.

Rykkamon's high gravity tugs at the sleek craft's suspension until the gyros compensate and the artificial gravity stabilizes.

The ship's drive spins down, and I spin my captain's chair to face Jordi, who is staring at the holo.

"They don't seem too impressed," he says, indicating the circle of heavily armed Rykkan thugs surrounding the ship.

"Maybe a delivery of forty-three tonnes of 3He will change their attitude."

"That's my girl." Jordi grins. "Always under-promising and over-delivering."

"I'm not 'your girl' any more, and if Papa was still alive, he'd slap that grin off your face." I point to the Rykkans surrounding our ship. "These guys are no joke. This time, watch your step and learn how to negotiate." I hold my glare at Jordi until he drops his smile and looks away.

I sweep my unruly red hair into a pony tail, and ready myself for my gravSuit. I hear Jordi grumbling. "Papa, Papa, Papa. Always Papa this and Papa that—"

I slap his head.

"Ouch!" He looks at me, hurt. "C'mon, Indy. It's true. No one ever measures up to precious Papa—"

I pull his head into an armlock. "If I didn't need you for this trip, I'd have left you back in that bar to fight your own way out.

Maybe I should have claimed the bounty on your head. Or let Santo keep you."

I release Jordi and stare at him for a moment. "But one more jibe at my father and I will make sure the Rykkans get a special bonus lackey with their helium three."

"Speaking of which"—he jerks his head at the holo—"looks like your man is here."

I look at the holoscreen. Walking up to my ship's ramp is a bulky Rykkan, complete with metran-reinforced armor and six similarly equipped bodyguards.

"He's either trying to intimidate us or he's scared of us," Jordi says.

"Of me," I say softly. "And so he should be. Let's get the gravSuits on. It's payday."

We make our way down the ramp and into the dusty clearing. We are clumsy now in our suits, battling Rykkamon's heavy gravity—almost double that of the standard "earth" gravity used across the Sector.

The Rykkan Chief swivels his thick, low-set head from side to side in the somewhat unsettling Rykkan trait. I'm not sure, but he looks annoyed.

I try to look as authoritative as I can for my twenty-six years, but the gravSuit's accelerators have a habit of overcompensating movement. Smooth and refined goes out the window. I go for bold and decisive, a much better fit to the gravSuit's inclination. I need to play this deal carefully, and even though this visit is my fifth to the planet—second if you only count the official ones—I'm only too aware I'm in a Rykkamon no-go zone, surrounded by shady characters, with my only backup a mouthy ex-boyfriend.

And I have to make sure the notorious Rykkan skill of reading human emotions doesn't give away the fact that I only just picked up this load of 3He from the other side of the planet.

The Chief is speaking in his clipped rendition of Galactic and I mentally shake away my distracting thoughts. Although I have what he wants, it doesn't pay to be flippant with Rykkans. Especially cut-throat Rykkan outlaws desperate to get their hands on a lucrative cargo.

"Madam Captain India Jackson," he says, dilating his eyes at me. "You are late."

I shrug. "What I bring is worth waiting for." I hold his gaze, though his pulsing eyes are disquieting.

He raises his laserRifle using both clawed and non-clawed hands, and I can't prevent the flinch. He laughs. "You have extreme tension. But real problem is not this, or desire to make me wait." He holds eye contact and swings the laserRifle around with one hand to point sideways at the horizon. I look to where he points the rifle. A dark mass grips the rocky and bare horizon. "Soon south-turning tornado storms lock down entire planet." He bares his square red teeth in a broad Rykkan grin. "Perhaps you like to establish new terms, as you must make hasty exit."

I step forward. "And if you would prefer not to make a hasty exit from life, I suggest you escort me to your camp"—I incline my head towards the shacks nearby—"and offer your guests suitable refreshments."

The Rykkan shuts his mouth and grunts. He swivels around on his stump-like legs, lifts his other arm, and beckons us to follow.

Jordi looks at me, eyes raised. "Nice job of building rapport," he says out the side of his mouth. I ignore him and do my best to march behind the Chief, against Rykkamon's nearly two-gee pull. I use my chin-tab to activate the suit's power boost, immediately feeling the energy increase to help me keep pace.

CHAPTER TWO

WE SIT IN THE LOW-BUILT shack on sturdy wooden stools, surrounded by the Rykkan's guards. The Chief uses his non-clawed hand to push my datapad back across the rough-hewn table. "Only forty-three tonnes. I order fifty." He opens his mouth to drive home a point when I stand up and grab the pad from the table.

"Come on, Jordi. Chief here wants to play games. I'm sure you remember as well as I do that our deal was for a minimum forty tonnes. I don't have time to waste. Or did everyone forget about the tornado?" I turn to walk out, but I only manage one step toward the shack's heavy door before I feel Jordi's hand grab me and pull me back.

He looks up at me with a serious face. "Pull your head in. No point in starting a fight. We have what he wants. Play his game and we're out of here, before this planet's freak weather kills us."

I turn back around and breathe a small sigh of relief when I see the Chief's red-toothed grin. Walking away from a Rykkan negotiation can create unpredictable outcomes.

He addresses me. "Your mate is wise—"

"He's not my mate. Nor is he wise. But go on." I hold his gaze.

The Chief continues. "Wisdom has no favorites. But maybe you insult my status. Maybe I claim agreement is void and I take what I need from your ship without payment." He stands, and so do four of his powerfully-muscled, gravity-evolved thugs, all of whom aim laserRifles at my head.

I ignore them, take my time to sit back down, briefly smile, and meet the Chief's eyes with a cool expression. "Rykkans can sense human states, yes?"

The Chief swivels his head to-and-fro. "This you already know. I speak of your tension and your desire to make a Rykkan Chief wait."

I nod. "Good. Then you know I am telling the truth when I tell you I have four drones equipped with the Sector's latest military-grade lasercannons. Cannons that are trained on your munitions store, and your not insignificant stockpile of illegal 3He cubes. Complete the deal as agreed, and when I return to my ship and see the credits have been transferred, I will disarm them."

He sits back down.

I lean in to the table. "And you also know I am telling the truth when I say I will keep my word and deliver on my promise. I will deliver all forty-three tonnes. I keep to my agreements."

The Rykkan's eyes pulse rapidly. I must be careful how far I push him.

He stands and bows stiffly as the Rykkans do, then sits again. "Madam Captain. You exceed your reputation. You discover what I make hidden and you use against me. Is not possible for Rykkans under honor system. Please share secret."

I maintain my cool. "Rykkans rely too heavily on their sensing abilities. We humans have no such skill. Instead we must depend on our own spies. But, let us return to our contract. I have to escape a tornado storm, and you must take possession of your cargo"—I tap my hand on my datapad—"once I see the funds."

The Rykkan's fat lips pull back slightly, revealing their red army. "Before we complete contract, I offer you information of interest"—his eyes widen rapidly—"for discount. A substantial one, because of personal nature of information and interest to

Madam Captain."

"Pfft. What information could be of interest—"

"It concerns your father's death."

CHAPTER THREE

"WHAT DO YOU KNOW ABOUT my father?" I glare at the squat outlaw.

The Chief licks his lips. "My discount?"

"Not likely."

"The Jovians made a deal with him."

I feel my blood rise. "Still no discount. Your information is a lie."

He gives what passes for a smile among Rykkans. "If you were Rykkan, I could show I do not lie. Information come from Sloper's men."

I stiffen when I hear my father's killer's name, then remember the Rykkan ability to sense emotions, and I quickly let it go.

The Rykkan appears not to notice, stands and motions to Jordi and I to do the same. "But is now too late for talk. You cannot escape tornado storm, and I cannot unload all cargo. We agree on stalemate. I pay twenty percent now, and the balance once I have all cargo." He shows his teeth. "In return, I secure your ship against the storm. After I pull down cabin."

I look out the shack's crude window at the incoming fury and see I have no choice.

The Chief laughs. "You have fear now. That is correct. Rykkamon tornado storms are big legend in this sector of Galaxy."

He is both right and wrong. I do have fear.

Not because of the tornadoes.

It's because of who I will fail to pay with only twenty percent of my predicted haul in my account. But first, I must head into town. Before the storm breaks. I have another deal in place that might win me a get-out-of-jail-free card. For now.

A shiver runs down my spine, and I get up and leave the shack in silence with Jordi. Together we battle our way through the rising winds and back to the ship.

CHAPTER FOUR

I STEP INTO ONE OF the cruiser's unipods and lower myself down to the landing zone, next to my ship. Through the pod's glass bubble I see Jordi standing on the ramp, fully suited, directing the Chief's runners to unload the 3He cubes.

The sight triggers a thought of Papa's vision: a future where races don't consume energy with the greed we have today. That day seems far off, and I sigh heavily, probably more from missing Papa's guidance than some utopian impossibility.

I pull myself together and look across to the other side of the dry and dusty camp. Rykkamon's short rotation and high gravity turns parts of it from a dusty bowl to a wet swamp. Tonight looks like it will be the latter, judging by the incoming tornado storm. At least in my pod and gravSuit, I'll be safe.

But safety is relative. Although I've hacked my pod to broadcast an anonymous ID signal, my long red hair gives me away. And since the last official visit involved a highly dubious getaway from Rykkamon's lower-orbit spaceport workshops, I suspect it would be better if I do not draw too much attention to myself.

Add that to Jordi's dubious warning. He insisted on repeating it over and over. He'd heard on Ganymede that a tall red-headed female pirate was apparently smuggling Rykkan mercenaries to Takao. Eventually I had to shut him up, telling him no matter what he said, I was still going into the supply center. He told me I never know when to stop. That I should lie low for a while. Be inconspicuous.

Yeah, right. On a high-grav planet, where most of the inhabitants have no hair and are two-thirds my height.

I steel myself and fire up the pod's mini-drive. I have about an hour to get to the supply center, order a refit of the ship's stocks, and pick up a highly illegal item. Which unfortunately dictates putting in a personal appearance.

I spin the pod around in a cloud of dust, throw a glance over my shoulder at the incoming mass of dark cloud, and spear off onto the west-bound mainway.

The pod maintains a steady one-meter hover. There are few other craft—not that I'm expecting many, since most Rykkans would not be in the outlaw no-go zone. Then there's the small matter of a super-sized tornado storm.

I concentrate on the mainway in front of me and watch the infrastructure increase in density around me as I approach the supply metropolis.

Around fifteen minutes later, the unipod slows. I look at the dash holopanel. I'm in a slowzone, approaching a checkpoint. I peer forward and note the lineup of vehicles—pods, flatbeds, a few hovertankers—stretching ahead. I don't have time to waste, and I'm surprised that the checkpoint is still running at this time of day. Especially with an impending storm. A prickling sensation runs across my neck and shoulders. One I've learned to trust. Maybe this checkpoint is looking for me.

I U-turn the pod and speed down a built-up side street. I'm not the only one to do so, so I feel safe that other pilots would think to avoid a traffic jam just as I would on my home planet. I've just never been in one on Rykkamon.

I follow the pods and hovercycles weaving in and out in front of me until we come to a halt at an intersection. I'm about to swing left to follow the general line into town when I see a crowd of Rykkans across the mainway assembled in an open space. I move past slowly and notice a group of eighteen or twenty young, tattooed Rykkans. They are surrounding another Rykkan, whose head is swiveling rapidly.

Curiosity makes me swing my pod around and pull up next to the crowd. Two of the tattooed briefly look my way, then ignore me. I see now that the circle is closing on the hapless Rykkan in the center.

I switch on my external mikes, not that I know much Rykkan. I soon realize I don't need to know any: what is occurring happens in almost any language. A group of males are about to take advantage of one female.

I know this is wrong. I cannot take my eyes off the unfolding spectacle, and I wonder why this scenario is replicated across the galaxy. One of them—presumably the ringleader—advances to the lone female. One thick arm holds a chain, the other a laserwhip.

He raises the laserwhip and in a flash I am no longer a spectator. It's as if I'm her, and I'm staring at an angry male about to deprive me of my liberty, and possibly much worse.

I feel my blood pounding and I'm already out of the unipod. My gravSuit protests at the pace I'm setting to reach the group before the ugly assailant reaches his prey, no doubt with his mates lining up to take turns.

Several tattooed squat heads swivel at the approaching sound of my gravSuit. Although my blood is boiling and my muscles scream against the two-gee gravity, even with a 'suit, I've remembered to close my helmet visor. And darken it.

The young thugs will see a metran-clad giant of unknown origin closing on them.

Looks like they're up for a fight.

I see bared red teeth everywhere as they turn as one and

advance towards me. I draw the gang's attention by stopping and raising both of my arms. One of which terminates in a metran-gloved hand holding a neuroblaster, the other a somewhat-illegal—okay, highly illegal—laserSword. Perhaps not quite as deadly as Papa's EMP-slug-equipped version my brother, Mitch, had stolen from somewhere on this very planet a while back.

To a gang of street-armed Rykkan thugs, deadly versus very-deadly might not be worth much thought.

But it is worth a fight. Their ringleader clearly sees an opportunity to lay his hands on an illegal weapon as a far more attractive proposition than a female Rykkan. Maybe he assumes he can return to his prey later. Assume away.

Now it is me they are circling.

I have a sudden attack of clarity. What am I doing? This was meant to have been a low-profile trip to the supply—

My thoughts evaporate when the leader lunges at me and lands the laserwhip on my leg. I'd forgotten how fast the hi-grav reflexes of a Rykkan could be. My metran suit deflects any damage, though my leg still takes enough of a shock to make me wince.

I don't wait to see what else eventuates, instead I take advantage of my gravSuit's stabilizer and I squat and twirl on the spot. My MMA training tries to kick in, but this is hi-grav suit brawling and I have to force myself to override my instincts. Firepower is the name of the game here.

I extend my arms, fire the neuroblaster with one, and thrust out the laserSword with the other. Both are set to high-impact damage, not pure-death, and cut heavily across most of the circle of thugs.

They'd underestimated my longer, skinnier arms, and half of them topple in my first spin.

By the second revolution a further five run away. The

ringleader is angry, his head bobbing and swiveling. Three burly, scarred street veterans remain with him.

They stand back, then spread out and flank me on all sides.

I change the laserSword setting to "cut" and advance on the ringleader. I figure without the gang's head, the body won't function. He runs at me—damn those reflexes—and I jerk my laserSword up in defense. But I don't adjust for the gravSuit's servomotors and I trip backwards, just as the leader reaches me.

Rather than the threat of my sword making him stop, it is now slicing up through the air, and I take his arm off at the shoulder.

He falls to his knees in shock, staring at his detached limb on the ground in front of him.

My adrenaline is peaking. I use it to rush—as best as my gravSuit allows—at the remaining thugs, who turn and run, jabbering loudly in Rykkan.

I stop and catch my breath. The Rykkan female, who to my untrained eyes appears a little older than her would-be captors, stares at me, her head vibrating in shock.

I walk up to her, ignoring the badly injured thug bleeding heavily behind me, and she flinches backward. Oh jeepers, she's afraid of me.

I stop again, and this time I raise my helmet visor, squat down to her level, and smile.

"It's okay. It's safe to leave. Can I take you somewhere?" I have zero idea if she understands Galactic, but I'm hoping my tone and body language convey the message anyway.

I also have no idea if my unipod will squeeze a big-boned, bulky-but-short Rykkan in the collapsible emergency seat, but I assume the language barrier means this will never happen.

The Rykkan female bows. Actually bows. Not like the Rykkan Chief's stiff trade-off, but a hinge forward from her hips. I'm guessing a full curtsy is only possible in a lower-gravity environment, but nonetheless, it's impressive.

She remains bowed. I am unsure of what to do. "Er, please be standing," I say stupidly.

She stands straight and looks me in the eye. "Please, no need to bend down or be feeling stupid," she says in perfect Galactic. "A plan of exit would be the most appropriate action." She points to the road.

The steady stream of traffic is at a standstill, and all manner of occupants are gawking from their vehicles. The neuro'd thugs pick themselves up and shamble away. Their leader is semi-conscious in a pool of dark Rykkan blood.

I switch my attention back to my newfound friend. "Follow me," I say.

Papa taught me to press my advantage in any situation, though I wasn't always the good student my brother was. This occasion requires me to continue to be the unknown, feared force.

I slap my visor back down, though not before I catch the ringleader blinking in and out of consciousness and staring at my face. He groans and his head slumps to one side.

I walk past him, my new Rykkan friend tagging behind.

"He has 35% chance to live," observes my erstwhile victim in the flat tone typical of most Galactic-speaking Rykkans.

I stop and pause. Then turn and pace back to the injured thug. I peel open one of the gravSuit's pocketflaps and pull out a supersized medpatch. I reach down and slap it onto the ringleader's bleeding stump, where the patch attaches itself and conforms to the shape of the wound. I wait briefly to ensure the bleeding abates.

"Now he has 85%. With self-repair, he will live."

Movement in my peripheral vision makes me look up. The crowd of voyeurs is growing in size and excitement. Maybe they don't see me as a threat anymore, now I'm apparently acting as a paramedic. Some are now inching forward, eyes bright for a closer glimpse at the spectacle.

Great. Don't attract any attention, Indy.

Time to be fearsome again.

I lunge forward to the crowd and wave my blaster and laserSword at the stopped traffic. Those already in their pods or hovers accelerate away; the others take a moment to absorb that they might be my newly acquired target before jumping back into their vehicles and speeding off.

I walk over and open my pod's rear gullwing. One punch and the emergency seat emerges from under a hidden panel. I look over at the Rykkan, doubtful she will fit.

"My name is Aktip," she says. "Do not worry, I will squash."

I can see I'll have to learn some new skills. Five visits to Rykkamon and I still don't grasp just how much a human gives away to the Rykkan sensing capability.

I tell Aktip I am "Indy," and I close the rear gullwing on Aktip's squashed-in form and head around to climb back into the pod.

I wonder just how much I unwittingly gave away to the Rykkan Chief. I realize I hadn't emphasized to Jordi exactly how tight-lipped he needed to be. Which, to be honest, for Jordi, is impossible. He talks a lot.

A voice from behind me startles me and I'm brought back to reality. My adrenaline is fading and I need to focus. What is she saying?

"You are having foggy-ness. Suggest continuing one block forward, then I will direct you to a safe place. For both of us. The storm comes very soon now."

I peer out of the clear bubble. Even with my visor down, I see Aktip is right. Darkness is falling earlier than usual, and there is only one reason: tornadoes. I've never been on Rykkamon in storm season. "How bad does it get?"

"If outside, is 90% chance of fatality."

"So this safe place is inside then?"

The Rykkan laughs, more like a gurgle. I'm surprised at her quick recovery. "Do humans always doubt?"

I grit my teeth as we accelerate down the long block, away from the carnage. "We're taught to."

CHAPTER FIVE

AKTIP DIRECTS ME INTO A built up area, populated by squat, solid-looking single-story buildings. Rykkamon is built low. For good reason. On Rykkamon I weigh twice as much as I'm used to, but I only have my normal muscle strength. For anyone born and raised in an old-earth one-gee standard, falling from anywhere in two-gee gravity hurts. Let alone from a height. Being underneath anything falling in two-gee is even less fun. I know this from previous visits.

The Rykkans, with their densely packed, squat muscular bodies don't feel the high-gravity in the same way I do. But they know not to construct high buildings.

We circle almost all the way around the next block, and Aktip points over my shoulder to a down-ramp. "Please descend."

I wonder if I'm just getting myself deeper into trouble, but one look into the sky confirms I have no choice. I guide the pod down the ramp, which as it turns out, zig-zags down for several levels, until we pull up in front of a several meter-wide metal roller-door.

I move to get out, but Aktip reaches through the pod and restrains me. "Please stay. It will be dangerous for you. Can you open my door from inside?" I nod and release the gullwing.

Aktip climbs out and moves to the right of the roller door. She lifts her non-clawed hand and places it on a nondescript area of the wall next to the door. A square under her hand briefly glows green and the door slides up.

Revealing a line of Rykkans assembled across the entry. All armed. And aiming their weapons at my unipod.

Aktip waves a greeting and walks over to them. She speaks at length, occasionally gesticulating to the unipod, and up into the air. Then the group breaks apart to allow space for the pod to slide through, and Aktip motions me to come through, stop and park. The door rolls shut behind me with a heavy clunk, and I take this as permission to exit my vehicle.

I open my door and stand out of the pod. I hear a collective gasp at the same time as I hear Aktip call out to me. "Please remove your helmet. You are anxious, but you are now with friends."

I wish they looked like friends. My experience with Rykkans up to now hadn't exactly produced a set of close buddies. But I remove my helmet and shake out my hair. I hear alien giggles, quickly shushed. I guess long red hair is funny on Rykkamon.

The building we are in is some kind of underground plasticrete reinforced bunker. The space extends far beyond this garaging area, and is utilitarian. And dimly lit.

I move closer to Aktip. "How long until the storm passes?" I sense momentary confusion. Her eyes dilate and close for a while, which I've learned means a Rykkan is deep in thought.

"You want to complete a task"—she pauses for a good half a minute—"but you do not know that the tornado front will take all night and some of tomorrow to pass. Is this correct?"

I nod.

"It is not safe for anyone to be outside in this season. I think it better to relax. We will all sleep here." Aktip casts her arm around, pointing at the group of Rykkans standing some distance from us, possibly curious, possibly protective, I don't know. My Rykkan facial expression recognition is underdeveloped.

She continues, "I will find us somewhere comfortable and we

can conclude my debt negotiation."

What?

I shrug and follow my new friend to an area clearly intended for an overnight refuge. She indicates a large cushioned bed topped with several animal pelts. "It should not be so hard for you."

I must be polite. "I'm not even sure if I can sleep once this suit's off. Last time I tried, I felt like I couldn't breathe. I may just pull an all-nighter."

"So sorry." Aktip's eyes pulse again. "May I conclude my debt negotiation now?"

I nod and sit on the edge of the large bed to equal out our eye heights. The bed barely moves, even under my weight and that of my gravSuit combined. It could be a long night.

Aktip bows again, then straightens. "You exhibited maximum bravery. If not for you, I would be on my way to be"—her squat body quivers—"a pleasure-body for the offworlders."

"Who are the offworlders?"

"I will explain after I conclude my debt pledge."

Debt pledge? Oh boy.

"I must now offer myself in service to you in any time of your danger. I will serve you to my death, or until my obligation is extinguished."

I smile. "I have no need of your service—"

Aktip stiffens, and her head swivels rapidly from side-to-side.

I am confused. "What is it?"

She opens her wide mouth, but only manages a squeak. She closes it again, her eyes pulse, and the stiffness goes away. "You do not know of the insult. You mean no harm. If you refuse the debt, then I must self-extinguish."

I start. "What? You mean kill yourself?"

She nods—a most human-like gesture.

"Then how is this debt concluded?"

"When you die." Aktip is matter of fact. "But not to be sad. This is not for a long time, I think. You are a powerful warrior, and warriors such as you learn to survive. Mostly they die in fierce battle—"

"Stop." I hold up my hand. "I'd rather us not discuss either of our deaths. I accept your pledge, and I hope to never make a call on it. Perhaps we could celebrate both of our escapes, and we can learn something about each other?"

The Rykkan positively bounces with enthusiasm. "You know of the celebration of a debt pledge? Then you must be my guest at my family home. Tomorrow evening. I will prepare food for human consumption."

Weary of further discussion of debt pledges and death, I agree. Perhaps a chance to learn more of the Rykkan culture might improve my subsequent deals with the outlaws. A light goes on in my brain. "Wait. Did you say that you'd be taken off-world as a pleasure-body? Who by, and where to?"

Aktip's face assumes a serious expression. "Rykkamon traders send mercenaries to Takao to fight with Resistance against the Scorpion. Rykkan males are strong and fast, and in Takao's low gravity, they are many times stronger than natives."

My eyes narrow at her. I've heard of the Scorpion and his inflammatory politics. But I don't want to get involved, and I certainly can't tell Aktip my secret, that I'm accused of brokering this illicit trade.

"I'm guessing these male mercenaries demand their pleasure needs are met."

She nods. "Yes. But you do not need to feel guilty. I will keep your secret."

Rykkans. Is nothing safe?

CHAPTER SIX

I GET OUT OF MY suit—with difficulty—and lie down on the makeshift bed. I close my eyes and try to sleep, but within minutes I am engulfed by an intense claustrophobia. There is a heavy weight pressing down on my chest and I cannot breathe. I've spent too much time in zero-grav and my body needs a training regime. Not double-gee torture.

I gesture to Aktip for help, and she gets me back into my suit. I lay back in an awkward assembly of limbs. The suit's systems relieve the pressure on my chest, and I decide my best bet is to talk.

"Why were you targeted by that gang, Aktip?" I stretch out on my back and turn my head to look at her using the gravSuit's assistance. "Isn't this region a no-go zone?"

Aktip is relaxing on a smaller version of a bed opposite me. We are at the end of a large dormitory-style room, left alone by the other Rykkans in the storm bunker. They seem to have accepted Aktip's care of me as enough of an indication that I am no threat to them.

"I am a communications officer for the Rykkamon government. I was tasked to visit this area and audit local equipment. I had finished this task, and it was apparent I would not be able to return home before the storm. I was searching for this bunker, which my friends use, when I became anxious and lost. Unfortunately, that made me easy to attack." The alien swallows heavily. "If it was not for your extreme prowess with your weapons—"

"Okay, okay. I got angry. I just hope word doesn't spread of a red-headed giant in a fight-suit on the loose. I was trying to keep a low profile."

I sigh.

"You are worried."

A Rykkan understatement of the obvious.

"Yes. Does our pact extend to our conversations?"

Aktip stiffens again. I waved my hand up at her from the bed. "Sorry, sorry. I presume that I can trust you to keep what happened between us?"

The Rykkan relaxes and nods. "The pledge requires it. The pledge is sacrosanct."

I carry on. "I'm not here ... ah ... officially. And you are an official. I don't want to make things difficult for you. Do you understand?"

"Yes. But official status matters not. I am now in your debt until the debt is extinguished, and—"

I cut her off. "I got it. So I have to tell you it's entirely possible there are people on Rykkamon who would like to question me about ... certain things. Tomorrow I have to organize supplies for my ship and pick up some ... other things." I concentrate hard on not thinking about specifics. What Aktip doesn't know won't hurt her. "Then I have to leave the planet quicksmart."

Aktip frowns. "Quicksmart?"

"Yes, it means—"

"I understand the meaning. But the pact celebration dinner?"

I'd already forgotten. I exhale to calm myself down. One more night won't make a difference. "Yes, of course. I'd love that."

"I sense your joy. We will share together in our delight!"

I smile weakly. I'd like to sense my joy. I really would.

CHAPTER SEVEN

I WAKE, LYING ON MY back, my joints stiff.

It's only when I try to move do I remember I'm still in a gravSuit. It takes a few more moments to work out that the low-frequency pounding noises I can feel through the hard Rykkan bed must be the continuing storm. I look across to Aktip, who is asleep.

I wonder how Jordi has found shelter. He's probably locked up the cruiser with himself inside and set the gyro to full stability. He won't even feel a thing; probably the safest place. Tomorrow—or today because it must be well past Rykkamon's midnight—I'll finish my trip to furnish the supplies, drop my special package at the ship and head to Aktip's home for dinner. My guilt rises as I realize I have no idea where her home is, nor who her family are. I guess I'll find out soon enough.

I adjust my aching body in the suit and try to drift off for what remains of the night, hoping the storm passes without incident.

The next morning reveals calm streets, and a palpable sense of relief in the way the Rykkans go about their business. Aktip chaperones me back to the mainway where she requests to be dropped off at a hoverstop. She assures me this area is safe; gives me her coordinates and bows her apologies, but she has to attend work.

I scoot away from the hover stop and in another ten minutes I'm at the supply hub—a drab, sand-colored, featureless building. Yesterday's tension seems a million klicks away and I relax into the procedures I've done hundreds of times: ordering dehydrated meal-units, clothing and boots, space-straps for Jordi's sweet-tooth, toiletries.

Even space travel has mundane elements. Papa would have called it, "Getting ready for another road-trip." Despite his inventive genius, he could be nostalgic for earth-like experiences, even though he'd never been there. Humanity's soul, I suppose. Which is rather ironic, when it occurs to me I'm buying these items on a very un-earth-like planet.

I complete my transaction with the indifferent and terse Rykkan at the accounts section, waving my holopad into his reader and confirming where I want the goods sent. He doesn't even raise a Rykkan eyebrow at the no-go zone location I give him. My kind of guy.

I leave and head a few kilometers across the wet and debris-strewn city blocks, populated by low-slung building after building, and pull up when I find what I'm looking for.

Fully armed, I step out of the pod and enter the code given to me into the doorpad. There is no response, and I glance to either side, fidgeting my weight from side to side.

I'm conscious of being the only moving entity in an otherwise deserted block; far taller than the average Rykkan, clad in a metran-equipped gravSuit ... and armed to the teeth. I'm guessing even in downtown Rykkamon no-hoper land, it could be a little suspicious.

The door slides away, and a voice barks from a hidden speaker.

"Disarm yourself and enter. Any armed weaponry will trigger vaporization of any person or people in the vestibule. You have been warned."

I guess I have. I step in, place my weapons in the rack provided, and power them down. The outer door hisses closed and I wait. I just hope Venik doesn't assess my suit as a weapon; technically it's an enabler and a defense system.

No matter what its classification, I'd still hate to fight someone wearing one.

The vestibule is well-lit and decorated in muted mahogany-tones. Scattered in the small space are plush chairs, and a small, black, coffee machine blinks a welcome. Venik's customers are not poor.

I remain standing, tapping my gloved hand against my suited thigh. I hate Venik's theatrics.

The inner door opens.

"India! How kind of you to visit. I trust all is well with you and Michelangelo?"

Venik loves his affected speech. And he insists on using everyone's full name. I motion for him to continue.

He grins. "You know, the last time I saw your brother—"

"It was you who sold Papa's laserSword to Mitch?"

"Technically, no. I merely brokered a deal for the Jovians."

The bald, portly man motions me into his building, all the while training a stunbolt at my neck.

"And took your commission," I say, following him into the sumptuous interior. "That's selling in anyone's language. But as much as I would love to see you rot in hell for handling anything of my father's, Mitch is very happy to have it in his possession. Shame we had to leave in rather a hurry."

Venik shrugs. "I take no sides." He indicates two padded tubchairs positioned next to a coffee table. "Shall we?"

I take a seat and Venik lowers the stunbolt, placing it next to him on the seat. "Now, what can I do for you?"

I grit my teeth. "No games, Venik. You have a special item for me. You know full well what it is. Pretending you don't, just to get me to beg, won't work. I'll pay what you ask."

His expression falls serious. I notice for the first time he has no obvious grav-assistance. Nano servomotors built into his clothing, perhaps? I meet his eyes.

"I have it. Your father would not approve of this."

"He's not alive to confirm that judgment, and you're not fit to pass it. How much?"

He tells me and I would have fallen off the chair if it weren't for my gravSuit. I hand over my holopad. "It's preset to transfer."

He stares at me momentarily before taking the pad and swiping his scanner. He hands the pad back and shrugs. "It's your life. Wait here."

He disappears through a door that opens at his approach, but closes when I attempt to follow him through. I stand and wait, looking around. Reproduction paintings, a full-sized wooden desk, a rack of holoscreens on one partition ... and armor-plating lining every wall.

Venik returns carrying a dark-gray plastisteel box-like container, roughly the size of a suit helmet. He sets it down lightly on the table. "Would you like to inspect the merchandise?"

"After what I've just paid?" I lean in to the man's pudgy face, and to my surprise he flinches. "Even a minor problem with it risks your becoming a quadriplegic."

I stand back. "If there is one thing you have a reputation for, Venik, it is for delivering. If you haven't"—I shrug—"then it's the last deal you'll ever do."

He licks his lips and swallows. "It is as promised. But I will suggest you keep it well out of sight until you are off this planet. My money was well-earned." He picks up the stunbolt and aims it at my face. "And I never want to see it—or you—again."

He motions me out, and in minutes I am in the unipod, flying back to my ship, my purchase safely hidden in the false footwell.

I wonder what has Venik so rattled.

CHAPTER EIGHT

Jordi narrows his eyes at me when I load the box into the ship's safe.

"You didn't see it."

He shrugs. "Sure. Where did you get to last night? That was a heck of a storm."

"Enacting some social justice. Speaking of which, we're both invited to dinner later tonight."

He grimaces. "Rykkan food? No thanks. Anyway, I have to see someone in town."

"I'm sure she'll be delighted. Meet a nice young man, a good future ahead of him as a space pirate." I wander into my cabin to get changed. Jordi follows.

"It's not a girl I'm seeing."

I twist my mouth. "Oh. That is a new development!"

He scowls. "It's not like that either."

"Then what is it like?" I hover my hand over the doorpad.

Jordi looks down at the deck, then flicks his gaze back at me. "Uh, I have to repay someone."

I stare at him for a while, then slap the pad and the door closes. I should have known. Not that he's the only one with a debt. But at least mine isn't from gambling.

I glimpse my tall frame in the mirror as I move to pull a new loungesuit from my locker. I look gaunt, hardened ... and unhappy.

I turn away quickly, hoping that Aktip's dinner distraction

will take me away from the knowledge I'm not fulfilling my father's legacy at all. Like Jordi, I'm just another space pirate.

Refreshed from my re-cyc shower, and experiencing mild—and rare—optimism, I resolve to enjoy my evening and try to deepen my understanding of Rykkan culture. I should be lucky to have a Galactic-speaking comms engineer at my service. Perhaps Aktip can teach me some negotiation tricks I can use on the outlaw Chief.

I review my ship's inventory and note that all the 3He has now been unloaded. I check my credits and to my surprise, I see the Chief has made good on his promise to pay the outstanding balance. I disarm the drones and hope that my optimism is not misplaced.

I leave a message on Jordi's holopad to maintain comms silence except in an emergency, and head out in the unipod, noticing the absence of the outlaw shacks. I make a note to ask Jordi if he witnessed their deconstruction before the storm. For some reason, I think this might come in useful. I have Papa's eye for odd detail.

I arrive at Aktip's dwelling complex, a low grouping of ugly gray brick buildings with hardly any windows, defined by wide darker gray walkways. Presumably Rykkamon building codes aren't conducive to palm trees and atriums. Or colored paint.

I park my unipod next to the building unit indicated, turn to the second entry door, lift my visor and raise my hand to tap the vidport, but the metallic door slides open to reveal Aktip.

She bares a wide red-toothed grin, one Rykkan expression I understand with no unambiguity.

"You came. Thank you." She bobs.

I feel my brow furrow. "Of course I came. Why wouldn't I?"

Her grin fades. "It is not important for our celebration. Come, my sisters have prepared a human feast."

I sincerely hope Aktip is unaware of her literal translation. I follow her through the foyer and into a low-ceilinged apartment, furnished with garish low-set futon-style loungers in all color variations, a rough canvas floor covering, and fluorescent-painted plasticrete walls. To my right, there is a long, low table, also rough-hewn like the Chief's, surrounded by low stools.

And a dozen Rykkan females, one to a stool, all staring at me.

I smile and remove my helmet.

My hair tumbles out around my shoulders, and there is a collective gasp. Three Rykkans actually fall off their stools, and everyone is talking at once, pointing at me. Or more specifically, my hair.

I'm taken aback at the odd reaction, and my face falls. Aktip tells me it is just curiosity, and motions me to sit on a stool next to her at one end of the table. I take a deep breath and remember to chill out.

I smile, sit down, and out of impulse, I grab my hair and fluff it up around my head in crazy gestures. One or two of the Rykkans chuckle, I join them in a laugh, and soon we are all hysterical, my hosts' heads swiveling in glee.

When I was a kid, I loathed my red hair. People would point and exclaim. Sometimes yell stuff. Not nice things. Papa used to say, "They're just jealous, Indy. They can't walk into a room and turn heads the way you do."

I didn't want to turn heads; I just wanted to fit in.

Now I'm turning alien heads. Literally.

I gather the group comprises Aktip's social network; similar status, similar mannerisms. Some also speak Galactic, so I find myself peppered with questions, punctuated by dinner, which surprisingly is a roast platter with a syrupy gravy, followed by a bittersweet pudding containing a bluish seeded-fruit I have not seen before.

"The food is very good, Aktip. Very human-friendly." I look over at Aktip, and smile.

"I sense you are telling the truth. But it was Vikra who provided for us." Aktip indicates a well-built Rykkan at the other end of the table. "She is fascinated by human culture."

I hold up my goblet to the other Rykkan in a universal gesture of acknowledgment, and take a sip from my sweet, berry-like beverage, grateful for the gravSuit's assistance. By now, my arms would be tired just from lifting food and drink—and from using Rykkamon's dense and heavy implements, engineered to withstand high-gravity accidents.

We discuss the last Sector War against the Blood Empire. Although not involved directly in the fighting, Rykkamon, like many other systems in the Sector, was under threat of the hostile takeover. With no common enemy since the war, the Sector has been in disarray, and not all news sources are reliable. Newcomers to any planet are often pumped for information.

"You saw these Blood Empire battles?" Vikra asks.

I shake my head. "I was on the other side of the Sector."

The question kicks off a memory: Papa had sent me on a lengthy exploration mission, and when I came back, the war was won, and Papa was missing. Sometime later, a Galactic official tracked me down to deliver his death certificate. Only recently did I discover his death was at the hands of a man called Sloper.

"All I know of them is what my parents used to say when they wanted to pull me into line: 'Better behave, or the Blood Empire will come to get you.'" I expected this to raise a smile or two, but it fell flat, and I found myself staring back at a table of confused Rykkans.

"Why do humans lie so easily?" The question comes from my

left, and I am taken aback until I remember the Rykkan predisposition to bluntness.

"I'm not sure we lie easily," I begin, but I am cut off when the Rykkan turns to her neighbor and engages in an excitable discourse.

Aktip intervenes. "Movvi believes you have just proved her point: to her, your answer is not truthful."

I try to come up with an answer, but I am still searching when the holoscreen comes to life. A news broadcast it seems.

"It is traditional among younger Rykkans to observe and discuss the news after dinner," Aktip informs me in a low voice. "I will translate for you if needed."

We have a saying in our blackmarket trading community: a holo tells a thousand textuals. There is no need for Aktip to translate this particular headline.

I am spellbound by grainy images of thug-like Rykkans lining up to board a dirty and dented spaceshuttle. The footage shifts to show Takao, and heavily armed Rykkans bounding into a war not of their making, using the low-density planet's low gravity to overcome an enemy not their own.

War in any form is ugly, but this is horrific. Whoever is using the Rykkan mercenaries as battle-currency has neither morals, nor ethics. Not to pass over the fact that interplanetary mercenary trade is illegal under the Aurora Treaty, passed more than fifty years ago. Contravention is serious. Fatally serious.

I stare at the holo, until a still image of a computer-generated, generic silhouette flashes up. A cold sweat breaks out inside my suit. The silhouette is a human female. With long hair. Jordi's warning, brought to me at great cost to him from Ganymede, is no longer just bar-room gossip.

Rykkan heads swivel to look me up and down. I hold my hands out. "It's not me. Ask Aktip." I turn to Aktip who is also measuring me with her eyes. I wait.

"She speaks true," my friend says, finally, though she sounds unconvinced.

"And also not," comes the flat retort from my previous interrogator. "What do you know of this trader?" I miss one of the words, but there is no mistaking the adjective's meaning.

"I know no more than you," I say.

"Why are humans so unreliable?" This from Aktip, and I flinch at her raw observation.

I stumble over my words. "We are ... different to Rykkans. We can hide from each other's thoughts and feelings, we—"

"Lie, cheat and steal?" My left-seated antagonist finishes my sentence.

"No. Yes." I shrug. "It makes us what we are." I manage a weak smile. "It's part of our mystery."

Our attention returns to the changing images on the holo, and I am grateful for the distraction. Then my jaw drops and I wish our conversation was back where it was. What projects from the screen is a jerky witness video. Of yesterday's fight in the park.

Our table erupts into a loud babble of Rykkan voices, arms variously pointing to Aktip. I cannot move, transfixed by the imagery, waiting for the inevitable revelation.

When it arrives, it's worse.

A handheld device has captured me advancing on the group of thugs and drawing them away from Aktip. A sudden swivel of Rykkan faces turn to me at the table. I keep my gaze on the holo, which follows my fight, my squatting and swatting of the tattooed gang.

Then the final horror: I appear to pause, adjust something on my laserSword (my illegal laserSword!), then as the gang leader advances, the filmed angle makes it look as if I take a considered step back, swing down then swipe up my sword to cut the Rykkan's arm off at the shoulder.

Someone at the table screams, others gasp, but the show must go on. On the holo, I advance to Aktip, who cringes, then I bend down and lift my helmet visor. Strands of red hair are clearly visible, even in the amateur footage.

I swear under my breath.

The table is now silent, and all large eyes are on me.

"This was you?" The question comes from my large chef at the other end.

I nod. Part of me is curious as to why Aktip did not tell her friends, but I assume it is to do with her pledge and my request for confidentiality.

"There is an alert out for you," Aktip says, trembling. "The boy whose arm you cut off is the son of an important Rykkan politician. Any Rykkan caught harboring you will be tried alongside you."

"Tried? What about your debt?"

Aktip is still. "My debt is mine only, and not honored by any other. It cannot be extinguished. Except by death. Which means we are now both wanted."

I open my mouth to speak, confused by the apparent mix of moral righteousness and injustice, but my antagonist on my left speaks first.

"I see your fear and your true heart. I sense you do not feel your actions were carried out for any other reason than to save brave Aktip. But now you must leave. Immediately."

I move to stand. "What about Aktip?"

"We will shelter her until you are caught. We too have friends in high places, and Aktip is a valued worker."

"Until I am caught?" I try not to be angry. "Those thugs would have shipped her off to—"

"It was not your concern, and it is still not your concern. Now leave this place before we are forced to report you."

I step back from the table, seeing only frightened alien faces. "And you think humans are unreliable." I turn on my heel and make my way to the door. Aktip follows.

"Be careful," she says in a low voice as we stand at the open door. The street outside is dark and silent. "There will be people looking for you now. The politician has offered a reward. Try to stay out of public view."

I pull on my helmet. "A red headed giant in a fight-suit? Sure. I'll just concentrate on blending in."

I bend down to her height. "Just so you know, I'd do it all again. Those grunts deserved everything they got. The arm might have been an accident, but he won't be bothering anyone again. Stay safe, Aktip. I'm sorry for stuffing things up."

I slide my visor down, take one look at Aktip's wide eyes and swiveling tremors, and head to my unipod.

CHAPTER NINE

My pod doesn't respond as it normally would; the last two corners had me run wide as if I was carrying an extra load. But, wrapped up in my thoughts, I realize too late.

I am about to pull over when I feel a neuromuzzle poke into my suit's underarm joints: one of its few vulnerable places. Only an experienced streetfighter would know this. I consider my options, but drop all of them as soon as I hear a familiar, coarse, high-pitched voice speak from the emergency seat behind me.

"Keep going. I'll tell you where to drive. Any moves other than piloting this pod without attracting attention, will get you this." He pushes the neuroblaster hard into my suit.

"I'm not exactly keen to attract any attention. Or haven't you heard? If that's really you, Darpesh, I'm shocked that you don't know I'm already on Rykkamon's most-wanted list."

Darpesh sniggers. "Good price on your head, too."

I look in my rearcam to see the wolf-like face of Sloper's assassin grinning back at me. I wonder what he's doing on the planet in the first place.

"How did you get into my pod?"

He shrugs his wiry metran-clad shoulders, all the while I feel the push of the blaster into my armpit. "You're not the only one who can hack Errikson's codes. But I doubt the Rykkans will care. Now you're muscling in on their gangs; killing their outlaws and taking over the mercenary trade, I'm seriously considering redeeming my bounty."

My chest tightens when I hear my captor's words, but I have no time to reason any of my spinning thoughts as he indicates we need to change lanes. I take the next two turns Darpesh tells me, and we head out of town, leaving the squat buildings behind us.

"I didn't kill any outlaws," I say, hoping Darpesh will fill in some blanks.

I feel a portable holovid attach to my helmet, and a video starts off to my right. I watch it while keeping one eye on the road.

The vision is of the no-go zone where I parked my ship. The action is horrific: the outlaws run out from their reconstructed shacks, straight into a volley of high-impact plasma fire. I cannot see who is the source of the firepower because it's the person wearing the holocam. But Darpesh's quickened breath and pleasure-humming behind me gives me a good clue.

Almost all the thugs die in the first barrage, and it's not until the Chief appears that they fall back to a strategic defense. A mini-grenade cluster thrown into their midst finishes them off.

The attacker now runs to my ship, and I am alarmed to see the entry port slide open, the wearer of the holocam obviously jumps in, and the video stops.

Darpesh snickers in the dark behind me. "Now you're a mass-murderer as well as an arm remover."

I shake some sense into my head. "What do you want? You have my ship. You've turned me into a wanted killer."

"I don't want anything. I'm only the courier."

His words send a shiver down my spine. "Sloper?"

"Oh yes. He's looking forward to catching up. It's not far now."

I tense up and struggle to keep my focus on the road. "He's here?"

Darpesh laughs. "I thought you'd be impressed. Pull over at the next ramp, you'll see a hovertruck in the bay. Stop next to the trailer. I think it will be quite a party."

Sloper. No wonder Venik was rattled. I never thought for one moment he would turn up on Rykkamon. The man I vowed to kill for what he did to Papa. Opportunity knocks.

I pull the unipod to a halt and don't wait for the gyrostabilizers to kick in before twisting violently in my seat—but Darpesh is too quick for me, and I experience the searing, intense pain of a neuroblaster at close range. The last thing I remember is slumping heavily in the high gravity and tumbling out of the side door onto the ground.

CHAPTER TEN

I AWAKE WITH A FUZZY head and a searing pain in one arm. I try to move, but I am pinned to something—a table?

"Save your energy."

Sloper? I stop struggling. Now it's between me and him.

I open my eyes and take stock. I have no recollection of being moved, but I'm no longer in the hovertruck's trailer. The room is sparsely furnished—just a few heavy Rykkan chairs scattered across a plain cement-like surface and one table, occupied by the prisoner.

Sitting in one of the chairs is the man I swore I would kill the next time I saw him.

Darpesh and three of his men stand against the walls, armed with neuroblasters, rifles and laserSwords.

Mistake number one: they left me in my fight-suit.

Sloper pushes his chair back onto two legs. A well-built man, with arms and legs forged from years fighting, he is also wearing a metran gravSuit, but has no helmet. I check around the room: my helmet is missing.

He gesticulates with his blaster. "You can say thank you, now you're awake."

I eyeball him. "I don't exchange pleasantries with double-crossers. You have anything useful to say before you die?"

Sloper laughs. "You've been wanting to kill me ever since I had a disagreement with your father—"

"Disagreement? That's rich. I'd call it murder. Either way, it's time for me to have my own disagreement. With you."

I wonder how Sloper knew I had set out to kill him. I've kept that off-limits in conversation. But that will have to wait. For now, I will stall him to give me time to figure out a way to dismember four assassins while tied down.

I lift my head to look up at him. "If you'd like a few last words, the floor is yours. As far as I can see, I'm persona non grata on Rykkamon thanks to you. Was that the thank you you were looking for? Or is this some strange way to begin your sadistic treatment?"

I flex my suit against the straps keeping me on the table. Not much give there. I wait for Sloper to make the next move.

He rocks the chair back to all four legs with a bang and allows the motion to bring him to stand over me. Grinning. The bastard. I'd happily take his head off right now even if it means my death. At least I will avenge Papa. I try to settle my ire. Anger will only get me killed.

An icy calm floods through me. I fix an impassive gaze on him. "What's so funny?"

He grins more. "What I have in mind for you."

I flop back on the table. My right leg has a tiny amount of movement against the strap. "You know how to string these things out, Sloper. Do we have time for a drink? Darpesh's blaster made me thirsty."

Sloper nods to one of the guards, who slips from the room. Sloper eyes me up and down.

"Get a good look, why don't you." I turn my face away, faking my surrender to the situation.

"Making sure the merchandise has survived. When I heard you were on Rykkamon, I took a calculated risk by coming here in person. As it turns out"—he glances over at Darpesh, who leans coolly against the wall—"events came together rather well.

Now Rykkamon has a price on your head. It's almost too good to be true."

Almost? What am I missing here? My mind races; I imagine torture, all my trade contacts given up to Sloper, then he throws me to the Rykkans. I'm in the middle of trying to connect the dots when the guard returns with a water bottle.

Sloper motions to the guard to give me the bottle. I shrug with my tied-down hands. "Is he going to hand-feed me?" I wriggle my left hand, feigning weakness.

The guard unties my left hand at Sloper's instruction. The other two guards and Darpesh raise their blasters at the ready as the guard hands me the water bottle.

I move to take it, but instead, I whip across to my right leg and rip at the loosened strap, using the gravSuit's chin-activated power boost. The strap breaks and my arm flies back. I use its momentum to smash my elbow into the guard's face and he goes down. As he drops, I grab his plasma rifle and spray it at full blast around the room. Both Sloper and Darpesh have already dropped out of range under my table, but I slice the other two guards and they too, drop in a violent spray of blood. The last image I have of them is their expressions of astonishment.

I'm yanking my right arm, but the strap is stubborn. My right leg is free, and I twist over to gain purchase and point the rifle under the table. My head explodes in pain when a heavy, blunt object connects with my skull, and I am vaguely aware of Darpesh lunging over me with one of the Rykkan chairs held over his head. I have no time to wonder how he swung it round so fast because another blow takes my lights out.

CHAPTER ELEVEN

I AWAKE FOR THE SECOND time, groggy and with a pounding head. I'm still on the table, and I try to move, but this time I'm heavy and my chest feels constrained. My breathing labors. My arms feel pinned down, and my head weighs as much as a Rykkan football.

It slowly dawns on me I'm feeling the crushing effects of raw Rykkan gravity.

They've taken off my fight-suit.

I'm only able to move my eyes, but they show me that Sloper is back on his chair. Someone has cleaned up the two dead guards and the bloody mess, and the water bottle guy is no longer present. Darpesh wears a murderous look, and with him are three more guards, leering at me. I realize I'm only wearing my off-white singlet and undies. No wonder the guards are ogling.

Sloper leans his bulky frame forward. "Mighty impressive. My sources did not tell me you've been training so hard."

"To kill you." I move to spit at him, but even in my rage I manage to check myself. The high gravity would make a mess of that. Better to save my revenge for when it is best served.

Sloper sits back and claps his hands on his suited thighs. The slap echoes off the room's hard surfaces. He laughs. "Just the person I need."

I frown. "Sloper, I give up. You're going to kill me, torture me, or give me up to the Rykkans. Which shall it be?"

I hope it's the first. Or maybe he wants to do all three. Not in that order, of course.

Sloper expresses mock surprise. "My dear girl, that would be such a waste."

I'm confused.

Sloper continues. "I'm hiring you."

I try to sit bolt upright, but the intense pain in my head, the lights flashing behind my eyes and the small matter of almost two-gee and a ton of industrial-strength straps all conspire to hold me down. I grit my teeth. "What makes you think I'd ever work for you?"

He holds up a portable holo to my face, and taps play. The video that springs to life has no sound, for which I am thankful. I look up at Sloper in horror. He shrugs. "He was on the way to Ganymede and took a wrong turn."

I look back at the holo, then look away. Mitch, my older—and only—brother is in a cage, covered in blood and wearing nothing but his boxers. He is crying.

Sloper switches the holo off and stands. "I take it that's a yes, then?"

"You bastard," I whisper.

He laughs. "Tell me something I don't know." His expression changes to serious. "But I will end his life if you refuse my job offer." He moves to leave, and one of the guards opens the door.

He pauses and looks back at me. "However, I believe in using both the stick and the carrot. So bring me back the prize and you will not only be reunited with your brother, but I will ensure someone else is caught for the Rykkamon atrocities and restore your reputation. I'll even pay your debts."

I have no words.

"I thought you'd like the employment terms." He turns to Darpesh. "Get the medbay to fix her up."

"Wait—"

Sloper turns back to me.
"What's the job?"
He grins again. "Salvage the Constellation."
A wave of shock slides across me. "What the—?"
But Sloper has already gone.

CHAPTER TWELVE

I'M IN A PRIVATE HOVERSHUTTLE with tinted bubblescreens and a driver who knows nothing. Sloper is sending me straight to the spaceport, where apparently there is a salvage vessel and a small crew at my disposal. Though Sloper's description of them as "a bunch of mercenaries," doesn't exactly fill me with confidence. I have no idea as to the whereabouts of my own ship, or Jordi. I'm wanted by the Rykkan authorities, my brother is being held hostage, and my trade is in tatters.

The only redeeming element in this list is the deal Sloper has offered to settle my debt.

The impossible problem is that first I have to salvage a battlecruiser no-one has been able to find for four years. That some say was destroyed.

Sloper told me the shuttle would get me past the spaceport's security—I imagine he'd bribed the guards—but once I was on the ship, getting off the planet was on me.

I glance out of the shuttle's dark plexibubble. Something catches my eye: it's a dark smear on the horizon. A dark smear rapidly getting bigger. I groan and slump back in my seat. The driver looks back at me. "We will be at the port before the next storm, Madam Captain."

We have to be, I think, since the entire city will be in lockdown, including the spaceport, and I won't be going anywhere.

The shuttle lurches to a halt.

The side door slides open in a swirl of dust and a gravSuited figure jumps in beside me. The door closes and we accelerate away at speed. The figure's visor lifts and I see a familiar smiling face looking out at me from under his helmet.

Jordi.

"How did you get here? I thought you were on my cruiser and captured after Darpesh killed the outlaws? Where have you been?"

Jordi's face drops. "Darpesh took out the Chief's guys? Sheez, that's bad news." He doesn't seem perturbed by the loss of my cruiser.

"Answer the question, or I'll kick you out."

His eyes widen. "Don't do that, please. Sloper will kill me. He made me join you on some salvage scouting mission."

"Made you?"

The shuttle bumps us around. The air is buffeting the vehicle badly and I see the driver fighting the controls, looking nervously at the approaching storm.

"It's a long story. So where are we going?" He looks at me, lips slightly apart, breathing fast.

I know Jordi well. Unfortunately. I sigh. I don't understand what I saw in him. But he does have some skills. Like talking his way in and out of anything. "You slipped out of my cruiser and went to town to gamble. Sloper found you."

Jordi shifts in the seat. "Sort of. Yeah." He avoids eye contact.

The shuttle lurches again, then steadies. I see the spaceport looming in the distance. I do some rough calculations. As long as Sloper delivers on his promise of a trouble-free entry to the port, we'll make it off the planet before the storm hits.

"So where are we going?"

I give him a quizzical look. "Sloper didn't tell you? Maybe he was worried you'd bail out. I—we—are going to salvage the

Constellation."

He jerks up and hits his head on the shuttle's bubble. "Moondog! That old myth? The Blood Empire destroyed it."

"Apparently not. It's just been missing for four years."

"Wait ... Don't tell me you agreed?"

I feel my mouth tighten and the smile vanish. "He has Mitch."

Jordi stares at me. I see the cogs turning in his head. "We're in deep."

I nod. "You could say that."

He screws his face up. "What's he going to do with it ... if it exists?"

But we have no time to discuss it further, because the shuttle careers to one side, making us both grab for support. Only this time, it's not the rising wind.

We shunt to a violent halt. Three unipod speedsters are blocking the mainway in front of us. In front of them are four Rykkans, armed with plasma rifles. One of them advances to our shuttle, limping badly.

"Hey!" I shove our driver. "Get us out of here!"

The driver looks to be paralyzed with fear and does not move.

"Darpesh didn't kill them all," Jordi says, stating the obvious as he watches the injured Rykkan Chief raise his rifle to shoulder height. He reaches down to his belt, unclasps two laserpistols, throws one to me. He throws me a quick questioning look. "The pleiades move? Or the epsilon?" He actually makes me smile. He's right. We've got out of worse.

"Pleiades. Got to be."

No more words are spoken as we simultaneously kick the emergency door latches on either side of the shuttle and roll out in opposite directions away from the vehicle, firing at foot level as we do. I keep rolling further away and firing. I'm a moving target, but they aren't.

Three of the thugs have already dropped, badly injured and hobbled. No way are they going anywhere.

But the Chief is nowhere to be seen.

I stop and stay prone. All four vehicles are stationary, locked in gyrohover standby, so I can see underneath them. The Chief, despite his limp, has moved around behind one of his pods. I call out. "Jordi! Status?"

"Green," he yells back.

"Shuttle," I call to him.

I scramble to my feet and bolt for the shuttle's door, but just as I'm about to vault into safety, the vehicle tears off in a flurry of dust. I am momentarily frozen.

"Drop, Indy!" yells Jordi, and I do. He fires over the top of me, and the pod in front of the Chief explodes.

I leap up and force my gravSuit into a power-boosted, but ungainly sprint for one of the remaining pods. I hear Jordi racing behind me. I jump into the pilot seat and Jordi takes the rear-facing emergency seat in the back. I thank the galaxies that the thugs left their pods running, and there is no code needed. I tap the pad, and we shoot off, leaving carnage behind us.

"Where are we going?" Jordi shouts over the noise. He has the rear gullwing open and his pistol trained out of the door.

I glance through the bubble up at the sky, then to the front. The pod is riding rough in the winds, which are whipping around us. One side benefit: the streets and roadways are emptying rapidly. One not so good side-effect: there's a good reason why everyone is running for shelter. A 90% fatality rate for anyone staying out in the open.

"Spaceport," I throw back to Jordi. "Hang on, it's gonna be rough."

"You're not wrong," I hear him say as he lets off a few shots through the rear of the pod. Some way behind us, and careering across the mainway like crazy is the remaining pod, presumably manned by the Chief, who has somehow survived the explosion. I'm guessing he isn't happy, but then again, I'm not exactly overjoyed.

I swerve from one side to the other, just in case our pursuer has drawn a line of fire, but none comes. However, he is catching us. Pods weren't designed to race with two occupants, and ours is the slower of the two.

I see the spaceport's entry gates some way ahead, just as another blast of wind almost pushes us into the warehouses on our left. I pull us back into line, and we're heading at speed to the gates, when I yank us around and to a halt, facing the rapidly oncoming pod.

"Indy, what the hell?" Jordi screams.

"We don't have access codes. The driver was supposed to get us through. And if you hadn't heard, I'm the most wanted person on this planet, so once they spot me"—and I think, for not the first time in my life, exactly how much I stand out in any crowd—"we're spacetoast." I steel myself. "We'll have to fight our way out of this one."

"You planning to fight the tornadoes, too?" Jordi gesticulates to the darkening sky. "Whatever we do, we need to do it fast."

The Chief's pod comes to a halt several meters in front of me. He may have survived, but there's a good reason for that: he's smart enough to take caution when needed. Caution over anger. I should learn that. I brace myself and ready the pod for our next maneuver. I hear the engines whine as I hold it back against the brake, building stored energy like a coiled spring.

"Indy!" Jordi is grabbing my shoulder. I shake him off.

"Indy, turn around!"

I quickly look back at him, blood rising in my face. "What?"

"Not you—the pod! Turn around! The gate's opening."

He's right. The gate is opening. The tornado approach means no-one is around to challenge us. I have just a few seconds to make or break. I unleash the pod's screaming turbine and throw the craft into full-lock. We spin wildly and fishtail toward the gate.

The gate stops, leaving an opening barely pod-width. "Hold on!" I yell back to Jordi, and I smash us through the opening, shearing off swathes of plastisteel on either side of the pod and throwing us around in our seats.

"The gate's closing again," Jordi calls over the turbine's whine. "I think we'll lose him."

I keep the pod pinned to full throttle, now searching the landing pads for the port-ID Sloper gave me. I hear a crash behind me over the wind noise. Jordi shouts at me. "He crashed. We made it."

I shake my head, and crouch over the pod's controls as we speed along. We haven't made it yet. I have to find the salvage cruiser fast. Our skirmish has cut our already tight launch window to nothing, and any minute the authorities will close the port to takeoffs before the storm hits.

I spot the landing pad ID and swerve around to park next to the run-down looking vessel. The wind drops in the lee of the ship's structure, but I barely register it as we lumber up the open ramp, our suits protesting. A movement catches the corner of my eye, and I look to see a speeding pod coming toward us.

"Hurry, Jordi. We've got company."

Jordi beats me up the ramp, and is already up into the helmroom with the ship fired up. I jump in beside him and punch the pad to bring up the ramp controls. I feel the ship shudder in the high winds. Simple physics means it won't blow away, but the movement is unnerving and adds to my panic.

I'm about to bring up the ramp when I hear a Rykkanaccented voice call up into the ship. "Wait!"

Oh jeepers. Rykkan port authorities.

"Close the ramp!" Jordi grunts.

I pause a moment. Shutting an innocent Rykkan in the ramp will kill them. I'm not against dispatching outlaws trying to kill me, but innocent victims? Not so much. My hesitation costs me, as the voice grows louder, and they are in the ship.

I tap the button, and the ramp rises. "Take her up, Jordi."

He needs no invitation, and we launch slowly to clear the port. Along with whichever Rykkan is now our hostage.

I turn around in my chair and level my pistol, waiting for the official to emerge from the ramp exit and into the helmroom.

A squat figure trundles up the passageway.

Aktip.

CHAPTER THIRTEEN

I POINT TO THE COMMS seat behind me and motion Aktip to fasten her harness. Talking can wait.

I punch up the holoscreen and wince at what I see. We're not going to avoid the tornado. "Looks like it could be a rough ride," I say to Jordi. He is momentarily preoccupied with the controls, then taps the input and we soar into the sky on anti-grav propulsion only.

He jerks his head back to Aktip. "Who's your friend?"

"You have suspicion," Aktip states. "But I am in service to Madam Captain. She will confirm this."

Jordi turns to me, and I shrug before looking at Aktip. "Why did you board our ship? Surely that is going beyond your debt?"

Aktip's head swivels from side to side two or three times, then she stops. "You were in danger—"

"I think we still are," Jordi mutters, but I shut him down with a wave of my hand. He's busy enough getting us out of here.

"Please explain." I fold my arms.

"I saw your approach to the spaceport."

"How did you know it was me?"

"There was an all-comms alert. I saw your predicament, and I opened the gate."

"That was you? But—"

"You do not remember? I am a comms engineer. My job is at the spaceport."

Jordi nudges me in the ribs. I shut him up. "Go on, Aktip.

Why does this mean you had to board our ship? I might not be able to set you back down ... for some time."

Jordi nudges me again. I spin back to him. "What?" He points up to the holo. We're about to dance with the tornadoes. "Aktip, hold on tight. We'll pick up the conversation shortly." I continue to stare at the screen. "Jordi, what are you thinking?"

He grins. "You mean, have I ever talked my way out of a tornado before? I survived my first encounter with you, didn't I?"

I shake my head.

Aktip makes a noise. "Excuse me, Madam Captain."

I look back at the distressed Rykkan. "Yes?"

"I also disabled all the port warnings and bypassed lockdown. The port authorities won't be able to track us."

I notice she says "us." I wondered why no one had set off any alerts, but I'd assumed Sloper must have paid off his spaceport contacts. "Thank you."

Aktip's eyes pulse. "We are invisible to the tracking systems."

"Yes, Aktip, I get it. Thanks again."

Jordi takes his eyes of the screen for a moment to look at us both. "I think what your friend is saying is that we're on our own with this tornado storm. We'll get no guidance from planet-side, and if we crash, no one will know where we are. Assuming you want to be rescued, that is."

He gives me a strange look and resumes his concentration for moment, then after a brief flick up to the screen, says, "Here we go."

I suddenly get the sensation we are upside down, as Rykkamon's deadly winds overwhelm the antigrav propulsion sensors. I am forced to grip the sides of my captain's chair as Jordi throws the ship around, and I hear the clatter of something crashing to the deck behind us. The ship flips again and the propulsion system whines in protest. I hope Sloper gave me experienced mercenaries. If they are even in the ship.

"Jordi?"

"I got this, Indy. Just hang on."

I see him punch up the fusiondrive and catch his eye. He grins. "I learned it from you, remember?"

"But I didn't fly around a tornado storm. One slip and we'll hammer ourselves into the planet."

He blows air noisily out of his mouth. "Always thinking of the negative."

"I'm no gambler, Jordi."

Aktip reaches a hand forward as the ship bucks and dives, taps Jordi on the shoulder and he flinches before looking back at her, eyes narrowed. "She makes trust with you, Captain Jordi."

He flashes a smile at me. "I like your new friend."

Then the lights go out and the ship takes a dive, and I see Jordi's furrowed brow in the glow of the helm controls as he works to save us. The cabin whistles and howls, and a jarring lurch throws my stomach into a somersault.

I briefly catch Jordi concentrating on the holoscreen in front of us, his finger hovering over the helmpad, waiting. He taps the pad, triggered by something he has seen on the screen, and we are thrown off to one side of our seats.

The fusiondrive kicks into life, and I am now pressed back into my chair as the ship's scream turns into a complaining howl.

I see a dark tornado cloud hurtle towards us on the screen, I am flung into the other side of my seat for several seconds like one of the theme park centrifuges on Gamma-4, then we rocket up into the sky.

We are clear, and heading to the upper atmosphere.

"Nice work." I look at Jordi. "Tell me you didn't just use the fDrive to fly into a tornado, surf the wind and slingshot us into orbit?"

"Of course not." He smiles.
"Captain Jordi is lying, Madam," Aktip says.

CHAPTER FOURTEEN

I INSTRUCT JORDI TO TAKE us out of Rykkamon's jurisdiction and into free space, using only the fDrive. I want to know if we are being tracked, which I won't if we use the hyperDrive.

The ship's systems tell us we are in the clear, and I order him to bring us to a halt, so we can remove the restrictive gravSuits and regroup.

I float down to the captain's quarters to change. The accommodation is stark and well-used. I glance around the cabin, and after donning a flightSuit, I collect the holocube left for me on the small desk next to the bunk and head back to the helm. I see no sign of Sloper's promised crew, but they could also be busy removing suits. Or smashed to a pulp by Jordi's reckless maneuver: one I try to convince myself I would never have done.

Jordi is already back and checking the ship's status. I boot him out of the pilot's seat. "Time to get acquainted with our crew. Find the NCO; assess any medical needs, and let them know you were personally responsible for the quality of their most recent flight."

He gives me a pained look and pushes off in the zero-gee. I call after him. "Jordi. Bring the NCO up here. I need to establish the ship's rules."

Aktip waits for Jordi to leave, then swivels to face me. "You do not trust him." Sometimes I find it hard to distinguish between a Rykkan question and a statement. This one is definitely a statement.

I chew my lip, wondering how much to share.

"He was your partner. Why do you no longer trust him?" Aktip's eyes are dilating and shrinking. Disconcerting.

"He and I were only together briefly at the start ... as partners." I emphasize the last word. "But he's been by my side for most of the last two years."

Aside from the time he spent on Ganymede.

"As for trust, it's not a question of 'no longer.' I actually never did." I shrug. "It was convenient at the time. But let's talk about you." I don't want Jordi in on the "lifelong debt" conversation.

I pause and look directly at Aktip. "Why did you risk your life to join the ship? Surely you must know I can't easily take you back to the surface." I don't tell Aktip we may not come back at all.

"We may perish," Aktip says.

Apparently I did tell her. I'd hate to play poker on Rykkamon. I say nothing and motion for her to continue.

"I have a debt for life. You saved me from being kidnapped and taken forcibly from my home planet."

I don't question the irony.

Aktip continues. "I saw the alerts, and I knew I could be in a position to save you. Now I can be with you—"

"Surely your debt is paid? You risked your own job and status to help us at the spaceport. You don't need to be with us."

Aktip's head swivels rapidly, and she stiffens. "You do not want me, Madam Captain? Then I must self-extinguish." She reaches down with her clawed hand and tries to undo her harness, but I reach over and hold her bulky wrist and gently pull her hand away.

"No, it's not like that. Help me understand."

Aktip relaxes, and I see just how affected she is by my mood.

"My debt is for life. It is not transactional. Because of my actions, even my friends cannot now prevent me from being pursued on Rykkamon. I am safest with you, where I can still fulfill my debt's obligations."

I regard the alien's features: the flat visage, large and wide lips, the squat head and powerfully muscled body. No wonder they are hired as mercenaries for lower-gravity environments. It dawns on me that, to outsiders, the very crime I'm accused of—taking Rykkans off Rykkamon and selling them for hire on other planets—I now appear to be committing. I shake my head quickly. "Wait. Of course. You've never been off-planet, or in zero-gee before, have you?"

Aktip shakes her head.

"Any side effects?"

She looks around, and shivers slightly. "I do not think so. But I will tell you if I do." She focuses back on me. "My presence here causes you stress?"

Even the Rykkan cannot decipher my cocktail of guilt, fear and anger. I open my mouth to answer when Jordi flies back into the helm, trailed by a grizzly and unshaven man in his mid-thirties, clad in space-fatigues.

"Don't worry, Aktip. It's my presence that causes her stress"—Jordi shoots me a grin—"in a good way. She's wondering when we'll get time to ourselves in this ship. But I've seen her cabin—it's big enough for two."

I roll my eyes. "In your dreams."

"You have them, too?" His eyes sparkle, but he quickly loses the cheeky face when I glare at him. I nod my head at the crew seat, and he pushes himself into it. Sitting's not really necessary in deep space, but it certainly looks more dignified.

In any case, I need our crew leader to witness my leadership. I look at the unshaven man and raise my eyes. "Please identify yourself."

The man nods. "Sergeant Danielli, Ma'am. At your service."

"Are you?" I catch Aktip's quick head-swivel out of the corner of my eye and feel the corner of my mouth twitch.

Danielli's brow furrows. "Yes, Ma'am. I do not follow your line of questioning."

"Let me ask you some questions, Danielli. On this ship, I am the Captain. You follow my orders, and mine alone. Is that understood?"

He looks confused for a moment, then squares me off. "Affirmative, Ma'am. And I vouch for all four of my crew. They're good people. Ex-Space Marines and a couple of pilots. We've been together as a unit for a while."

I regard him coolly and bide my time before asking my next question.

"Tell me of your loyalty to Sloper, Sergeant."

"We were hired only for this mission, Ma'am. I have not met Mr. Sloper in person."

I notice he avoids answering the question. A politically savvy fighting man. I cross my arms. "If I offered you double what Sloper is paying you, would you and your men leave Sloper's service?"

Jordi's head comes up quickly. "And women. Men and women." He looks offended at my scowl. "You told me to check out the crew. Make sure they were all okay." He adopts a lopsided grin. "Some of them are definitely okay."

I look back at the NCO, who has kept a neutral face, waiting for Jordi to finish. "We have only been advanced twenty percent of our money. We get the rest when you return." He looks uncomfortable. "May I speak plainly, Ma'am, since you have?"

My nod gives him permission.

"We were stuck in that hellish heavy-hole—sorry, miss"—he glances at Aktip—"and I needed a job to get us off the planet. I would have taken anything ..." He hesitates.

"But?"

He gives me a defiant look. "My crew and I all saw your fight on the holo. When you rescued that spinhead and cut the jibber's arm. We agreed that if anyone could get us off the planet, it would be you. We all voted. I knew Sloper had a job available, and Plexi guessed it was you from the subnet chatter. We're—"

I hold up my hand. "First order, Danielli."

He salutes, smartly tucking his feet into the grabrail. "Yes, Ma'am."

"The Rykkan over there?"—I point to Aktip—"Her name is Aktip, and she's the 'spinhead' I rescued." I stare the man down until he is visibly uncomfortable. "And Danielli ... don't ever call a Rykkan a spinhead ever again."

Danielli collects himself, tells me 'yes, Ma'am,' then turns to Aktip and salutes. "At your service, Ma'am. I apologize for any unintended offense given."

"You did not intend offense," Aktip states.

"That is correct, Ma'am, I did not—"

"She is telling you what you intended. She's not asking for clarification, Danielli."

"I see. Sorry, Ma'am." I see a thought cross his face. "May I ask where we are heading, Ma'am?"

I smile. "You may not, Sergeant. And please do not call me 'Ma'am.' You may use 'Captain' when on duty, or Indy when you are stood down. Speaking of which, we are shortly going into hyperDrive. Do any of your crew need assistance before we jump?"

"No, Captain. Just a few bumps and bruises."

"I can rub medcream on the lady's bumps." Jordi smirks, then ducks as I throw the holocube at his head.

I turn back to Danielli. "Sergeant, you are dismissed. Please be ready for disembarking, fully armed and suited, on exit from our jump. I appreciate your offered loyalty. I hope to actually earn it one day."

The Sergeant salutes, executes a perfect twist-and-turn, and sails back down the passageway.

Jordi let's a scornful whistle escape. "Pfft. Loyalty, my ars—"

"He speaks truth, Mr. Jordi," Aktip says.

Jordi shuts up and sulks.

I lean back the best I can in my weightless position and look over at Aktip. "Thanks. Now let's talk about a certain mythical battlecruiser, what the hell Sloper wants with it, and our plans to find it."

I pause for a moment to look around at my new crew.

"And stay alive at the same time."

CHAPTER FIFTEEN

I PUNCH UP THE HULL'S holoscreen, and I point to the simulated image of a staggeringly large X-class battlecruiser on the screen.

"This is supposedly what the Constellation looks like. I asked Sloper for a description, and he confirmed what we're looking at here. It was built in secret to fight the Blood Empire. Ten years ago, when Oberon's Circle of Seven started to amass significant cruisers and weapons stores on the fringe of the Sector, someone very high up escalated the design and construction of the Constellation. General—"

"Wait," Jordi interjects. "How do you know all this?"

I make a face at him. "Papa, of course. He followed all this stuff like it was all that mattered." Maybe it was at the time, I think. "I got this image from his cube store—who knows where he got it from. As I was saying"—I glare at Jordi—"the Constellation was crewed by General Garnek and his marines. It was rumored to have experimental weaponry onboard, which is why the Sector kept it from general knowledge. They thought trade partners in the region might get upset, or pull back from cooperation."

"Why would they behave this way?" Aktip asks, raising her brow protuberance. "I do not understand."

I sigh. "Human relationships can be complicated. Everyone has an agenda. I guess they were worried that someone might get wind of the Constellation's power and switch sides."

"Back the Blood Empire? That's a pretty serious

transgression." Jordi says.

I purse my lips. "It's happened before. Maybe they were worried history would repeat itself. But it never mattered. Oberon launched his play on the Sector and we responded. According to the myths, it was only because of the Constellation that we overpowered the Circle of Seven and they retreated."

"Then where is this ship now?" Aktip swivels from the holo to me. "It is surely valuable and symbolic? Would this Blood Empire not return if they knew the ship was no longer in use?"

"You got me. I don't know. It was supposed to have been destroyed in the last great Sector battle. Then the Sector fell apart, and it's still in disarray." I stare at the image for a while before switching it back to an external view, and I linger on the sparse starfield in front of us. "But Sloper has wind of it." I correct myself. "More than that. He gave me the exact hypercoordinates."

I look at my crewmates and shrug. "I have no idea how he got them."

"He paid for them," blurts Jordi, then, realizing what he had just admitted, reddens. He looks at me meekly. "Oops."

"Your gambling debt was with Sloper? You knew he was on Rykkamon and you know I would go after him, yet you kept it from me. What kind of friend are you, Jordi?" I stare at him, feeling my temperature rising, and pushing it back down. Jordi has his faults, but this is going too far.

He holds up a laserpistol. "Good job he gave me some firepower, eh? Your friend helped get you out of a tight spot with these."

I seethe at him. "I'm tempted to eject you into space right now." I push up and fly past him to retrieve the holocube I threw. I tap the sides and flick the image across to the hull's screen. I'm pretty sure there is only one reason Sloper put the cube in my cabin. "I told you Darpesh took out the Chief's gang. But I didn't tell you he posed as me. Now tell me if you can work out why we needed the pistols." I press play.

I'm proved right as the video shows the ambush on the Rykkan outlaw camp. I see Aktip's discomfort next to me and switch it off.

Jordi's face is white. "I ... I—"

"Stow it for later. For now, you owe me. Big time."

For once Jordi says nothing.

Aktip's face is unreadable. "Why did this man do this?"

"Because he wants the Constellation."

Aktip looks at me, confused. "Why did you agree?"

"Yeah, why does Sloper think you can do what nobody else has been able to do?" Jordi says.

"Did you forget?" I tap the holocube again and the video resumes. It's the same imagery Sloper showed me before, and just as difficult to watch the second time around. I feel my eyes moisten as I look at my brother, reduced to tears himself, near-naked and bloody in Sloper's cage.

I look at Jordi. "Do you think I had any choice?"

The video finishes and we sit in silence. Eventually it is Aktip who breaks the spell. "Then we must find this battlecruiser and bring it to Sloper as requested. He will then return your brother."

"If only it were that simple. Space pirate gossip has it that many salvage crews supposedly located the Constellation, and not a single one has returned. Even the fact that Sloper has given us coordinates means nothing. Most spacers say if it is still in existence, it's a ghost ship, hunting for new victims."

"What garbage. Surely you don't believe that?" Jordi recovers his composure. "A ghost ship? Nup." He scratches his head. "But what does Sloper want? He'll have the entire Sector out for his blood if he really has found it." He frowns at me. "Will you really give it to him?"

"There's more to it than meets the eye," I admit. "At this point I'm not able to make a decision. We have no choice but to go to the coordinates given." I look at my two crewmates, lost for words. What if Sloper lied? Just to get rid of me? Am I about to take my friends (which is debatable in Jordi's case) to their death?

Then I think of my brother and what he would do in my position.

"Boot up the hyperDrive, Jordi. There's only one way we'll ever find out the truth."

CHAPTER SIXTEEN

WE EMERGE FROM HYPERSPACE INTO what should have been empty territory, devoid of any nearby planetary systems, and immediately the proximity alarm shrieks. I shut the salvage cruiser's alarm down as I've already read the holo-warning:

LARGE MASS, METALLIC-ORIGIN IN CLOSE PROXIMITY. RISK OF COLLISION.

We are not at risk. I have halted our motion, and engaged the ship's cloaking function.

I flick on the cabin's holoscreen to panoramic mode and zoom in.

However many credits Sloper had paid for these coordinates, it was worth it.

There before us, drifting in space in all its glory, floats the massive hulk of the Constellation. Sloper hadn't lied. The nagging doubt that he had invented this entire scenario simply to dispose of me vanishes, replaced by an icy tingle up and down my spine.

I turn to Aktip, sitting in the navigator's chair beside me. As a skilled comms engineer, she offered to man the navigation and general communication. I was grateful for any help. Especially if it came with undying loyalty, unlike Jordi, who only seems to know how to look after himself.

The squat alien's brow protuberance rises, and her eyes pulse at me. "You have indecision." It is not a question.

I glance at the holoscreen, then turn around to Jordi, who sits behind me. He is glued to the screen, his mouth slightly open. He shakes his head to clear it and focuses on me. "It's massive."

I nod. "We'd better be cautious. Anything tries to attack, we can only run away." Silently I curse Sloper's insistence on a salvage cruiser with no weapons. I guess that means he's still scared of me.

Aktip speaks. "No other salvage vessel has returned from a search for the Constellation." The Rykkans have a tendency to state the obvious, often when you least need to hear it. But Aktip is right to remind us. Not only are we unarmed; history suggests we have a 100% chance of not surviving.

"Aktip, how far do your senses extend?" I ask.

"Your question is considered taboo on Rykkamon. But since we are in special situation, I answer—"

"Bit like asking a guy how long his di—"

I turn around and swat Jordi's grinning face to shut him up. "Go on, Aktip."

The alien lifts one clawed hand—the Rykkan equivalent of assent. "In clean space such as this; perhaps 500 meters. Possible it is 600."

I grimace. Not far enough. "Let's circle and take readings. Jordi, you're on standby for an instant jump. At anyone's call."

I urge the ship forward gently using only impulse power. To any observer, we'd be an unidentifiable dark mass, moving silently through space.

We circle the giant battlecruiser, like a small moon orbiting a planet. The vessel rotates majestically below us, so I match its motion first, then gradually speed up.

"No electromagnetic radiation." Aktip states flatly.

Unusual. An abandoned ship will usually have some chatter. Then again, the Constellation was—is—no ordinary vessel. Lit only by our ship's spotlights traversing the huge ship's structure, the Constellation is intimidating even when powered down. Turrets bristle at regular intervals; laser-ports pepper the matt-sheened plasma-resistant surface, and numbered locks big enough to swallow ten of my own ship sweep past our viewports with clock-like frequency.

Whoever commanded this oversized warship could probably take on an entire planet.

Jordi taps me on the shoulder and points to the edge of the holoscreen.

I realign our ship to where he is pointing, and we all fall silent. I reduce our propulsion, and we slow down to approach one end of the giant ship. There is a massive gaping black hole at the stern—one we hadn't spotted, since we'd arrived at the blunt bow.

"This is ship power units?" Aktip looks at me and smooths her wide lips back with her large, flat tongue. That's one nervous Rykkan.

"Was the ship's power unit; singular," I correct. "Except by the look of those cuts, this power unit wasn't destroyed by firepower or an explosive device." I look from Aktip to Jordi, whose expression of curiosity has changed to a battle-hardened visage. He meets my eyes and waits for me to finish. I continue. "The Constellation's engines have been surgically removed."

"Who can do such a thing?" Aktip asks.

I pan the holoscreen across the chasm, picking out the precise lines where hundreds of meters of war-grade, plasma-resistant hull alloy has been sliced through. "If we knew that, then we might have an idea why no other salvage vessel has returned."

But Aktip is acting strangely. Her head is jiggling. She gives me what I assume is an intense look. "Ma'am, we must leave immediately—"

I am already reaching for the controls to reposition the ship when a swarm of fiery-red projectiles streak toward us from deep inside the battlecruiser's exposed interior.

We are sent scrambling into action.

"Jordi, hyperDrive. NOW!" I hit full-speed reverse, hoping the fDrive on this ship has more thrust than the missiles bearing down on us. The acceleration throws us all forward against our harnesses and we watch the cruiser's image dwindle to a speck on our screens.

But the missiles are outpacing us.

"Jordi?" With difficulty I twist around to see Jordi slumped forward against his belt. The idiot has left his harness loose, and he's passed out when the upper strap has caught his airway. I turn back against the high-grav thrust and try to reach with an impossibly leaden arm over to the hyperDrive module, but Aktip is too quick for me. Her Rykkan body is unaffected by the thrust and she is out of her harness and has climbed behind me. She grabs my hand and pulls me forward. I hit the hyperDrive command, hoping that Jordi's preset is programmed.

We jump into hyperspace, and for all intents and purposes vanish from normal reality. I pass out.

When I come to, Jordi is in front of me and has me by both shoulders. He peers at me.

"Damage report?" I manage to whisper.

He shrugs. "I'm okay. I just couldn't breathe for a while."

I push him away and rise up. "Not you, you idiot," I say through gritted teeth, "the ship."

"The ship is functioning at 100%, Madam Captain," Aktip says, thumbing her non-clawed finger at the helm functions. She stops and swivels her head toward me—an aspect of Rykkan physiology I still find unnerving. "One crew member reports a possible broken nose."

"And one crew member is still risking one." I glare at Jordi.

"What were you thinking—"

He waves my comment away. "Let it go, Indy. We escaped, thanks to Aktip. I'm sorry. I was caught short. No electromagnetic broadcast; no signs of life—who would have predicted a plasma attack?"

Jordi is right. I smile weakly at Aktip. "Thanks. Without your high-grav conditioning we'd be galactic gas."

Aktip inclines her squat head and raises a hand. "Thank you, Madam. Shall I complete the damage report?" I nod. The Rykkan continues. "My sensors did not register any lifeform ..." She scratches what passes for a nose.

I raise my eyebrows. "Do go on." I think I'm about to find out why the alien was able to give me a warning when my ship couldn't.

"It is embarrassing in our culture to be boastful, Madam Captain. I provided false information earlier. I can sense up to 3000 meters if there is no obstruction. I confirm there are no lifeforms on that ship. The attack was 100% automated, which is why at first I did not understand."

"Understand what?"

"There are no lifeforms ... but there are. I take sense of something I have never sensed before. Just before I recommend we must leave. Sorry, Madam Captain. I am failing my debt obligations."

"Hardly, Aktip. We're still here, thanks to your early warning, as well as your strength. I'd say your obligations are more than being met. But that would explain why no other salvage ships have come back. None of them would have had a Rykkan's long-range senses on hand to save them. They'd have assumed that no power equals no threat. But why didn't we register any EM radiation? There must be something activating those plasma launchers."

Aktip shrugs, one of her more humanlike gestures. "I cannot provide the answer, Madam. So sorry." Her head swivels back to the controls.

"Why don't we send in a drone?" Jordi sounds hesitant. Better a dented ego than an overambitious Jordi, I think. I decide to flatter him.

"Smart thinking." I run some rough calculations in my head. "Let's jump back in to one klick out from the Constellation, and send in two drones; one after the other."

Jordi furrows his brow. "Huh? Why two?"

Aktip swivels back. "Madam has superior tactical intelligence. She plans to sacrifice the first drone. The second will be cloaked and carry an emergency salvage power unit."

I laugh. The Rykkan's sensing capability at close range is almost like mind reading. "Exactly. Let's put a spy in there. I plan not only to come back from this mission, but with the Constellation in tow."

Jordi lets out a low whistle.

CHAPTER SEVENTEEN

I RETURN TO THE HELM after personally preparing the drones. Our ship might not be armed, but I don't plan to damage my rep. So far, India Jackson has delivered on all her missions. Both legal and illegal—maybe that was why Sloper chose me. A vision of Mitch writhing in agony flashes into my head. I'd pushed my brother's plight out of my mind, but for him to survive, I have no other choice except to bring the Constellation to Sloper.

"You must leave brother-worry in hyperspace," Aktip says quietly.

I take a deep breath and focus on the helm panel. "Let's do it." I swipe my finger and we hyperjump. No proximity alarm this time, and now the Constellation shows on the holoscreen as a small, computer-labeled object.

"Launching both drones," I say, and hold my breath. The screen tracks them both, one invisible to the Constellation, the other metaphorically waving its hands and exclaiming, "Shoot me, shoot me."

"Hang on," Jordi says, frowning. "Our own ship was cloaked before, but whoever shot at us still knew we were there."

I smirk. "You forget I have"—I make quotation gestures with my fingers—"'superior tactical intelligence.' It's not whoever, but whatever. That attack was automated. To the Constellation, we are a large, slow-moving mass showing traces of power. In other words, something to shoot at. But they can't program it to auto-fire at any small unpowered object, or they'd be waving a flag to anyone watching. A small asteroid is of no consequence."

"But—"

"Just watch."

I fix my attention on the screen as the two drones approach the massive man-made wound in the battlecruiser's stern. As predicted, more plasma missiles launch from the bowels of the ruined ship's engine bay, and Drone One vanishes in a ball of fire. Drone Two sails down into the hole.

"How?—"

"Magnets," I reply. "Old science. They wouldn't have planned for that. I had Drone Two under power until it was close to the ship, then cut all systems. I left it magnetically locked onto Drone One at a short distance"—I flash a look at Aktip—"using old school solid, plasticized magnets. Aktip knew about them from her days at the spaceport and reminded me. All salvage vessels carry supersized magnets for retrieving iron and steel from flammable environments. When Drone One was destroyed—"

"Drone Two lost the attraction to Drone One and instead directed itself to the nearest large semi-ferrous object."

I clap my hand on Jordi's shoulder. "You do have a brain in more than one member after all."

He smiles, then screws up his face. "Then why aren't the missiles firing on Drone Two?"

I sigh. "Belay that last compliment. One, Drone Two is not under power, ergo the footprint is inert, and two"—I shoot Jordi a look of despair—"why would they fire plasma missiles inside their own ship?"

Jordi's face falls. I continue. "Aktip, take us a little closer and boot up that drone to battery power. Let's plug it into the Constellation's network." I whip around to Jordi. "Before you ask, Drone Two is running several of my blackest-hat hacker routines. I plan to out whoever programmed those attacks."

Aktip switches the holoscreen to split view. The left panel now shows the derelict battlecruiser slowly coming closer into view. On the right, using the drone's low-power infrared for vision, we are descending—or ascending, who knows—through the rear decks of the massive freighter's engine bay. I notice the razor-clean cuts across supposedly impenetrable structures; the neatly sealed conduits and pipes ... and the complete lack of human or alien remains.

This was no fight scene.

"You are experiencing a realization, Madam Captain," Aktip states.

And then some, I think. Someone has undertaken the seemingly impossible task of removing the starship's main power unit—bigger than twenty of my salvage cruisers put together—with some kind of oversized cutting beam.

The drone enters a small passageway—now cut open to space—and winds its way through a labyrinth of interconnecting bulkheads, descending several decks until it stops in front of a complex control panel attached to a bulkhead.

"How did it know where to go if there is no EM leakage?" Jordi whispers.

I reply at normal volume, and he jumps. "No need to whisper, there's no one on deck to hear us." I point to the right screen. "That's a remote control panel. In theory, only the ship's captain and authorized officers can operate it."

Or hackers, I think. I tap a button on the helmpad next to me, and the left-hand screen changes to show a schematic.

Jordi sucks in a breath. "You had a blueprint?"

"Schematic, strictly speaking. Yes. For a couple of years now." Not that I'll tell him where I got it. "I traded a cargo of laserwhips for it on a whim. I was never completely sure it was authentic, but remember when I said I asked Sloper to provide a specific description of the Constellation? He may have thought I only needed to know for visual confirmation." I look at Jordi squarely. "But even his limited information was enough for me to confirm that this file is the real deal."

I flip the view back to the ship. I sense Aktip fidgeting beside me.

"You lied to Sloper, Madam Captain." Again, this is not a question. "How are you managing this?"

I give Aktip a wry smile. "Sloper isn't a Rykkan, Aktip. Lying comes easily to humans. As your friends were quick to point out."

I turn my attention back to the drone, waiting for its next command. I'm running it on low-grade battery power so as not to attract any more automated attention, but this next step will need all my skills: I must fire up the drone's fusion-power; connect to the remote system; hack the ship security controls on a galactic-grade battleship; disable the bizarre auto-defense system; boot up the ship's network using the drone's salvage fDrive power unit, and—

There is no "and." Before I can do anything else, I need information.

"Wish me luck," I mutter under my breath.

Aktip's loud reply startles me at first, then helps me relax. "Madam Captain, luck is an unnecessary emotional condition and will lower your superior tactical intelligence by introducing illogical variables." Shorthand for, "Indy, concentrate on the task at hand."

I do just that and the helm room goes silent.

Using both hands, and with my throat-mike in place, I ready myself.

"Drone Two, acknowledge your Captain." A text appears on the right-hand screen. CAPTAIN AT THE CONTROLS.

I tap the drone's power button on the helmpad at the same time as ordering the drone to connect to the remote control panel. "Engage security override. Run helper-sequence A and report." I hold my breath.

The remote control panel we see in the left split screen bursts into life. At the bottom of the screen I can barely make out the drone's telescopic arm connected to the panel, now injecting my code into a secure battlecruiser's command system.

Text appears on the right-hand screen. CONSTELLATION BASE SYSTEM READY TO BOOT.

Phase one completed. I hover my finger over the helmpad and look at Jordi, who I notice has a sheen of sweat on his brow. He nods. I tap the bootup icon now appearing on my helmpad.

Our ship shudders, the drone's remote image shifts violently; spins and flickers, then goes dark. A piercing klaxon erupts and we are all forced to clamp our hands over our ears.

I quickly let go one hand to slam my ship's "all mute" button, and we plummet into silence. My ears ring. Aktip yells at me, her sensitive ears still in recovery. "MADAM CAPTAIN—THE SCREEN."

I have been momentarily distracted by the noise and I look back up at the holo. The entire screen now displays one single warning.

YOUR SHIP'S SYSTEM HAS BEEN COMMANDEERED. UNAUTHORIZED AND ILLEGAL ACCESS REJECTED. FULL AUTHORITY IS REQUIRED TO REVERSE YOUR SHIP'S DESTRUCT SEQUENCE. PLEASE ENTER DNA AND VOICE PRINT OF AUTHORIZED CONSTELLATION PERSONNEL IMMEDIATELY.

I punch commands into the helmpad, but it's no use. I'm locked out of the flight controls. "Crap. Aktip, any ideas?" I look at the alien, whose head is rapidly swiveling from side to side.

"Sorry, Madam Captain. I have insufficient tactical capability."

"Jordi?"

He stares at me and throws his hands in the air.

The screen changes to a countdown message: ATMOSPHERE VENTING OCCURRING IN 120 SECONDS.

The cabin lights turn red and the large 120 flips to 119. Then 118 ... 117.

"I thought they were going to auto-destruct the ship?" Jordi says.

I shrug. "Death by asphyxiation or death by explosion. It's all the same to me."

"Can't you hack in?" Jordi looks desperate.

"I already tried that with the drone." But he was right. No sense sitting back and doing nothing for ... 109 seconds.

I swipe my holopad into life; gesture for the ship's controls, and request admin-access. ADMIN ACCESS DENIED, flashes the holo. PLEASE ENTER DNA AND VOICEPRINT CREDENTIALS.

Images of Papa and a bloodied Mitch swim in my head. The heat rises in my face. "I will not die like this!" I scream at the top of my voice. Aktip winces and swivels her head back and forth rapidly. In fury, I slap my hand on the helmpad.

A red outline of my hand appears on the helmpad where I slapped it, briefly pulsates, stops and switches to green. The cabin lights also turn green, the holoscreen changes to bright white and a text message appears.

<<**DNA authentication and voice ID confirmed**>>

What the—?

A soothing voice issues from the now un-muted comms system:

"*DNA and voice print authorization confirmed. Full access*

granted. Captain India Jackson has the Constellation's helm."

"What the ...?" My mouth drops open.

"CAPTAIN India Jackson?" Jordi stares at me. "Captain of the Sector's most revered battlecruiser? Indy, is there something you're not telling us?"

I shake my head slowly. "I've never stepped foot on it."

"She speaks true," Aktip says.

I bark out a laugh. "Never truer." I sit back in the helmchair, put my hands behind my head, and try to piece together the unsolvable.

CHAPTER EIGHTEEN

My mind is reeling. I hear Aktip and Jordi arguing, but their words do not register.

How can I be the captain of a long-lost secret battlecruiser? The most sought-after mystery and the sole reason for the defeat of the Blood Empire's attack. I allow the zero-gee to float me back into my captain's chair and try to sort out my thoughts.

I hear my name. "Indy?" It is Jordi. I turn to him and stare blankly.

"Madam Captain?" Aktip peers at me. "You have distress."

I shake my head. I have to stay focused. "Not so much distress as disbelief."

"How can you be the captain of this ship?" Aktip asks.

"I have no idea. But the more I think about it, the more ludicrous it seems. Impossible actually." I shrug. My thoughts are finally starting to form. "We'll need to be cautious. Who's to say this is not just another trap. Maybe all the salvage crews had their ships hacked. Maybe they were all given supposed 'authorized status' and it's just more bait to lure us. Give us a false sense of security."

Jordi frowns. "Strange way to do it."

I look at him. "The Constellation is supposed to be capable of extreme battle tactics. Maybe this is its auto-protection in play. Artificial intelligence?"

He shakes his head. "I don't buy it. But there's one way to test."

I raise an eyebrow.

"Login and ask for a report of previous boarding or salvage attempts and current defense status. If you're its authorized captain, it should be an open book."

I take Jordi's suggestion and slap my hand onto the helmpad. "Constellation, this is Captain Jackson." The pad glows green.

<<**Affirmative. Captain Jackson at the helm.**>>

"Report previous boarding attempts. Summary list on screen."

The holoscreen changes to a black background, and green lines of text appear. The list of vessels—some names, some with "unknown" tagged against the list scrolls for several pages until I order it to stop.

"Report defense status."

<<**Defenses currently disabled.**>>

I lift my hand off the pad to logout and look at Jordi. "Could still be a trap."

Jordi gives me a lopsided smile. "So do you plan to sit here all day and debate whether or not the Constellation's syscom is lying? One way or another, we have what Sloper wants. He gets his ship, and it comes with a free captain. Doesn't matter if it's true or not, does it? Seems convincing enough to me."

As Jordi speaks it dawns on me that I can't allow Sloper to possess the Constellation. Maybe I shouldn't have taken on the job, even with my brother's capture. Then again, Sloper will eventually find someone to do his dirty work. He probably has a long list of debts he can call in. Other people with families he can beat and torture. I take a deep breath.

"You have sadness." Aktip states.

I give her a resigned smile. "I'm stuck, Aktip. I can't take the Constellation to Sloper, whether I'm the true captain or not. It's not the wreck I thought it would be, even if Sloper's coordinates worked. Whoever has the Constellation is in a powerful position. Sloper is almost the last person in the galaxy who should be granted such power."

"And you're the best choice?" Jordi mocks me.

I scowl at him. "I'm here, and I'm not going to let this get into the hands of a power-hungry crook."

Jordi holds out his hands. "So what's the plan, then? Sloper won't give up Mitch unless you return with the Constellation, and you're intent on being the Constellation's first rogue captain."

Mitch.

I tap my fingers on the arm of the chair and try to calm my thoughts. What would Papa do?

I slap my hand on the pad again. "Constellation. Report power status."

<<**Standby power available for ship's systems only. All other sources non-responsive.**>>

"Run standby power and boot up all systems with full health check. Report status on completion."

<<**Affirmative, Captain.**>>

The green pad switches to an orange and green rippling wave.

I look at Aktip and Jordi. "The Constellation isn't going anywhere. Sloper will expect me to return with something, but what I need is an fDrive to run the ship somewhere. I have no physical way to fly the ship." I tap a button on the commPanel. "Danielli, report to the helm."

"*Affirmative, Ma'am.*"

Jordi raises his brow.

"We're going to review our position and follow a plan."

"A plan? Whose plan?" he says.

I smile. "Mine."

CHAPTER NINETEEN

DANIELLI JOINS US AND WE gather around the helm's small fixed table.

"Here's where we're at. We've found the Constellation"—I see Danielli's eyebrows lift, but I keep moving—"however it has no propulsion, only standby power available. The good news is that it's not a wreck. If anyone finds out we've located the galaxy's most powerful battlecruiser, which is possibly still functioning, we'll have every pirate in the Sector jumping into hyperDrive looking for the coordinates. However, we appear to have control of the cruiser's syscom." I turn to Danielli, hold his gaze while I place my hand on the still-rippling pad. I wait.

<<**Captain Jackson logged in.**>>

Danielli reacts with a brief flicker of surprise, smiles briefly and gives me a nod.

I continue. "So we have a quandary. If the Constellation can be made to run, it's still potentially a powerful weapon in the wrong hands. Sloper is definitely the wrong person. But if the Circle of Seven discover its existence, we might accidentally trigger a fresh Sector War."

"Why is this?" Aktip says.

It's Danielli who answers. "Oberon was defeated by the Constellation in the last war. If he knew the ship was still in existence, he'd want to gain control of it."

"To destroy it," I add.

Danielli looks at me. "Or force its Captain to work for him."

I hadn't thought of that.

"Then what do we do with it?" Jordi says.

I give him a cool smile. "We won't be doing anything with it. You will go back to Sloper to cut a deal."

"What?" Jordi forgets he is in zero-gee and tries to stand up, but instead shoots up to the hull's overhead bulkhead, where he grabs a rail. "You can't be serious!"

I level up at him. "Was I mistaken in thinking that you owed me one? Time to pay up. You can use the escape hyperpod to return to Rykkamon's orbit. Find Sloper—"

"How the hell will I know where he is?" Jordi is fuming.

I stare at him for a moment before continuing. "You had no problem finding him before, when I didn't even know he was on the planet. It's your problem, anyway. I have a battlecruiser to command, or did you forget?"

"Yeah, with all your vast experience—ouch!"

Danielli grabs Jordi's ankles and yanks him back to the table. "*Captain* Jackson is issuing an order. Failure to follow a Captain's orders is both mutiny and treason under Sector legislation."

Jordi glares at him, then turns back to me. "Suppose I find him, without being picked up by the Rykkans. Then what do I tell him?"

"You tell him to wait for a hyper-relay message. Tell him we have the Constellation and I will meet him to agree an exchange in return for my brother."

"But where are you going?" Jordi creases his brow.

I lean forward. "Now why on earth do you think I'd tell *you* that?"

Jordi looks around, agitated. "What do I offer him? To use your words, what deal am I supposed to cut?"

"The Constellation has an impressive reputation for experimental weaponry. Make something up." I laugh. "You've always said you can talk your way in and out of anything. Time to live up to the talk. Get suited up and into the pod."

He gives me a filthy look and heads back to get ready. I look at Danielli and Aktip. "We need to investigate the Constellation. In person. Something doesn't smell right. Maybe we can find out why its drive is missing, and why it was abandoned."

Danielli lifts his chin. "If I may speak, Ma'am?"

I gesture for him to go ahead.

"You were pretty rough on the kid. Seems like no reason for it, and we might need all the help we can get. Aren't you risking unwanted attention from Sloper?"

Jordi's voice issues from the commPanel. "*Escape Capsule One ready for escape launch.*" His voice is sharp through the comms.

I chin my mike. "Copy that, Capsule One. Jordi?" I wait for his acknowledgment, which comes in the form of a grunt. "If any of your actions cause any harm to my brother, I will hunt you down. Prepare for launch in 3, 2 ...1, launch." I hear the hiss as the capsule detaches. The limited hyperDrive will take Jordi a few hops to reach Rykkamon. Maybe up to a full Earth day.

Before I can resume our conversation, Aktip swivels her head to me. "You are suspicious of Jordi."

I nod. "But I might be wrong." I look at Danielli. "Does that answer your question? Either way, my plan will still work."

"What is your plan, Ma'am?" Danielli waits.

I grin at him. "I don't have one. But I've just bought us some time to work it out."

CHAPTER TWENTY

I LEAVE AKTIP AT THE helm comms, along with a private message, and tell Danielli to take me to his team. I might have *his* loyalty, but when you've been on the wrong side of legal as long as I have, you get to know that winning over each member of your gang could mean the difference between life and death.

We float along the passageway to the mess. "I didn't have time to ask. Was anyone injured in our defensive reverse from the missiles?"

Danielli pulls himself along the rails with the practiced ease of a zero-gee fighter. "One bruised nose, Ma'am. As requested, we were strapped in and awaiting orders post-jump. With all due respect, Ma'am, they don't need me to tell them basic spacedust."

I raise an eyebrow. "Then what caused the incident with the nose?"

"An unsecured panel, Ma'am. The ship is not in prime condition."

"I guess your team aren't invincible then."

"Permission to speak freely, Ma'am."

"Again? Permission granted. Indefinitely under my command, Danielli."

He looks uncomfortable. "My crew are well trained, Ma'am. There's no need for you to—"

I hold up my hand. I know what Danielli's inferring, so I call him on it. "You don't think I should be telling them how to do their jobs?"

He stops and turns back to face me. "No, Ma'am. If you want me and my crew to back you, let us work our own playbook."

I break out into a smile. "I fully intend to, Danielli. But first, I want them to know they can trust me, too."

The wiry sergeant sums me up for a few moments, then turns back down the passageway.

The crew are not in the mess, but in their quarters, already in space gear and checking each other's equipment. They turn almost as one when Danielli enters, and in one flourish, they simultaneously salute him. "Ready for combat, sir," they say. In unison.

"Stand down," Danielli says. He introduces me to all four, and I note the looks of curiosity, especially at my height. As far as I can see, none appear to harbor any resentment. I hope Danielli is right when he told me they voted as one.

"Captain India Jackson." I glance at each of them, holding a smile and brief eye contact. "I wanted to meet each of you in person and make you an offer." I see Danielli look sideways at me, surprised, then resume his poker-face. He leans against the nearest bulkhead.

I continue. "From what I can understand, we are possibly the hottest property in the galaxy, if only they knew it. We've just found the Constellation."

I wait for the looks of surprise to fade before I continue.

"We're simultaneously sitting on a bomb; a 3He-power goldmine; a weapon sufficiently powerful to bring the Blood Empire to its knees ... and levels of danger unknown to me and potentially inestimable. I understand you are paid soldiers. If anyone is unwilling to continue, then you'll be sent on your way in the next Escape Capsule. Once I have funds, I'll pay out your job quote two-fold as promised, no questions asked." I wait for a response. There is none. "Does anyone wish to take this option?"

I watch Danielli. He does not shift, nor does he look at his team of men. And one woman, I now realize. Jordi was right. Short black hair and a pixie-face, with what looks like a lithe body under that space gear. No wonder he wanted to "assist" her. She catches me assessing her and speaks in a low drawl.

"With respect, Captain Jackson, we haven't been advised of the alternative."

Danielli was right. They do know how to take care of themselves.

"What's your name, uh ..." I look at Danielli.

"'Soldier.' We all respond to that." Danielli has the slightest hint of a smile on his face. He's waiting to see how I handle this. I incline my head.

"Thanks." I turn back to the woman, who is actually grinning at me. "Your name, soldier?"

"Plexi, Captain." she says.

"No family name?"

Her grin vanishes. "No family, Ma'am."

Jeepers. I shift my mass to one side. "Apologies, Plexi."

I clear my throat and look at all of them. "You asked about the alternative? Before I present you my offer, you need a little background." I tell them of the Constellation and my apparent status as its presumed captain. I explain my quandary, and Sloper's treatment of the Rykkans ... and of my brother. Then I ask Aktip via the commPanel to run a holo showing our recent survey of the Constellation, including the missile attack.

I pause to let it all sink in.

"My plan is to investigate the battlecruiser in person, gain control and work out how in hell we can hide a moon-sized cruiser while I establish who to return it to." I take a deep breath. "I'm not certain that this isn't still just a trap. Anyone with me will be risking their life. But here's my offer: All my life I've traded

He and weaponry. Whatever happens, I know I'm possibly the best person in the Sector to get a seriously good deal for giving up the Constellation. Well into trillions of credits, maybe a quad. Whatever I get, I'm willing to share equally among every man, woman and Rykkan on this ship." I mention nothing about needing help to rescue Mitch. No point introducing another complication this early into the relationship.

The soldiers grin and look at each other. Still no one speaks. Plexi coughs. I raise my eyes at her.

"Captain Jackson, you said our galaxy is doomed if the Constellation falls into the wrong hands. What if the person with the wrong hands turns out to be the highest bidder?"

My ploy is burst. Plexi is right. The Constellation is not for sale at any price—to the wrong buyer. I try to recover.

"Um, yes. Good question. I would try to find another way to reimburse you, because under those circumstances, the Constellation is not—"

Plexi interrupts. "Ma'am, we're used to hearing false promises. Be very careful what you say, and what you expect to deliver."

I smile. Plexi has me cornered in exactly the same way I would if I were her. I straighten and stand tall to address everyone, not just my pixie-faced interrogator.

"You are right. The Constellation is not a tool for someone to play power games in the Sector. We've already suffered enough since the last war ended, and I will not allow it to be used merely as a ship for profit or power. I will stake my life on it. Some things are more important than money."

I look Plexi in the eye. "Does that answer your question?"

"Captain, I'm pretty sure I speak for my squad when I say we are with you all the way." I hear an "Aye, Captain," from all the others, including Danielli.

The woman launches forward with precision and arrives in front of me, holding out her hand. "Corporal Plexi at your service, Ma'am."

"*They speak true, Madam Captain,*" I hear Aktip say in my private commchannel.

CHAPTER TWENTY-ONE

I REMEMBER THAT TWO OF Danielli's squad have pilot training, so I leave one of them—Ortiz, the one with the bloodied nose and still suffering embarrassment—at the helm, along with Aktip on comms. I have my remote datapad with me in case I need to access my ship, but not because I don't trust Ortiz—or Aktip for that matter.

Danielli, Plexi, a really big guy called Herg, and I, each take a podPlate after suiting up. Although we could spacewalk by cable over to the Constellation, I figure the podPlates will give us way more mobility, given the size of the battlecruiser.

I step up on my plate and grab the control bars. "Ready?" I say over the commchannel as I look at the others. They nod, and we propel ourselves out of the airlock and across open space to the Constellation.

I almost lose control of my plate as I see the cruiser through my helmet's faceplate with naked vision for the first time. If I wasn't physically seeing it for myself, I would think its vastness incomprehensible.

"You wanna go in through the drive region?" It's Plexi, who has scooted up next to me. To those left in the salvage vessel, we must look like a row of four ants sliding on microcards across a puddle of black ink, up against the looming bulk of the giant we're about to board. I sense the tension in my stomach, and focus on my breath instead.

"Captain?"

"Yes. But before we head all the way in, I'll login again from a physical commPanel. Just to be sure."

We "land" at the edge of the enormous open-cut wound at the Constellation's stern. Our magboots clamp us to the ship's exterior and we leave our podPlates floating just above the hull. I've deliberately touched down a few meters from the edge of the immense man-made incision, where my schematic shows a commPanel. I spy it and head over.

"Wait—"

It's Danielli.

"Let me lead. Just in case."

I motion him past me and he approaches the panel. He signals the all clear, and protects me as I kneel. I wear a commglove, enabling fingerprint recognition—even DNA if requested, but it isn't. The panel flashes green a few times, then solid. I hear a voice in my ear.

<<**Captain Jackson present on exterior mission.**>>

So far, so good.

"Disable local security. Four crew members returning to the ship, including Captain Jackson."

<<**Request identification of additional crew members.**>>

"Voice recog requested."

<<**Affirmative.**>>

One by one my team identify themselves by speaking into the panel. The panel flickers.

<<**Confirmed recognition and identification. Captain Jackson to authorize override of criminal records of Private Herg and Corporal Wilcox required for access to the interior.**>>

I look at Danielli.

"Wilcox was my family name." It's Plexi. Her voice is strained.

Danielli speaks up. "Captain—"

I wave him away. "It's okay. You should see *my* record."

I see him shrug in the bulk of his suit, and I turn back to the panel, though I'm not entirely sure why I'm looking at it. The ship's computer can communicate perfectly well through my headset. "Authorization for override confirmed."

<<**Affirmative. Access granted.**>>

I look at the others, the massive hull with its frequent clusters of weaponry extending behind them, silent and deadly, glinting gray-black against a sparsely starred backdrop.

I move to step back on top of my podPlate, but again Danielli holds me back. "We should go in first, Captain." I nod and Danielli, Plexi and Herg position their podPlates in front of mine. Once I'm aboard, we all descend the blackness in silence, our headbeams sweeping from side to side as the black closes in over us.

"We'll follow the drone's path. It's on your schematic." I say, watching the others in front pausing at every opening, one on watch, one sweeping light into the unoccupied rabbit warrens, and the other covering us all. We all have laserRifles, but I wish I had more. Cannons preferably.

Our descent through the gloom is slow, but uneventful. Again I notice the lack of any evidence of a firefight: no charred walls, no old, bloodied stains. No debris or abandoned weaponry, let alone decomposed bodies—or perfectly preserved bodies in the freezing vacuum.

The scale of the ship alone is intimidating. The hole cut in the drive bay is as deep as a tall skyscraper, and as dark as the blackest mine. I stop to engage a commPanel and ask the ship to turn on the lights.

<<**Emergency lighting already active. Main lighting unresponsive. Power reserves critical.**>>

I see no emergency lighting until we arrive at the mouth of the passageway the drone entered. There is a faint light strip on either side of the deck. Or is it the overhead? It's not until I see lettering on the passageway's bulkhead that I realize it is the deck. The lettering says C126-A.

"Do you wish to proceed, Ma'am?" Danielli asks over the comms.

Despite my growing unease, I know we must get into the ship proper; find the helmroom and try to work out what we can—or can't—do. Though my nose so far tells me it doesn't matter where we go, the outcome will be the same. This is a ghost ship, and it's going nowhere. "Head in, Danielli. Let's find the drone first. Stop when we reach it."

I float up next to the sergeant and together we swoop down into the eerie passageway side-by-side on our plates. Plexi and Herg follow.

"Any thoughts so far, Danielli?" I ask.

He continues forward next to me, stopping from time-to-time at any airlock or door, ever watchful. He answers without looking at me. "No plasma missiles. Maybe we're too small to trigger them."

"Or maybe whoever fired them is waiting somewhere else?" I think I hear him shrug.

"We'd pick up the energy traces. No, my guess is that your Captain's status has shut down any autodefense."

"But?"

He stops in front of an open door, pushes it open with one hand while pointing the rifle in with the other. "There are never any buts, Ma'am. Only vigilance. Just because one threat has gone away, it doesn't mean there isn't another round the corner. But it does seem strange. There's no sign of any—"

"Life. Or that there once was life here," I say.

Danielli says nothing and beckons me on. We descend the ladder to the next deck. I can't imagine the number of decks and ladders in a cruiser of this size. Then again, with full power running, I guess we'd all be using the gravtubes.

We drop a dozen more levels and Danielli stops again. He points up the passageway. "Drone should be up there."

"What's left of it."

The four of us advance more slowly now, though I'm not sure why. I feel like a kid, walking through a pitch black forest, expecting an ugly giant to burst from the trees at any minute.

The drone is split in two, burned out and lifeless, both parts skewed away from each other in mid-air where they had come to rest. Its extension arm drags on the deck.

There's no point in picking over the pieces, so I tell Danielli to move on. We enter a long, much wider passageway, with multiple doors on either side.

"Looks like flight crew assembly points," Danielli says. "We must be heading to one of the Constellation's hangars."

Plexi is looking at a schematic on her plate's pad. "Yeah, got it, right here."

Herg opens the bulkhead door at the end of the oversized passageway ... and we stop. We emerge into a massive hangar. The emergency lighting is barely enough to see that the space is huge.

And almost empty. We sweep our suit headbeams around. Nothing. Just one z-wing barely visible in the dark, laying in partial disassembly on the far side of the cavernous space. It's the first sign of anything left behind I've seen so far. I try to imagine what it must have been like in full battle. Hundreds of fighter craft of all descriptions; squads in formation; military organization. I can just make out the hangar's exit and oversized lock to my left.

Danielli looks over at me.

I shrug. "Nothing to see here. But I have a very bad feeling."

"You're not the only one," Plexi says. "But let's look on the bright side."

"What?" I say.

She grins at me through her faceplate. "I've found the armories on the schematic. Reckon we should go get us some bigger toys. Might help negate that bad feeling." She says negate with an accent: knee-gate.

I like Plexi.

"Lead the way."

CHAPTER TWENTY-TWO

A FEW MINUTES LATER, WE'RE in what I estimate is the middle of the ship. I wonder why the armories are here, and not in a more convenient spot. Danielli seems to sense my question. "My guess is the cruiser is designed to be impregnable. Looks like these armories can be sealed in. There are probably gravtubes to distribute to the hangars and turrets."

There seems to be a dozen or more doors to various weapons stores leading off the passageway. I peer through the viewport of Armory One. It is empty. Even in the dim emergency lighting, we can see it's stripped bare. I open the door, just in case, but a quick sweep over with our helmet beams reveals only exposed bulkheads and empty racking.

"Nothing to see here," Plexi says, turning to go, but I put my gloved hand on her arm.

"Don't you think that's odd? Why would there be absolutely nothing left?"

She stops, confused. "Yes, Ma'am. That's correct. In all the armories I've seen, even those cleaned out for restocking, there's always something left. Straps, old shells, empty battery casings. Plasti-crates. But you're right. This is different. Gives me the heebie-jeebies." She jerks her head to the exit. "Come on. Maybe we'll get lucky in number two."

And we do. Apart from the lone broken down z-wing, Armory Two is the first evidence I see of the Constellation's fitout. Plexi squeals when her headbeam reveals an entire bulkhead of racked weaponry. She rushes over and tries to remove a handheld plasmacannon from its fixture. The codepad next to it flashes red, and I hear a muted alarm, which quickly fades. The emergency power is clearly limited.

I float over and place my glove on the glowing pad. It turns green and Plexi rips the cannon from its rack. She looks at me, and I can see her eyes gleaming even through her faceplate. "Thanks, Captain." I leave Plexi to check the weapon over and move next to Danielli, who is pulling laserwhips out of a rack. Evidently their security doesn't require captain-level permissions.

I train my beam over the equipment. There's more than enough to equip our small group. "I wonder why this armory still has weapons?" It's more of a rhetorical question, but Danielli answers anyway.

"They may have left a small team onboard. Running the shutdown procedures. Maybe the same folks involved in removing the drive. Captain, we should try the helmroom. You might be able to access the ship's log directly."

I nod. I've had no luck with any remote requests, which was one of my motivations for boarding the hulk. But curiosity would have brought me here, anyway. What captain wouldn't want to inspect their vessel? Especially when it's the galaxy's baddest battlecruiser. "Let's kit ourselves with what we can carry to the max. We can come back for the rest later."

"I like the way you think, Ma'am." I hear the amusement in Danielli's voice pipe into my helmet.

"Plexi?"

"Yes, Captain?"

"Can you get us to the helmroom from here?"

"Sure thing, Ma'am. May we clear Armory Three first?"

What the heck. Probably empty anyway. "Sure thing. Head on in."

CHAPTER TWENTY-THREE

THE EMERGENCY LIGHTING IN ARMORY Three is out. Though it contradicts what we've seen up to now, perhaps after four years unattended, parts of the Constellation need minor maintenance.

I follow the others into the darkened store. "Danielli, can you light up—"

"*Captain Jackson.*" Aktip breaks into the comms. "*Captain Jackson. I am again sensing something odd and we are discovering electromagnetic traces from the center of the ship. Captain, do you copy?*"

"Copy that, Aktip—"

I have no time to finish as the room erupts in a flash of plasma fire from Herg. I drop to the ground with the others, grateful for magboots that keep me from floating up into the air.

I see Herg at the ready, laying on his stomach; boots and magbelt holding him to the deck. My headbeam reveals an inert body just ahead of him. Danielli holds a laserpistol in one hand, and with the other, motions us to push backwards on our bellies. Our podPlates are outside in the passageway.

We retreat, worming our way backward, wary of the silence and the dark.

My body is tense and I recoil when an explosion rocks the overhead, blasting debris and smoke across the room. Shadowy suited figures descend from the newly created aperture. I fire my laserRifle, but the lack of visibility, and the headbeams flashing everywhere, make it difficult to hit the targets. The room is filling with smoke. Luckily my suit's filter removes any smell of burning flesh.

I shuffle back further and come up against an obstruction behind me: the entry door. It has closed behind us. I'll have to come up to kneeling to palm the exit control. I have a flash grenade I picked up from Armory Two, so I activate it, throw it over the battling figures, and yell over the comms. "Eyes closed! Flash grenade."

The searing flash burns bright red through my closed eyelids. I jump up, and slap the doorpad by feel. The door slides away from me. I yell again. "Exit open. Fall back, I'll cover. Stay down."

I back out behind the door's edge, spin around, stand up, wedge myself against the door jamb and lean around with my laserRifle. I aim high, but my team are on all fours and I fire easily over their heads. Strangely, the return fire is wildly inaccurate, and through the drifting smoke, my headbeam plays across stumbling figures.

My brain finally makes the connection. I keep firing until everyone is clear of the room, and shout into my suit mike. "Danielli, Plexi, Herg. Anyone have an EMP stunner?"

Danielli and Herg both reply with a "no."

"No stunner. But I have a Pulse bomb," Plexi says. She's already understood my intention, nods to me and throws the package into the room. I slap the door closed. I can only hope that the armories are EMP-sealed. It would be crazy on a battlecruiser like this for them not to be. EMPs are soundless and emit no light, but I see Plexi has the bomb's remote in her hand.

She waits for my signal, which I give. She thumbs the remote, pauses, then holds up her other hand. "Clear to enter."

"Enter?" Herg doesn't speak much. "You want to fight more?"

Danielli laughs over the comms. "Captain Jackson is smarter than the lot of us, Herg. It's a SIM ambush cluster. That EMP would have disabled the lot. But we'll take the usual precautions." He motions to Plexi to ready herself, then to me to operate the doorpad.

The door slides open and we peer in. Smoke curls around our feet. Someone points their headbeam into the armory and I see five figures held by their own magboots on the deck. One is still sparking and jerking. There is no other movement, but we venture in carefully and spread out.

I move across to the first inert simulacrum, part android, part organic. No wonder Aktip wasn't sure what she sensed. There are no SIMs on Rykkamon.

It is lying on its side, eyes open and unblinking. I kick it. It does not move. I reach down around its back with a laserdagger and slice in deeply through its suit, drawing an opening from the back of its head. The skin pulls apart, exposing artificially grown cartilage and, lower down its back, various organs. Which spill out. I put my laserdagger away, stuff my hand into the mess of guts and rummage around, in close proximity to what in a human would be a spine. I hear a groan of protest from Plexi, which I ignore. I find what I am searching for and pull hard.

A sucking vibration travels along the stringy sinew I yank out of the SIM. I tug harder at the end, and the entire, meter-long neuronic entrails and its bulbous terminal shoot out, spattering liquid on my suit. I stuff the gruesome assembly into a suit pocket.

I look up to see the others gaping at me through their faceplates.

"I needed a souvenir." Which triggers an idea.

"Danielli—can you subdue that one?" I jerk my head at the SIM still moving. He nods and heads over, placing one boot on its chest. I trail behind him, one eye on the gap in the overhead above me, but we are not troubled further.

I bend down to the SIM. "Roll it over."

Danielli obliges. I unplug my diagnostic multiplug from my belt and attach it to the SIM's rear neck terminal.

Herg keeps watch and Plexi joins me. "Whoa, sister—uh, Ma'am, I mean—that's some major geek skills you have there. This time, let me know when the autopsy starts so I can look away."

I say nothing and concentrate on the task. I tap into my armpad. My time with Errikson not only taught me how to hack into his ship, but I learned more than a thing or two about SIMs. Probably why I was the first to recognize their disorientation from my flash grenade. SIM optics in night vision mode are vulnerable to irreparable damage from extreme light blasts. They were literally firing blind.

"Stand back and cover me. I'm going to hack it. Hopefully download some data, if it's not too fried." The others retreat a little, but Danielli keeps his foot on its back and gestures for me to continue. He keeps his headbeam trained on the disabled SIM's neck, and a laserpistol on its head.

I tap the run button, and immediately the SIM straightens all limbs and tries to push itself up, but Danielli kicks it down, using a nearby grab rail for leverage. Smoke pours out of all its joints. The SIM's bionic optics must have melted because there is a disgusting thick rivulet of yellow fat coming out from underneath its face.

My armpad flashes a warning, and simultaneously I hear the pad's comm system in my ear. "*SIM destruct sequence initiated. Evacuate the area.*" I rip the connector from its neck.

"Everyone out, fast. SIMs are blowing up. MOVE IT PEOPLE!" I yell the last three words, and the comms system shrieks in protest.

We turn as one and push off the deck, flying into the

passageway. I catch the jamb with one hand, swing myself around violently and knock all my breath out when I slam into the bulkhead.

But not before slapping the doorpad to seal the room.

The door's plastiflex viewport flashes red and I feel the thump and vibration of the explosion through the deck's alloy. I look down at my squad, all gripping the passageway where they landed after clearing the room. Herg is partly on top of Plexi. She pushes him off with one elbow. "Get off me, Herg, before you start enjoying it. I don't give free feel-ups."

Clearly my team are in one piece.

"Captain?" Danielli looks up at me. "Sitrep?"

I must look worse than I am. "A-OK. Winded, s'all. Team sitrep?"

Herg gives me a thumbs up. Plexi kicks up from the deck and somersaults. "Primed and ready for fightin', Ma'am."

"Sergeant Danielli?"

"Humiliated, Captain. That's twice you've saved us. It's supposed to be the other way around. Other than that, no serious injuries. Did you get the data?"

I'd almost forgotten. I punch into the armpad, then realize the podPlate has a bigger screen, so I push the data over to the plate's system and step on. The screen flickers to life.

"They're Errikson's SIMs. Ganymedian origin." I see a protected file and brute-force it open. Errikson had a bad habit of using junior coders for some of his SIM basic functions, and they almost always left a poorly protected back door. I stare at the information on the screen, tapping back and forth to make sure I haven't made a mistake. I look over to the others. "I don't know how much you know about Errikson and the Jovian mafia, but they aren't exactly the best of friends."

Herg makes a spitting noise through his suitcomm. "I

wouldn't work for those Jovian crazy bastards if you killed me," then he realizes what he just said and starts laughing, as does Plexi.

I snort. "Neither would I. But Errikson was on a paid commission. And not a small one either."

Plexi and Herg are still finding it hard to keep a straight face.

But Danielli and I are not laughing. If the Jovians have Errikson in their pocket, then our mission has just become an entire dimension more complicated.

CHAPTER TWENTY-FOUR

I TELL MY SQUAD WE'LL head—cautiously—to the helmroom. After our last skirmish, they appear to have a new regard for me and do not question my direction. We float off on our podPlates and negotiate almost thirty decks before we emerge in a wide multilane passageway.

"This is it," Plexi tells us. "The central connection to the helmroom's outer ring."

"Copy that," I say. The last time I looked at the schematic I noticed the unusual outer and inner ring configuration of the main helmroom. I still have no idea why the Constellation was built this way. "Danielli, Plexi, Herg—your best assumptions about the helm design?"

I figure it might help us either avoid more traps, or better understand how to use the Constellation—or both.

"Negative, Ma'am," Danielli says. "Not seen anything like it."

"He's seen a few," Herg adds. He seems more talkative after our last run in with the SIMs.

Plexi looks at me and shakes her head.

We continue along the wide passage until we reach one of the outer ring bulkhead doors. I place my hand on the doorpad.

<<**Authorization required.**>>

Apparently my authority is less automatic here. "Captain India Jackson entering the helm."

The doors slide apart and we enter a dimly lit, and much smaller passageway, leading off to the left and to the right. Our podPlates will not fit comfortably into the confined space, so I order our team to disembark and leave them outside the bulkhead door on standby.

"Port or starboard?" Danielli asks.

"Makes no difference. Port." We push around to the left, and I re-anchor my magboots so I can almost walk.

"What are we looking for Ma'am?" Danielli says.

"I'd like a recon of the entire helmroom's outer circle. Resources, entry points, exit points. Match them up with the schematic and note any changes. Just because I have a schematic doesn't mean it's correct."

I lead us around, weapons at the ready. We each sweep our headbeams carefully into all alcoves, doorways and commPanels. This time, I take care to include the overhead.

I open my comms. "Aktip? Captain Jackson to Salvage One."

"Yes, Madam Captain. Aktip at the helm."

"Any more changes in EM background?"

"No, Captain. But your signal is reduced by 22db since you entered the last section."

"Shielding," I murmur.

"Sorry, Ma'am?" It was Danielli.

"Shielding, Danielli. The outer ring is already shielding some comms."

We continue until we complete a full circuit. I re-open the bulkhead we entered through and am relieved to see our podPlates where we left them, hovering in waiting.

"Let's attempt entry." I take us around to the nearest doorpad and slap my gloved hand on it, expecting the suit to transmit my biodata as it usually would. But instead of glowing green, the door is unresponsive. I look at the others.

Danielli shrugs in his suit, and points past me. "Maybe another equipment failure? Try another."

The next doorpad responds in exactly the same way. With nothing.

At the third pad I decide to try a different approach. I place my hand on the pad and speak. "Captain India Jackson requesting access to the helm."

The pad glows green, and I look over my shoulder at the other three and smile. "Needed to be more assertive, obviously—"

<<Please enter secondary authorization.>>

Huh? I look at the others, while still holding my hand on the panel. Danielli holds out his hands. "Request override?"

Good idea. "Captain Jackson requests override of secondary authorization."

<<Request denied. The Captain is required to enter secondary authorization in all cases.>>

What the? What kind of Captain is denied access from their own helm? Maybe I'm not the real Captain after all?

I try one more approach. "Provide information list of secondary authorization requirements."

<<The Captain does not have the required security level for this request.>>

I remove my hand and look at my squad. "Seems like we've gone as far as we can. We'll fall back to the salvage ship and regroup for our next move."

We exit the outer ring and mount our podPlates. I am lost in thought as I follow behind Danielli and Plexi, with Herg providing the rearguard. We ascend and descend endless decks; traverse ghoulishly lit and cavernous workshops—empty of any equipment—and everywhere we pass, there's no sign of any fighting, defensive activity, scorch marks on bulkheads ... nothing.

"Captain?" Plexi calls back. "Look at this." We all stop and crowd around Plexi's podscreen. "I've been looking through that

SIM's data. They weren't the only cluster in place."

I frown. "Then why haven't we been re-engaged? Where are they—can you tell?"

Plexi swipes across to another view, zooms in and taps a zone on the schematic. "They're in Armory Five."

I chew my cheek. "Then my bet would be Armory Four or Six have weapons left in there as bait."

"It might not be wise to—"

"Don't worry, Danielli. We can leave them there. I'm certain they are human-triggered. Think about it. We got excited in Armory Two and then wanted more, so we went to Armory Three. Prior to that we'd had no electromagnetic traces until Aktip alerted us. Someone left a trap—a crude one at that. Probably the same people who set the plasma missiles. I'd also lay a strong bet that any salvage teams who made it past the missiles met their demise this way."

"They didn't have their own Constellation Captain, either," Plexi says.

"Still ..." I pause for a moment. "It begs the question: who took away the bodies and ships of the other failed attempts?"

CHAPTER TWENTY-FIVE

WE BOARD OUR SALVAGE VESSEL without incident and I order a command meeting in the limited space of the mess. All seven of us anchor at various points around the bulkhead—there'd be no room if we all mag-anchored to the one table.

I have Danielli give the sitrep. I figure his authority over his own team gives him that right, and confers me some assumed leadership. When he gets to the part about the battle with the SIMs, I see the two crew members who remained on the salvage ship looking at me with increased curiosity.

No one has a clue why there is no evidence of previous salvage attempts. Maybe the SIMs doubled up as forensic cleaners. Aktip just watches everyone, entranced by the discussion.

We end up agreeing that the plasma missiles must have caught the other ships, and maybe the one that slipped past them and supplied coordinates to Sloper never attempted to board. Sloper would have killed the returning crew and destroyed the evidence.

But the mystery takes us around in circles, until there is silence.

Finally, I get to speak.

"I can't deliver on my promise with what is left on the Constellation. Yet. But my offer remains. If anyone wants out, speak up." I look around the room—some heads are upside down, peering at me from the overhead, but all seem to be waiting on my next move. I give it to them.

"I'm going to Ganymede."

I see a few exchanged glances.

"I plan to find out from Errikson what the Jovians want. In the meantime, I have to stall Sloper, send a hyper-relay message to Jordi to confirm our meeting place, and discover where my brother is being held. I need a good team—belay that—I need the best team money can buy. From what I've seen of Danielli, Plexi and Herg, I already have that team. And I'm willing to bet all of you believe you'd beat anyone in a street brawl."

I see grins and hear a few suppressed whoops. I pause and look around. "So is anyone up for a fight?"

The room erupts, and I catch Plexi looking at me, her eyes sparkling. I smile at her, and while holding her gaze, I hold up my hand for silence.

"Here's my next question. Does anyone have any good ideas about how to hide a battlecruiser?"

Plexi laughs.

CHAPTER TWENTY-SIX

I'M NOT REALLY SURPRISED THAT it's Plexi who devised a plan. It worked, and now we're already almost three days into our series of hyperspace hops to Ganymede.

Which means in the next two hops, I'm heading into a hornet's nest. My hyper-relay would have reached Jordi two days ago, and he in turn may have already found Sloper. The cogs are turning. There's no turning back, despite what my body might scream.

I ignore the fear and meet with Danielli and Aktip in the helmroom.

They wait for me to speak, datapads in hand.

"Here's how we roll."

"Roll?" Aktip says.

"It means how we'll work together. The Jovian mafia controls Ganymede, and it's not the most healthy destination. I'd rather not draw undue attention, so we'll dock at Ganymede's trading station. Danielli and I will head down in the public shuttle."

I turn to my Rykkan companion. "Aktip, you'll stick out like a Rubidian arm-digit on Ganymede. So you'll stay here and station the comms. Comms will be dark, except for our emergency beacons. Plexi will be the acting captain, and what she says, goes, unless I order you otherwise. Clear?"

"Yes, Madam Captain."

I furrow my brow. "I think we'd better avoid calling me 'Madam Captain.' Just in case."

"With all due respect, Ma'am," Danielli says, giving me an odd look, "if we're not going to draw attention to ourselves, purely showing yourself might be a giveaway." He taps his own cropped hair, and points to mine.

I grin. "Don't worry about me, Danielli. I have it handled. Now ... we'll head into the social district. I have some trading contacts I can pull favors with. Our objective is only to discover as much information about Errikson as we can. Low key recon. Then we'll pull back and make a plan, depending on what we uncover. Questions?"

"Yes." Danielli leans forward. "Weapons. I've no experience with the Ganymedian authorities. What can we rely on slipping in?"

"Anything we can hide on our person. But if we get stopped, it will cost us." I shrug "They might have Generals and a superficial military order, but it's still a mafia-run outpost. Everyone carries. Even so, tucking Plexi's plasmacannon under your arm might attract the kind of new friends we don't want."

I hold Danielli's gaze for a moment. "And if we find ourselves using them, something has gone wrong." I don't tell him about Jordi's warning. My reputed status as an illegal trader of Rykkan mercenaries originated on Ganymede. Probably in the very bars we're likely to be heading to. Then there's the fact that my last exit from the moon wasn't exactly tidy. There might be a few people taking an interest in my return, but the last thing I want is a gunfight in the heart of mafia-town. I only just avoided the last one.

I let our other pilot—a wiry, taciturn youth called Zhang—dock us to Ganymede's outer trade station, where we will board the central shuttle hub. I am busy elsewhere on my ship with Plexi.

As soon as we dock and we confirm transportation access, I check in with Aktip and Danielli on the commPanel. "Status check from Ruby. Ready for action?"

"Yes, Ruby." Both Aktip and Danielli confirm.

Ready for action is exactly how I look. Though maybe not in the military sense.

I draw up the plastizip on my black leather skintight and float awkwardly down to the airlock. Not drawing attention to yourself on Ganymede is counterintuitive: everyone is a wannabe. Me? I'm a wannabe rock star from Ribas, or an aspiring actress from Actiron, here to see her new manager, "Django." It won't matter what I am, as long as I look the part. Where we're going, narcissism is the norm. No one will pay much attention. Except if I have flaming red hair.

Danielli's eyes practically fall out of his face when he sees me at the airlock. He nods approvingly at my full-length leather outfit. "You came prepared." He inclines his head to my jet-black hair, tied in a long and tight braid.

I shake my head. "Plexi's dye came in useful. The outfit is another story." As is what I've hidden in it.

I catch his inquiring eye. "For later. Right now, I need to be in character. We on the same page with that?"

He nods. "Sure thing, Ruby. You're here to get hired, and I'm your sleazy manager."

"And that means you act like it. No deferring to me: act like you're in control. I'll let you know when I have a specific request."

He grimaces. "So I have to treat you like crap, order everyone around, but behind the scenes, follow your lead. Sounds simple."

"Then let's party."

CHAPTER TWENTY-SEVEN

"Sheesh, Tyrone," I say to Danielli as we enter the station's main hub and feel the grav-simulation kick in, "it's about time you finally brought me to somewhere with gravity."

I adjust my breasts in the leather jerkin, throwing a flirty smile at the guard lazily checking everyone out at the shuttle entrance. "At least people here can see these are real."

Danielli does well to disguise his slight shock at my newfound persona. "Loudmouthed as always, Ruby. I think you'll fit in just perfectly." He winks at the guard and looks back at me. "You and Ganymede are made for each other. Now move your butt. From what I hear, Django is desperate to see his newest recruit."

He pulls my elbow roughly and I make a show of ripping my arm away from his and scooting into the shuttle on my high-heel mags.

If the stakes weren't so high, this would be a comedy.

We descend to Ganymede Central in the shuttle. I adopt a bored look typical of wannabes secretly seeking fame and fortune. But what I seek is much darker and my stomach turns at the thought.

"Ruby!" I finally twig that it's Danielli calling me. The shuttle has landed without me realizing.

"Yeah?" I give him a sullen scowl.

He jerks his thumb at the exit. "We gotta guy to see. Pronto."

I bound past him in Ganymede's 15% gravity, and look down my nose at him. And anyone else looking. Though I see my leather skintight has collected a few views. Good. I'd rather be lusted after than ousted. The latter has far worse consequences.

A change of shuttle pod and a couple of beltways later, and we're inside the T-Dome.

I stop and gaze, like a starlet in awe of movieTown. Despite being three-quarters the size of Mars, Ganymede has proved stubborn to terraforming. The colony engineers believed they could build on the existing traces of oxygen and, using Ganymede's geothermal resources, form a neutral gas base. But with very low gravity, and dominated by Jupiter's massive magnetosphere, Ganymede's atmosphere production is still in its infancy.

The only way to survive the daily dose of Jupiter's fatal radiation is inside one of the many shields, most of which double-up as pressure domes. Some for housing, most for work, some for the energy transfer plants monopolized by the mafia ... and some, like the T-Dome, purely for entertainment. Of any variety.

If I have my bearings correct, this dome houses the Xpress district where Jordi and I tangled with some of Ganymede's lowlife. And the scene of a fight. So it's not exactly salubrious. Then again, not much in the Xpress district is.

I strut—a kind of hip-swinging bounce in lo-grav—in front of "Tyrone," scowling at anyone who tries to hit me up. My height—exaggerated further in the mag-heels, my jet-black braid and the black leather skintight seem to do the job. I need to be intimidating, but also a wannabe.

Tyrone pushes me roughly. "Hey!" I protest, but he pushes again, making me skip forward a few meters. "Leave it out, you puke-jockey. I know where we're heading." A few bystanders smile at the interchange and carry on as if it's a normal day on a Jovian moon. Because it is.

Soon we are heading down the Xpress mainway. A place I remember leaving in a big hurry on my last visit. My mag-heels with their "enhancements" don't always grip as I wish, so "walking" comes with a frequent majestic slo-mo hop. I try to make it part of my act.

A string of grimy blue lights lead us down an alley, and we arrive in front of an unlabeled door.

Which is open. Revealing a small mezzanine entrance foyer, and a bar room and dance floor set below.

Tyrone growls. "Get inside, babyface."

Babyface? Danielli needs a heads-up on the current lingo. But I throw him a nasty look and enter the mezzanine.

Unchallenged, we descend the slo-lift, a cloud of fun-gas envelopes us, and we're blasted by driving drumtrax. Danielli hands me a filter and I slap it over my nose and mouth. I don't need fun-gas to know when I'm having fun, and I'm not planning on any fun anytime soon.

I scan the crowded and large, cave-like room, as if I'm looking for the cool people. Not far from the truth. The forgotten-era throw-back strobe lights and loud music are pounding my head and make recognition difficult. I spy the face I'm looking for, surrounded by a gaggle of his preferred furry aliens, in a booth on the far side of the dance floor. I grab Danielli's arm. "Darling—I've seen just the man you need to hook me up with." I drag him behind me as we push aside the slo-mo heaving, sweaty crowd, most of whom have inane fixed grins from the fun-gas.

I'm halfway across the room when I notice a face staring at me from the bar over the gloom. I spin around, pull Danielli into me, yank down our filters—and kiss him hard. He flinches momentarily, then leans into it. I pull away, noticing his red face. "Ah, Tyrone. Has it been that long? Poor darling. Never mind—

they'll be plenty of willing victims for you here."

I sneak a glance at the bar. The staring face has moved on, apparently satisfied. I pull our filters back up, let go of Danielli and flounce across the rest of the floor. I stop at a throng of fur-groupies surrounding the man I've come to see. I put my hands on my hips and wait.

Slowly the man's attention comes to me. His bald head glistens when the colored roving spotlights hit it; lank brown hair descending either side of a face with high cheekbones. He smiles and opens his mouth to call my name, but I give my head a tiny shake. Instead I push through his furry friends, ignoring their protests, and float down onto his lap.

"It's Ruby, darling. Or did you forget already?" I lean in as if to kiss him on the cheek and whisper in his ear. "That hard object in your lap? It's not you being glad to see me." I dig my laserdagger into his solar plexus to reinforce my meaning. "But I'm sure you'd still love to get a private room."

The man's eyes widen for a moment, then he breaks out into a wide, toothy smile. "Ruby. How long has it been? Will your friend accompany us? Or will our time together truly be private?" He flicks his eyes briefly at Danielli.

I flutter my hand behind me. "Tyrone, why don't you find yourself a playmate? There should be someone young and furry enough for you here. Pedro and I are going to have a little private fun. Come back in five minutes. If you last that long." I rise up, dragging my dagger suggestively up Pedro's lower chest. He just grins wider, stands and beckons me through a guarded door, which hisses closed behind us.

Pedro bats the laserdagger away and hugs me. "Ah, the 'divine one.' But what on Europa are you doing back here? There's a price on your head. Are you mad, Indy?"

I feel a brief smile flick over my face at Pedro's use of the honorific nickname my father used to use. "Apparently."

I pull down my fun-gas filter. There will be no gas or fun in here, but my lips are still tingling from Danielli's kiss. I'd let go of any notion of any such action years ago. I shake the thought free, but the tingle remains. "What can you tell me about Errikson?"

Pedro sinks slowly into the plush tubchair behind him. I follow him and slide onto his lap. Just in case someone pokes their head in. He sighs. "So that's the risk payoff. I should have known." He looks me in the eyes. "It's still all about Papa, isn't it?"

I shake my head vehemently, but deep down I wonder if he's right. Then I remember Mitch. "Not just Papa. Sloper's got Mitch holed up somewhere and he'll kill him if I don't bring him what he needs."

His eyes narrow. "Must be big if you'd rather do what Sloper asks than kill him. What's Errikson got to do with it?"

"Can't tell you. For your own good. Actually for the Sector's good."

He leans back and regards me carefully. "Word is that Sloper went after the C—"

I put my hand over his mouth and whisper. "That's what I mean. Forget you ever had that thought."

Pedro's eyes widen and I remove my hand. He collects himself. "Errikson's been holed up in the yards."

The shipyards in Jupiter's orbit, and in Ganymede's shadow. Easier to contain Jupiter's fierce radiation wind that slays delicate equipment.

He continues. "He's hired the biggest hangar cloak you've ever seen. Street-talk says he's bringing in a big salvage op."

I shift on Pedro's knee. "Hmm. Who could get me in there?"

"Spacedust, Indy. You're as tough as they come, but even your moves won't help you if they find out you're here."

I bring my lips together in a tight smile. "Are you forgetting something? Indy's not here." I stand up and wiggle suggestively. "It's Ruby. And I'm looking for action. Let me ask you again: who can get me in?"

Pedro exhales noisily. "Might be time for me to repay my debt to your father. 'Specially if you've found what I think you've found."

You don't know the half of it. If anyone other than Danielli learned about my new captain credentials, I'd be spaced in a picosecond.

"You have someone in mind?"

He nods. "You won't like it."

My face falls. "Bruno?"

He nods again. "If there's anyone who knows Errikson's Achilles heel, it's BB." He looks anxious. "But have you got anything that will interest him?"

I give Pedro a wicked smile, unzip the front of my jerkin, reach all the way down to my abdomen and pull out the long neuronic entrails, capped with its small graphene-encased headunit. I dangle it suggestively. "Ruby's got a toy for Bruno the Bad."

"Oh Jesus." Pedro looks up at me with wide eyes.

"That old urban myth? Didn't know you still believed."

Someone knocks at the door and it slides back. A small furry face pokes in and speaks in a peculiarly incongruous deep and sexy female voice. "There's a Tyrone looking for Miss Ruby."

I look at the creature. "Tell Tyrone Ruby's almost finished. And so is Pedro."

CHAPTER TWENTY-EIGHT

PEDRO TAKES US IN A wide-bodied, three-seater flaretrike, unique to Ganymede. I introduce him to Danielli, but I refuse his request for more information.

"It will only put you in more danger," I tell him. Sounds noble, but I know the fewer people I share information with, the less likely it is to leak. Papa always said, "*You don't want it found on the netcom, you don't put it on the netcom.*" The Sector War saw the demise of the netcom as a flawed security risk, but Papa's principle remains: people can't give up what they don't know.

I glance at Danielli. He has said little since the club, but I'm pretty sure he's one hundred percent soldier, and his repressed desire to talk has nothing to do with the giant smooch his captain gave him. I only hope I wasn't ID'd.

Danielli looks over at me. "Ah ... Ruby. What is our mission objective?"

"We trade this"—I reveal a little of the neuronic entrails I'd cut out of the SIM before it autodestructed—"for information about Errikson. Access to his hangar cloak if we can. Depends how bad Bruno wants to cut Errikson's SIM market down."

I shiver. Even though we are under a geothermal-powered heatdome, a leather skintight wasn't the most practical choice for a moon with an average outside temperature of -121 Celsius. I have to find the location of the Constellation's drive. Once I know that, I can lure Sloper into a deal to get Mitch released. Sloper's greed will take care of his motivation. I just need to take care he doesn't quite get what he wants.

We jet across an empty drone park and into a long, low building, designed with one convex wall and tucked into the edge of the dome. Whoever chose this location was streetsmart. Finding defensible strongholds in a domed environment takes planning.

Pedro pulls the trike around to the building's main door and we slo-mo off. He calls up the doorpad on the main access and punches in a code. I raise my eyes at him when he looks at me.

He grins and entwines his first and second fingers. "Me and BB? ... We're like this."

The door slides back and twenty or so armed goons rush out at us. We're surrounded.

Pedro looks at me and slowly disentangles his fingers until they point in different directions. "Or like this."

We follow the armed platoon into the building and down a brightly lit corridor. I pick up sounds from the closed doors we pass—laughter; a girl's high-pitched squeal, some males arguing. Yep, Ganymede. Satellite of love, as it's known.

We turn into a larger, sparse, windowless room. Three guys stay outside. There's one hefty square table in the middle. No chairs. Leaning against the wall at the other end is our man. Bruno the Bad.

"You've put on weight," I say as I come to a stop in front of him.

He had, too. Never a slim man, Bruno's brown jowls now droop almost into the folds of his neck. His arms are trike-jet thick, maybe flabby, but still strong. He wears a satchel slung over one shoulder.

I smile. "You should try setting up shop on Rykkamon. Put some muscle on you."

He doesn't return my smile. "I heard you have ops with

spinheads. But cut chat, pretty face. You want something from Bruno, you give something to Bruno." He leers at me. I see food stains spattering his plastivest.

I start to pull down my jerkin's zip, but Bruno grabs my wrist. "Not that. Bruno not interested in women."

I regard him coolly. "You think I don't know your ugly pleasures? Please. I'm not unzipping for your carnal delight, believe me."

He stares, and drops his hand, holding his eyes on mine. I keep up the staring contest and drop the zip down to my panty line. I reach in and pull out Bruno's prize, whipping it back out of his reach when I see his eyes light up. I pull the zip up.

"I've got more where this came from." I watch him carefully, and I sense Danielli shift behind me. I'm confident of my deal, but we're on Ganymede.

"Where?" His eyes fixate on the SIM headunit.

"Classified. But I'll bring 'em ... when you give me the info Pedro tells me you have."

He hacks up a spit, and the gobball sails majestically down to Pedro's feet. Pedro is unmoved. Then he laughs, his belly wobbling in lo-grav empathy. "Okay, Miss Rooby. I play your game. You want information of Errikson, yes?"

I nod, and hold up the neuronic unit. "This should more than pay for it."

Bruno laughs again, and reaches into his satchel. He pulls out a handful of identical SIM units, complete with their long neuronic tentacles. "Trouble is, already have units." I feel my face fall. He leans forward, snatches the device from my hand, looks up at me and says, "I think, you want information from Mr. Errikson, better to ask him yourself."

Crap. Looks like my attempt to avoid my cover being blown in the bar was all in vain. At least it earned me a kiss. Time to play games.

I fall to my knees—slowly in the gravity—and beg Bruno. "Please! Sloper has my brother. I need to know what Errikson is—"

As I settle, I sit back on my heels, reach back with both hands and snap each high heel off.

In a true ninja move, I duck my head, whip both arms around in front of me in a wide pincer-like movement, and I bring them forcefully together to stab the two neurowhips concealed in each heel into Bruno's ankles.

Bruno's eyes glaze over in pain, but he's paralyzed. I grab his satchel off his shoulder as he sinks down. I hear the sound of laserpistols firing behind me. I spin around on one foot and stay low to the floor.

Danielli has already cut down almost ten of them, Pedro is wrestling a guy at the door ... which leaves five goons spreading out to take me down. I wonder why they haven't killed me yet, then I realize my trump card: the price on my head is for me alive.

Something else strikes my awareness. These guys have all spent a lot of time on Ganymede. Maybe too much to keep their muscles in trim. I drop Bruno's satchel, hold my hands out in pretend surrender, and cower. They come closer. I crouch more.

I wait until the first is almost on me, reaching out to subdue me, when I spring into the air and somersault over his head. Stabbing one neuroheel-whip in as I do so. He drops in slo-mo, but I've already hit the ceiling with my feet, rebounded and am diving into the two in the middle with both arms outstretched. They break my fall, or rather, my neurowhips do, and I slide down using the whips on their bodies as a brake.

At the last minute I twirl head over heels and land on my feet to face the final two on my right.

One of them feints to my left, but I see it coming and I've

already pushed off from my last victim. I give him a straight metal-toed kick where it hurts. He grunts and goes down.

One to go. This guy's big though—he even towers over me. He has a massive, outlawed plasmacannon strapped to his back. Plexi would be drooling. I throw my snapped-off heels to the ground. "Alright, I give up. You're way too big for my tricks." Then I slip my hand down through my skintight's zipper, pull out the microlaser pistol I'd tucked inside on the ship, and splatter the guy's knee to sausage meat. He howls and topples. Slowly.

Microlaser in hand, I turn to the rest of the room. Pedro now has his guy on the floor and Danielli's already taken out his assailants. I look at Danielli and jerk my head at the door. He holds up three fingers, but Pedro is waving us away, his foot on the other guy's chest. "We go out there, we're dead."

I look at Danielli.

"He could be right, Ma'am. The element of surprise is gone, and we'll be fighting our way out of a tunnel."

I point at the plasmacannon on the giant's back, who has passed out.

Danielli's eyes widen. "No."

"Yes," I say, and cut the cannon off the guy using his own beltknife. I waste no time, and I turn to face the wall next to Bruno's limp form and pull the trigger. The wall partially disintegrates, but I can see the dome barrier beyond it. I fire again, and blast the dome barrier into a hole into Ganymede's partly formed atmosphere. The icy cold penetrates instantly.

"We have 10 seconds to get out and back in again!" I yell over the noise of our room's air whistling against the pressure. I fire again to widen the aperture, and jump through.

Hell's neutrons, it's so cold I'm not sure I can move, but I have to. Holding my breath, I bound along a few meters next to the dome, stop, turn and fire the plasmacannon into the dome's surface. Repeatedly. A ragged hole appears, but I am now too cold to understand what to do next. I cannot move. My hands stiffen, and will no longer grip. I let the cannon drop slowly through my fingers. Shit.

Then I feel myself manhandled though the hole, followed by Danielli, then Pedro, who turns and throws his jacket over the hole. It doesn't work, and the jacket flies out. I hear alarms and sirens from the dome breach, and I'm in danger of passing out. The lo-grav helps us again, and my two companions drag me away. We crawl back far enough into the dome's atmosphere to collapse, exhausted.

The shock of the sudden freeze is wearing off. I'm hoping the ten seconds of exposure to Jupiter's deadly rays won't kill us, but if we don't get to Pedro's trike, we're dead anyway.

My judgment for the re-entry point was good: we're in an alley I'd noticed when we arrived, running parallel to the building. The trike is not far away. With the thugs inside preoccupied with closing the breach and / or working out what the heck went down in that room, we might have some time up our sleeves.

Danielli's eyes meet mine. I think I can get to my feet. We nod at each other briefly, then I stagger along the side of the building, staying close to it, Danielli loping ahead of me, Pedro behind.

We turn the corner to Pedro's trike.

There's a short figure astride it. He turns and beams.

"India! So good to see you again," Errikson says.

CHAPTER TWENTY-NINE

ERRIKSON'S MEN CLOSE IN AROUND us. Bruno appears from his building, rubbing his head, his eyes blazing. Errikson laughs, and bounds off the trike. "I told you she was dangerous, but no, you told me no girl would trouble you."

My passionate kiss with Danielli was for nothing. Well, almost nothing: it had intrinsic value. But, someone alerted Errikson, that's for sure. And now I can't believe my eyes. Clearly Errikson has some deal going down with Bruno. Last time I was on Ganymede, they were at each other's throats. The Sector has truly turned upside down.

Errikson stops laughing and stares at me. "Let's take our three heroes somewhere else. Those sirens are giving me a headache."

We're bundled into a hovervan and whisked away. I look at Pedro. His eyes fill with despair. I lean over and whisper. "I'm not done yet." He manages a brief smile which quickly fades.

I'm not entirely sure how confident I am of my statement, but something inside me refuses to be beaten. I'm the captain of a battlecruiser, goddammit. I still have a trick or two up my sleeve.

Danielli catches my expression. "Impressive fighting skills back there, Ma'am." I know he's trying to make me feel better.

"Didn't work though, did it?"

We sit in silence while the van bumps and bounds along like a beach ball in the low-gee. We jolt to a halt and I sense us being lifted. I hear voices outside, but not what they say.

Then we all feel the gravity briefly intensify, pressing us into our seats. "We're leaving the surface," Danielli says.

"The shipyards?" I look over to Pedro, still with his head hung low. He lifts it up and nods, then drops down again.

We journey for what feels like thirty minutes, then a distant clang confirms what we suspected: we're docking in the shipyards. The van doors open, and I see the entire van has been lifted into a cargo hold. One of Errikson's crew throws in three suits. "Put these on, unless you're contemplating suicide."

We suit up in silence. I float out of the van and let the mag boots connect me to the deck. Errikson is over by a gantry; surrounding us are cranes, gantries and other locks. He motions for us to come over and our guard pushes us forward. Unnecessarily in my mind. Where else was I going to go?

Danielli accidentally bumps into me, as if his mag boot snagged on something. I hear his voice quietly through my faceplate when we bump together. "E.B. active."

I do not acknowledge him, but keep my eyes trained on Errikson. He turns to greet me. "Ms. Jackson. Always a delight." Most people imagine Errikson to be some Nordic-descended blonde, heavily muscled and big-boned. But I am almost double his height. Errikson is a dwarf: stunted from birth by radiation. No doubt Ganymede's environment suits him.

"You're working for the Jovians."

He waves my statement away and shrugs. "Everyone works for someone. I heard you were working for Sloper." He points to Danielli. "He works for you. I also believe you owe me a lightCruiser. What's your point?"

What *is* my point?

"You want me for something. You're under the Jovians' thumb. Therefore *they* must want me for something. So let's cut to the chase. What is it?"

The small man's face breaks out into a broad grin. "If only

Frederic could see you now—"

I lash out and plant one kick into his groin before I am restrained. Not that it will hurt much in almost zero-gee.

"If Papa could see me now, *you* would be dead, not him."

He throws up one hand, the other rubbing his groin. "We'll all be that way one day, darlin'. I'd prefer not to arrive as quickly as some, of course ..." He looks me up and down.

"What?" I glare at him.

"You're going to help me."

"Of course I am. And the Blood Empire are nice neighbors. Any other fanciful ideas?"

He sighs and holds his hand out to one side. A man next to him puts a holocube in it. Errikson holds it up to me. I reach to grab it, but he jerks it away and taps play. The video shows my brother. Not near-naked anymore, but dirty, haggard and wild-eyed. I reach for the cube again, but Errikson pulls it from my grasp. "Ha! See ... I do know what you want."

"It's none of your business."

"Oh but it is. You see, I have something you want, which in turn is something Sloper wants, and Sloper has something—or someone—you want."

I screw my face up. "Then what do you want from me?"

"Access to this." He manipulates the holocube and an image of a massive starship drive fills the space over our heads. Danielli and I exchange glances. Errikson nods. "That's right. The drive from a certain not-so-mythical battlecruiser." He flicks the image off. "A little robofly told me you might hold a clue to the drive. Help me access the drive and I might even let you go. With the drive. Once I'm done. A parting gift, you might say."

I push aside my confusion. "Where did you get it?" More to the point, how did he cut that thing out?

"My dear. I thought that much was obvious. But I see by the

look on your face you are more interested in how we did such a fine job extracting this ... monstrosity."

I say nothing.

He smirks. "You have no idea, do you?"

I let out a breath. "Enough with your games, Errikson. Do share your magnificence. How did you liberate this thing—if it's what you say it is?"

He looks up at me, beaming through his faceplate. "Ah, but that's my point. I didn't. Your father did."

CHAPTER THIRTY

I AM SPEECHLESS. BUT WHAT I don't understand is this: if Errikson needs me to access the Constellation's drive, why would he let me go? Why would he give me the drive to refit the Constellation for Sloper? I'm certain he has no idea I'm the Constellation's slightly hobbled Captain, or that I've found the legendary battlecruiser, so why does he think I can access the drive? I realize I'm back to square one: why would he give it away, once accessed?

And then it dawns on me. The technology in the drive must be worth more than either the drive itself, or even the Constellation. The realization is crushing: that if the Jovians get their hands on a technology powerful enough that it trumps the galaxy's most revered battlecruiser, we're all in a pile of Bellatian excrement.

All this rockets through my head while I look Errikson in the eye. I collect myself and take stock. Danielli is on my right, Pedro behind Danielli. We're all about fifty meters away from the airlock. They are all heavily armed. We are not.

"What makes you think I can get you access?"

Errikson laughs. "Let's just say I have inside information. A simple job. Then you are free to leave, once I have taken what I need." He sees my expression. "Oh yes. Like I said, you can take it with you. A big chunk of scrap alloy like that? Might be credits in it for you. Good luck finding all the other parts though."

He confirms he doesn't know I have the Constellation. I feel goosebumps on my neck. I have seconds to play this out before the action starts. I can only hope Aktip and Plexi have been meticulous in their investigation of the shipyards.

"I won't do it."

Errikson is caught with his mouth open. He closes it slowly and narrows his eyes. "Well. You leave me no other choice. I wasn't going to spoil a pretty girl, especially after your father so generously helped me out." Two men walk up carrying a coffin-like box at each end. Errikson motions them to stop. He lifts the top and beckons me to look inside.

I gasp. In the box is a SIM. A female SIM. An exact replica. Of me.

He smiles and my blood runs cold. "All I need now is some of your skin, your neuro-impulse pattern, and a working voiceprint. I was quite prepared to do the right thing. I'd like to say that it won't hurt a bit." He shrugs. "But it will."

And then all hell breaks loose.

The hangar lock behind us shatters in a barrage of automatic lasercannon fire. Errikson's men scatter and take shelter behind the various crates and boxes in the small entry hangar. But it doesn't save them from the shooter's ire. Danielli pulls Pedro to the starboard bulkhead and I boot myself off the magnetic surface and fly to the overhead.

I risk a quick look at the destroyed hangar's airlock. Just beyond it hovers our salvage vessel. I can't quite believe my eyes at first. Strapped to the nose of the sizable vessel is a small, suited figure brandishing a lasercannon in each hand. Our unarmed salvage ship just went military.

Plexi is firing at anything that moves ... and anything that doesn't. A voice hacks into my suit's helmet. "Ma'am? Is that you up on the overhead?"

"Copy that. Danielli and Pedro are directly below me. Cover

us to your port side and we'll make our way out."

"Affirmative."

Errikson's men are now returning fire, but something is causing them to miss Plexi completely. I'm not sure why, but I'm grateful, nevertheless. I pull myself across the overhead using the various mounts and gantries. I see on the deck Danielli has spotted my movements and mirrors my trajectory, elbowing Pedro to do the same.

The amount of firepower being exchanged is staggering. I see two D5 plastisteel containers completely melt under Plexi's sustained barrage. Errikson's men, surprised and overwhelmed by an unusual and unprecedented attack are falling back. I see no sign of Errikson.

The three of us make it to the edge of what's left of the large airlock, and I push down to join the others. On the side of our ship I see a squat suited figure tethered to the sidelock, aiming a rescue line launcher at us. I wave to attract attention, and the figure fires the line at us. The line lands at Danielli's feet, the autoclaw tears into the deck's alloy and grips. Danielli looks at me and motions frantically. "Go. Move it!"

It's not a time to think, but to take action, so I obey his orders and throw myself out into the stars. I hook one arm over the line to steady myself, then pull as fast as I can with both arms across to my ship. I sense firepower around me, but none hits. I reach the ship and heave myself into the lock. I turn straight away and help Pedro, then Danielli enter the ship.

The squat figure pulls a laserknife from a utility belt, ready to cut the line. Aktip, of course. She leans out and at the same time I hear a crackle and a familiar voice in my ear comms.

It's Errikson. Where is he? Then I spy him across the space between us, crouched at the edge of the airlock.

He speaks. "*I thought you might be difficult. I have backup. My second choice. Shared DNA you see. I'm told he's for sale, too. Shame you ruined a good deal. I think Michelangelo will probably agree with me."*

I watch horrified as Errikson raises a lasersniper, and takes aim as Aktip cuts the rescue line. There is a flash right in front of me, and Aktip screams and falls back into my arms. She is still holding the cut line. I cannot help myself and I howl. "No!"

I hold Aktip tight as Zhang speeds us away from the shipyard and we depart Ganymede's hellhole.

CHAPTER THIRTY-ONE

I CLUTCH AKTIP IN MY arms, halfway out of the open airlock. She is shivering and I can feel her head swiveling inside the custom-fitted suit someone had cobbled together. A scorched rip in the suit across her waist is already self-sealing, but it only emphasizes the extent of her wound.

A voice breaks into my helmet comm. "*Hey ... I know relatively speaking I'm going the same speed as you guys. But I'd still appreciate a hand bringing me back in.*"

It's Plexi. In all the agony of witnessing my friend cut down in front of me, I've forgotten Plexi. I turn to Danielli, knowing how my face must look. "I can't ..."

He knows I won't leave Aktip. He grabs a line from the lock, attaches it to his belt and heads around the front of the ship to bring Plexi back in.

Eventually the two come back in to discover Pedro and I manhandling Aktip—whose mass is sizable—back into the ship's airlock. Plexi sails in through the door. "Cool shooting, don't you—" then her face drops when she spots Aktip being floated inside between Pedro and I. "Oh crap."

We take the Rykkan to the medbay. I remove my helmet, and I gently slide Aktip's off fearing the worst, but she is still breathing. The wound is on her lower hip where she caught Errikson's fire. She's lost a lot of blood—dark red blood, which I guess must be due to Rykkamon's high iron content.

After cutting her suit from her, we strap Aktip to a bunk.

Pedro takes my hand. "We need to stabilize him."

"Her," I say, looking at my protector, barely alive. An alien I'd never known until a few days ago, who has left her home to defend me. "She's my friend."

Pedro acknowledges my correction. "Her. But you're in shock, so let me close the wound. You have patches on board, right?"

Danielli rummages in a med unit and holds up a pack. Pedro rips them open and without any hesitation, slaps as many patches across Aktip's bleeding hip as it takes to cover her up.

"What if they don't work on Rykkans?" I ask Pedro.

His face is grim when he looks at me. "Then she'll die anyway. In this situation, my guess is she's no different to a human: first we must stem the blood loss."

"And second?" I ask, hearing the weakness in my voice.

Danielli replies. "We get the hell out of here and find emergency help. The nearest friendly planet, preferably."

Aktip convulses, and it shakes me into sharp focus. I draw myself up and punch the commPanel. "Captain to helmroom."

"*Helmroom. Zhang at the helm.*"

"Zhang. We have a medical emergency. Find the nearest friendly planet one hyperDrive hop away. Criteria: known to possess fully equipped and advanced medical facilities. Don't wait for my order, as soon as you find it, take us there."

"*Affirmative, Ma'am.*"

I tap the commPanel off and place my hand on Aktip's leathery brow. "Stay with us, my friend. Your debt is not ready to be extinguished."

CHAPTER THIRTY-TWO

ZHANG PROVES TO BE ANOTHER gem in Danielli's squad. In just over ten minutes we are requesting permission to descend to NewSwiss12. An Arctic planet with a near-earth-level gravity, NewSwiss12 has an enviable reputation for putting officers back together after battle. I'd never heard of it, but Danielli tells me Zhang chose wisely. Though not cheaply.

We touch down at NS12's spaceport to find a medEvac team awaiting us. The leader steps forward, holding a datapad. "Chief Surgeon Meredith Vysl, head of admissions. We need credit transfer authorization before we proceed."

She extends the datapad out and I place my hand across it. The doctor pulls the pad back once it flashes green, examines it briefly before shooting me an odd look. "I understand you have an injured crew member?"

I jab my thumb back behind me where Plexi and Herg are carrying Aktip on the medbay's gurney. "Female Rykkan. Age unknown. Significant laserRifle injury to right-side hip area. Unconscious since the injury with what looks like major blood loss."

The doctor eyes me. "Treatment to date?"

I shrug. "Medpatches only."

The doctor nods and motions her team to take over from Plexi and Herg. She looks at me. "We don't have Rykkan biomapping. I'll have to request an emergency hyper-relay transfer from Rykkamon." She holds my gaze. "If we're to save her."

I feel my shoulders tighten. "Can it be done anonymously?"

The doctor holds out the datapad again. "Additional credit transfers can make anything anonymous."

I place my hand on the pad. "Do whatever it takes to save her. Just don't ID anyone."

The doctor just looks at me. "No problem with the latter. But the former? I can't guarantee it. We're already reducing our chances given the time it will take to obtain the mapping." She turns around and hurries after the rest of her team into the nearby green-glass clad building, stark against the snow backdrop.

Plexi takes my hand. "Ma'am? We should head in there too."

"We should. Bring Pedro and Danielli. Things are heating up."

I comm the ship and tell Zhang and Ortiz to ready for a fast exit, and walk off to the building, leaving Plexi behind me. Aktip's injury had kept me from my thoughts waiting in the wings, but now they flood in. Why did Papa help Errikson? What's in the Constellation's drive that is more valuable to the Jovians than the Constellation itself? And now Errikson wants Mitch in place of me? I shake my head. This isn't what I signed up for.

CHAPTER THIRTY-THREE

I SIT IN A WAITING area around a table with Danielli, Plexi, Herg and Pedro.

Danielli gives me an empathic look. I hope my actions in Pedro's club haven't given him the wrong idea, no matter how pleasant it was. But I underestimate him. "Ma'am, I'm sure you feel bad. As it was, we were lucky to get out of there with as little damage as we did."

I look over at Plexi. "How did you deflect their firepower? They barely hit anything." Except Errikson.

Plexi picks at her nails. "When I blew the hangar lock doors, I threw in a little bonus. Literally."

I raise one eyebrow at her.

"It's a thing we, uh ... liberated in a previous mission. A small weapons interference grenade. Long name for a simple thing. It deliberately interferes with any electronic weaponry and creates a distortion path in the telemetry. We only had one, and I didn't know if it would actually work."

"I guess it did."

"Almost." Plexi gestures to the corridor the medics took Aktip down. "I'm sorry, Ma'am."

I heave a sigh. "Let's hope she pulls through. In the meantime, there's plenty we can focus on to distract us." I look at Pedro. "Tell me what you know."

Pedro sits back in his chair. "This might be a hyperleap too far, but I'm betting that you already knew Errikson had the drive of the long-lost Constellation. Why you came to Ganymede I don't know, but my guess is that you want to relieve Errikson of his new booty." He leans forward and places both hands on the table. "Tell me straight. Have you found the Constellation?"

I stay silent for a while. The less people know about it, the better. But Pedro is my father's old friend and my mentor. The others say nothing and wait for my lead. I might have gained this crew by accident, thanks to Sloper, but so far, they are my guys. And girl. I decide to play it safe.

"Hypothetically, if I had, what would you advise?"

He claps his hands together and smiles. "I'd advise you to tell no one. But hypothetically, let's look at the situation—"

I hold my hand up. "Wait. Let me outline where we're at." I want my team to follow my lead, not Pedro's. "Sloper took Mitch hostage. He sent me to find the Constellation. He clearly knew something I didn't."

"Your father's involvement."

"Yes. What we've pieced together—and the less who know how we know this, the better—is that Errikson had removed the Constellation's drive, and we presumed he was bringing it to Ganymede."

Pedro rubs his chin. "You were right about that. But Errikson and the Jovians? What's going on there?"

I look around at all of them. "I'm betting the Jovians know something about the technology used. Somehow they've found out I might be able to access it, and they've paid Errikson to secure the drive."

Danielli looks confused. "But Errikson says he had help from your father?"

"Papa is dead," I say abruptly.

Pedro shrugs. "Then he used information he got from him when he was alive. Doesn't matter. What matters is—"

"What matters is that I rescue Mitch. Errikson is the Jovians' hired hand, and he seems to think my brother will also grant him access to the drive. But Sloper won't want to give him up, and he's waiting to rendezvous with me. Unless I give Sloper what he's after, he'll kill Mitch."

The room falls silent. Then the parts floating in my head come together.

I take a deep inhale and look around at the others. "Here's what we do: We steal the drive from Errikson. We find out why Papa helped him remove the drive. We refit the Constellation"—I glare at Pedro to make sure he knows the sensitivity of the information I've just confirmed—"then we persuade the Jovians to rescue my brother."

Herg splutters. "Anything else, Ma'am? Sounds like quite some plan you have." Plexi just stares at me. Danielli wears the beginnings of a smile.

I look at Herg. "Yes. I'm glad you asked. From what I hear, Oberon and the Circle of Seven are showing signs of being active again. It's time this Sector put aside its differences and combined forces. If it's true, we need to be ready."

I don't really know where all this has come from, except that just maybe, discovering I'm the Constellation's Captain unlocked a deep desire to free myself from my space pirate's existence. Or perhaps it's just that I feel the weight of Papa's hand from the grave on my shoulder. Exactly what he's asking me to do, I have no idea.

"And?" Danielli says. "You want us to be a part of that?"

I smile. "I can't think of a better crew for it."

"I'm confused," Pedro says.

"Then let me spell it out for you. We're going to force the Jovians and the Scorpion to combine forces, and we're going to make sure the Blood Empire comes out second best in any discussions about who runs this Sector."

Pedro sucks in a noisy breath, but Herg and Plexi exchange worried looks.

Danielli looks over at me. "You should know the previous mission Plexi referred to was against the Scorpion. I wouldn't exactly say we'll be welcomed with open arms."

Pedro ignores them. "What makes you think you're in any position to bring this about?"

I give him a cool look. "Because I'll be in command of the only battlecruiser ever to take down Oberon's forces."

His eyes almost pop out of his head, but before we get any chance to continue our conversation, the door opens, and the doctor looks around for me. She looks me in the eye. "I think you'd better come with me."

CHAPTER THIRTY-FOUR

SHE LEADS ME INTO A white and sterile recovery room, where Aktip, now clad in a medirobe, is lying on a bed. My heart leaps—she is awake. Her head swivels to me and she smiles. "You have worry, Madam Captain."

I stand next to her. "Thank you, Aktip. You've more than fulfilled any obligation. Let me get you back home as soon as I can arrange it."

"Actually she'll need to, if she's to survive." The doctor looks over at me. "We did the best we could. But even with the Rykkamon biomapping, there are treatments your colleague needs that are only available on Rykkamon. There's some bone and nerve damage, and Rykkamon has the specialized equipment for that. More to the point, she's lost a lot of blood. Blood that we don't stock. I've already told her this, but I estimate if she is not able to have a blood top up in the next two or three days ..." She shrugs.

I feel myself deflate, and try to smile at Aktip. "Then I guess we'd better get moving. I'll inform the crew."

Aktip is not capable of walking, but she assures me she is in no pain. I do not believe her. She is wheeled back on board, but insists on being in the helmroom with us. "You need my sensing, Madam Captain," she says.

"Really?" I smile at her. "You think after what we've all been through, anyone here is going to be anything less than honest?"

Aktip swivels to me. "Not here. For your negotiations."

Crap. She knows I'm planning to leave her on Rykkamon.

"How long will your treatment take?"

She regards me with troubled eyes. "I do not know. Less than one Rykkan week. But I am not specialist."

"You know I have to find my brother. I can't afford to lose any time." I almost said "any more time."

Aktip nods, but her eyes are bright. "This time, I have plan."

Everyone turns to look at Aktip.

CHAPTER THIRTY-FIVE

AKTIP'S PLAN IS AUDACIOUS. It could work.

We spend some time refining and filling in the holes she didn't see. Pedro volunteers to find his way back to Ganymede, suggesting that his underground network can keep it's ears to the ground for more information about Errikson's movements. He says he'll be able to stay out of Errikson's sight by calling in some favors. I make it plain to him that the information he is now privy to is a matter of life and death.

Pedro nods. "Your father and I went back a long way, divine one. I trusted him with my life. You can trust me with yours."

I hug Pedro, and he heads back onto NewSwiss12's surface.

"Divine one?" Danielli raises an eyebrow.

"If only it were true. But it's a long story. For when we are out the other side of this." I look over at our pilot. "Zhang, do you have an estimate of hyperDrive time to Rykkamon?"

"We should make it in under two days, Captain," the young man says, then continues. "But I already have the course plotted. Ready to commence at your order, Ma'am."

More and more, Danielli's team impresses me. I make a note to ask Danielli how they came together and what motivates them to be just mercenaries for hire, when they could be a valuable part of any organization.

"A few minutes, Zhang." I turn to Danielli. "Will the crew be ready?"

"I'll make it so, Ma'am." He leaves to prep everyone, and I

focus on my next task: construct a new hyper-relay message to Jordi. We need new coordinates and a convincing story. I ask Zhang to find options for coordinates that will suit the plan, and I concentrate on my words to Jordi.

It takes me almost twenty minutes before I am ready to send. Danielli is back and we are ready. I hand him my pad. "I value your input, Danielli. What is your response?"

He reads the message quickly then looks up with a smile. "Yes, Ma'am. That will do the trick, no doubt about it. Knowing Sloper's reputation."

I take back the pad and hit send. I open the shipwide comms. "This is the Captain. Our destination is Rykkamon, estimated time of travel"—I look down at the helmpad—"44 hours, 36 minutes. Sergeant Danielli has already given orders for our arrival." I pause. "Make sure you are well-rested."

Plexi gives me a strange look and I shrug. "Based on recent experience, we need all the rest we can get. I hear it's a soldier's best weapon."

She grins.

CHAPTER THIRTY-SIX

WE ARRIVE IN RYKKAMON'S OUTER orbit after an uneventful series of hops. Now we are at risk. If the Rykkan authorities pierce the thin disguise I'd managed to hack into our ship's ident, then we'll need to escape fast. But I have to find where Mitch is being held. Any mistake will come at a high cost.

Aktip cannot walk, so we dock at an orbit-station where one of us will wheel her to the shuttle. My hair is still jet-black, but my crew convinces me that my height, build and general "attitude," as they put it, might be too risky to expose to any Rykkan official. After all, there is a price on my head.

So we send Danielli to be the Captain of our purported exploration vessel. I'm hooked into his comms system in case they ask any tricky questions. Based on what I've seen of Danielli so far during both our training sessions with Aktip, he won't need my help. But I watch from his suitcam, anyway.

He enters the port pushing Aktip. The official stops them both and I hear Danielli request the shuttle as soon as possible, due to the serious injury sustained by a Rykkan native on our research ship. From the cam view I see the official enter notes into his pad. It's hard to see when a Rykkan is suspicious, so I hold my breath that Aktip's first step in her plan will work.

The official looks hard at Danielli for a few moments, then waves them both through to the shuttle station. I exhale and look at Plexi, who has just done the same. "Genius," she whispers. I nod.

Danielli returns to our ship, and Aktip is now on her own, accompanied by the advance medEvac team we have ordered for her. I feel responsible for the poor alien's plight. My impetuous actions earlier with the Rykkan gang may have saved her life, but the price she has paid has been excessive.

We disengage from the spaceport and after a short impulse drive flight, we exit Rykkamon's strong gravitational pull.

I order Zhang to punch us into free space using the fDrive. Once there, I tell him to cut the drive and bring the ship to a halt within comms range of the planet, but outside their authority.

I call a meeting in the helmroom.

Danielli and Plexi take the chairs, Zhang remains in the pilot's seat, and Ortiz is asleep, on an off-shift. Herg secures himself to a bulkhead and gets busy disassembling part of my ship's maneuvering system on a temporary worktable. I frown at him, but he doesn't look up.

"Don't worry about Herg, Ma'am," Plexi says. "He don't miss a trick. Just prefers playing with his hands."

I smile. "In the same way you like playing with weapons?"

Plexi's face reddens.

I look around at my crew. "Let's assume that Sloper's spies have worked out we briefly entered Rykkamon. My hyper-relay message should have him distracted for at least a day." *If Jordi did his work as promised.* "We have to work out how to get the data we need for the Constellation's drive. Does anyone here think it can be refitted?"

Danielli breaks the silence. "Logic says no, Ma'am. But there has to be a reason why it was so painstakingly removed." He lifts a shoulder. "Those cuts would have taken weeks. If whoever took it only wanted to disable the ship, there are faster ways."

I tighten my lips and tap my hands on the small helm table. "Which means that someone knows the plan for refitting it. But who?" I look around the ship's small bridge. Danielli, Plexi, Zhang and Herg look back at me blankly.

"Wouldn't Errikson?" Danielli asks.

"I'm not so sure. I think he's just been paid to get the Jovians access to what is in the drive. Maybe neither of them care about a refit."

"Is that why he wants your brother?" Plexi says.

Mitch. He is my main priority now we have taken care of Aktip. Plexi is right: Errikson wants Mitch. Or me. There's some reason Mitch is also the key. "I'm guessing that's the case. As far as our plan goes, that's our next step. We have to rescue Mitch from Sloper before Errikson either buys him or finds out where he is."

"So we wait." Danielli is calm.

I nod. "We wait. As terrible as it feels to me, we have to allow Aktip to do her work, and for my message to Jordi to reach Sloper."

As it turns out, we don't have to wait long. Sloper initially employed Danielli's squad, so I'm just about to ask for ideas about where he could have stashed my brother when the comms panel indicates a private incoming call.

From Jordi.

I tap the comm to allow the call to start, and to show only me to the caller. I allow the others to see Jordi on the holo and hear the conversation, but he won't hear or see them.

"You got my message."

After a delay, he inclines his head. "We're just under a day away. I called as soon as we could get live relay." He looks around furtively. "Sloper knows you're on Rykkamon."

I smile. "Then he would be wrong." I feel my expression turn serious. "Where is Mitch?"

A brief emotion crosses Jordi's face. Not long enough for me to pick it up. "I can't tell you, Indy."

I half rise out of my chair. The lo-grav straps hold me back. "What do you mean?"

Another figure enters the comm view. "Because if he did, I'd have to kill him." Sloper grins at me and I slap the comms connection closed.

I thought the delay sounded fake.

Someone leaked our visit to NewSwiss12. They aren't one day away at all. They're on Rykkamon.

CHAPTER THIRTY-SEVEN

"Zhang—how quickly can you get us back into Rykkamon?" My voice is urgent and Zhang picks up on it immediately by punching codes into the pilot's helmpad.

"On our way, Ma'am. Fifteen minutes tops."

I feel the sudden surge of acceleration as the fDrive cuts in and we're all pressed into our chairs. I open the ship's comms. "Captain speaking. All hands on deck for descent to Rykkamon. I'll need a small guerrilla party ready on landing to engage in tactical operations. Volunteers only."

I slap the helmchair's arm. How could I not have foreseen this? Of course Sloper would expect me to double-cross him.

"What is our mission, Ma'am?" Danielli says. "Plexi, Herg and I are all volunteers."

I level my gaze at Danielli. "I want Sloper. He knows where Mitch is. I won't be his lackey anymore. Not now we know what's at stake."

"Your plan?" From Plexi. She often forgets to address me.

"I don't have one." I'm hoping Aktip can help me enter Rykkamon's communication systems to locate Sloper's vessel, but it seems a long shot. And another reason to place Aktip in danger. In any case, she might be in the middle of critical medical treatment.

Danielli breaks the silence. "Then don't hunt him down. Make him come to you."

"How?" I furrow my brow.

"Tell him you know where the Constellation's drive unit is. Tell him when you help him liberate it from the Jovians, he'll have more power in the Sector than he ever dreamed of."

I let out a whistle. "That's risky. What if it comes true?"

He shrugs. "Think about it. The only risk we all have is if you—or Mitch—give him access to the drive."

"And I'd rather die than do that. Do you think Jordi has told him I have Captain status on the Constellation?"

Danielli shakes his head. "I'd say not. I think Sloper's bluffing, hoping to intimidate you. If he knew that, he'd have Mitch here, ready to trade. No, I think he thinks he holds all the cards."

"He holds my brother. And Errikson won't wait around for an invitation."

"Even more reason we let Sloper come to you. From what I know, he hates Errikson."

I bite my lip. "Alright. Zhang, take us only as far as Rykkamon's outer orbit. Let's make sure we all know what we're doing."

Several minutes later we emerge into Rykkan airspace. And into pandemonium.

The comm flashes and we come under rapid fire.

"Two cruisers approaching port and starboard," Zhang yells, "shields holding."

Our vessel is unarmed. We have no ability to return fire. Only shields. I'm not expecting this and am momentarily lost.

"Ma'am?" Zhang hesitates.

I snap to action. I look at Danielli and Plexi. "We don't have any defense. I'm taking us planetside." I turn back to Zhang. "Take us down to the surface." I give him the coordinates where I want us to land, and he glances back, a confused expression on his face. "I know what I'm doing, Zhang." I've given him my previous no-go zone landing area as our destination.

He blushes. "Yes, Captain. Taking evasive action now."

Zhang is turning out to be a real asset. He spins the salvage ship in a way I never expected, then drops us like a stone out of the clutches of whoever is attacking us, and we approach the planet's surface at a frightening pace. At such a speed I brace myself for impact, and I see the others doing the same.

But it's not needed: Zhang waits until the last moment, then I see him tap a brief instruction into the fDrive interface. At first I don't believe what I am seeing, then I come to my senses and try to reach across, but a sudden thrust of gravity pins me back in my chair.

We come to a violent halt, enough to whip my head back and I feel a stabbing pain in my neck.

Everything stops and we are all shell-shocked. "Clusters, Zhang. What were you thinking?" Plexi says, rubbing her shoulder where the harness had cut into her.

I move my neck around. It's painful, and I have a headache, but I don't think anything is broken.

Zhang looks sheepish. "Sorry, Ma'am. It was the only thing I could think to do."

I look at him, and smile, rubbing my neck with one hand. "We're alive, and we're not being shot at. So far, so good."

I tell Danielli to get crew and ship damage reports underway. Then I notice the comm flashing again. I tap the answer icon. The holo springs into life to reveal ... Aktip. Strapped into a Rykkan chair. Standing next to her, sporting medicasts on both his arms and a legbrace, is one Rykkan Chief. The background shows they are also in the outlaw's no-go zone, in the Chief's newly reconstructed cabin.

I'm still not very good at Rykkan expressions, but he does not look happy.

CHAPTER THIRTY-EIGHT

I PEER AT THE COMM. Aktip is already looking better. Has her treatment already taken effect? I am weary from the constant changes to every game plan I try to follow, but I must once again take control. I cut to the chase.

"What do you want?"

The Chief bares his teeth in a red Rykkan grin. "You are in a hurry."

I sigh. "Unless it escaped your attention, I landed somewhat hastily, in a ship that is not welcome on this planet. Even in a no-go zone. We were attacked in Rykkamon's outer orbit." I furrow my brow. "How did you know we would land here?"

"Questions, questions. All to be answered. Your friend here already give me helpful answers." He pats Aktip's shoulder.

"It is alright, Madam Captain. I am prisoner, but I am not in pain," Aktip says.

I don't understand. I look over at Danielli. He gives me a hand signal to indicate that I should keep the Chief talking.

"Chief, you've always been a straight talker. Help me out here. Unless you tell me what you want, I have to find a way to get off this planet and avoid two very aggressive fighter ships."

The Rykkan Chief waves his hand dismissively. "They will not pursue you. You are safe from Rykkan's police. For now. While we talk."

I am definitely missing something here. "How do you know they will not track us down?"

The Rykkan spits on the ground in front of him. "Your brain shaken from bad landing. Fighter ships are under my control. You understand now?"

Several connections close in my mind. "You wanted to force me here? To take revenge? You must know that it was not me who raided your camp. That was—"

"Sloper's assassin. Yes, I know this. Your friend here told me truth."

I slump down—easy in the hi-grav, though our ship is trying to compensate. "Let's start again. What do you want?" If the Chief isn't holding Aktip as revenge for me supposedly destroying his camp, mowing down his people and stealing his loot, then what does he want?

The Rykkan speaks. "I think we talk in opposites. What—or should I say, who—is it you look for?" Once again he grins.

I feel the blood run from my face. He knows about Mitch? I see Aktip's eyes pulsing. I realize both she and the Chief are in range sufficient to sense my state. I calm myself down and concentrate on my love for my brother. It's hard to stop the recent imagery of his capture, and I can't help letting my pain influence my emotions.

The Chief nods and I see Aktip visibly relax. "Yes, your brother."

"Sloper has him. So what's new? I came to Rykkamon to bring Aktip home for medical help. But I also plan to find out where Sloper is holding Mitch. Someone here has that information, and as soon as you let Aktip go, we intend to discover where he is and leave."

"Now you know what I have for you." He is grinning widely now.

I freeze. "You know where Sloper took my brother?"

"Oh yes." He can't stop grinning. "Also know where Sloper docked lightCruiser." His grin disappears abruptly. "So here is deal. Which you take or your friend dies."

Danielli catches my attention. He motions to himself and Herg. Should they head back inside the ship and don gravSuits? I shake my head and focus back on the Chief.

"I want verification of your information before I agree to any deal," I say. "Prove you know where my brother is and we can talk. But I have a deal for you: let me exchange places with Aktip. Take me hostage instead. Aktip is innocent."

The Chief's eyes bulge. "I accept offer. But we don't wait. I show my truth to your friend here. She will say I have truthful information. Then you come here and I let her go."

I don't get it. This is too easy. "Fine. Verify your information. Now."

The Chief turns to Aktip, looks her in the eye and steadies himself for a moment. Then he speaks in a rush of Rykkan. I watch Aktip nodding. He stops and waits. Aktip looks into the comm cam. "He is speaking the truth, Madam Captain. He told me where your brother is imprisoned."

I stare at the male Rykkan. "Why do you tell me this?"

He bares his teeth. "So you do want deal. Good. You swap with this one"—he points to Aktip—"then I take you to lightCruiser and we go to Takao—"

"Takao?"

He nods. "Your brother hidden there. Sloper has trade with this Scorpion, but Scorpion not know of brother situation."

I realize what he has just said. "We go? What do you want on Takao?"

"I don't want anything from Takao. I make you deal. I give you ship and help you find brother." He smiles, revealing a wide expanse of red. "Then you give me battlecruiser."

I hear Plexi's sharp intake of breath, then everyone starts talking at once.

CHAPTER THIRTY-NINE

Despite the protestations of my crew, I put on my gravSuit and head down the salvage vessel's ramp. I stomp across to the Chief's cabin, where the door opens. Aktip confronts me. "Madam Captain, this is not good idea."

"I know, Aktip. But what other choice do I have? I must rescue Mitch. Without him, all is worthless anyway. At least you are healing. Why was that so fast?"

Aktip regards me. "It is how things work on Rykkamon. I am weak, but I will self-repair."

The Chief appears behind her. "We must leave. My people make way safe, but does not last forever."

I step aside and watch Aktip limp off to the salvage ship's ramp. I turn back to the Chief. "Where to now?" He motions me to another door—a larger one—in the side of the cabin. He taps a panel, and it slides up, to reveal a duopod. I climb in, with one brief look back at the ship, the ramp now closing. I wonder if it is the last time I'll see my friends. I try to shake off my despair, but it sits heavy in my heart.

As soon as we are under way, I quiz the Chief. "How did you know of the battlecruiser?"

He laughs—a grating noise to a human. "The whole Sector speaks about cruiser rumors." He swivels back to look at me behind him in the pod's inline two-seater format. "But only I guess correctly."

"How did you find my lightCruiser?"

"I have informers in dock. Your friend told me about Sloper and his assassin. As soon as two meets two, I know who to ask." He shoots me an expression I do not understand. "Is good your friend injured and come to Rykkamon. Otherwise I would kill you. Big price on your head, too."

Is my bounty now "alive or dead?"

I remain silent for the rest of the journey to a remote shuttlepad. When we arrive at the pad, I see there are no buildings nearby, only a mountain range visible faintly in the light-purple atmosphere. "Where are we?" I ask.

"Better you do not know. Is outlaw landing pad."

There's a lot of things about Rykkamon I still do not know. The underground is more established than I'd ever imagined, and the corruption must be widespread for the Chief to orchestrate my passing through without question. Yet Aktip and her dinner guests were the epitome of integrity. Two distinct cultures. I make a note to ask Aktip. If I ever see her again.

A shuttle descends and the doors open. I suppose I will soon find out if the Chief really is taking me to my lightCruiser. The Chief utters some Rykkan into the comms and we disembark from our pod. He points to the shuttle, brandishing a laserpistol. I climb inside, feeling my suit power me up, and am immediately manhandled by some Rykkan thugs and pushed into a seat. I feel cuffs wrap around each wrist and to the seat. I offer no resistance. My plan is not to fight. Not here.

The Chief takes a seat close to the cabin. His goons sit around me. No one speaks a word until the Chief gives the okay to lift off.

As the hi-grav relinquishes its control, I sit back a little and gauge the Rykkan crew. Rykkans are hard to recognize with only one glance, but I'm sure I've not seen any of these guys before. They obviously know me though, as I occasionally catch one or two of the eight or so discussing something, then making slicing motions, after which one of them inevitably swivels his head back at me and grins. Not in a friendly way.

In less than an hour we dock at an unfamiliar spaceport. Presumably another blackmarket-controlled outpost. When we step through the airlock, I see it is dirty and run-down. Definitely not Rykkan tourism class. After I remove my gravSuit, someone cuffs my hands together. We leave the shuttle, and take a travelbelt across the port's large space to an airlock opposite. To one side is a large plexiglass viewing screen. I adjust the angle of my walk ever so slightly so I can see the side of the ship docked at the port. Enough comes into view that I can recognize the Slingshot. I actually manage a smile. So far, the Rykkan Chief has shown he really does speak the truth.

"Now you have trust, yes?" Once again, a Rykkan almost reads my mind. I'm thinking with enough training, a human could communicate directly to a Rykkan without a word transpiring between them. But not the other way around, as I've never been close to understanding what any of them think.

I stare at him. "Trust is always earned and easily burned." The words that leave my mouth are the same ones I've heard uttered more than twenty times over by Papa, but it's true. I hold up my cuffed hands. "So now that you see I trust you, will you trust me?"

He laughs and gestures to one of his thugs, who raises his brow protuberance. The Chief growls at him. The thug flinches, and removes the cuffs. I shake my wrists out and give the Chief what I hope is an engaging and transparent smile. Aktip's training had better work. I'd done well at learning to transmit false signals, but repressing my state under stress was a different matter. I do my best to relax, but the tension in my jaw suggests otherwise.

The airlock to my ship opens, and we all file in. I take a quick look around on the way to the helm. Everything still looks as shiny and new as the day I relieved Santo—Errikson's SIM—of the tricked-out ship. I take my place in the captain's chair. My Rykkan accomplice seats himself in the chair next to me. He swivels to look me in the eye. "We both take big risk, no? I give you your ship, now we find your brother. So far my promise for deal is carried out. Now is your turn. Any funny human tricks, and my men will remove your legs." I notice two of his men stationed either side of me, chairs turned and laserwhips primed.

I hold my gaze on the Rykkan and try not to hold my breath. Aktip told me that breathing is the key to what I am about to do: trick a live lie-detector. Sort of. "You help me rescue my brother and I will give you the Constellation."

He lets out what a human might think is a giggle, but I know enough about Rykkan negotiation that this is an accidental admission. The Chief cannot contain his excitement. "And we kill Sloper and the Darpesh-thing."

I suck in a huge lungful of air. I hadn't planned on a full-scale battle. But what is it to me? Sloper has already ruined enough of my life, and I'd always planned to kill him. Perhaps it just wouldn't be at my own hand.

I nod, then I lean forward and hold my finger over the helmpad. "Do I have your permission to set course for Takao?"

He nods and grins. "We are team now. The Scorpion must watch out, I think."

From what I know about the Scorpion, it's we who need to watch out.

I tap the pad and we slide away from the lock. Takao here we come.

CHAPTER FORTY

THE CHIEF ASSURED ME HE'D paid off enough people that Sloper would never know my lightCruiser was no longer where he left it last. We both agree to send the salvage vessel on ahead with a deliberately high number of hyperDrive hops. Sloper will think we are running and set pursuit. He will realize we have discovered Mitch's location.

Meanwhile, I will run the Slingshot at maximum capacity to arrive at Takao before them all.

But I will not underestimate Sloper. He'll send a hyper-relay in advance. There'll be a welcoming party.

I have a plan for that.

Even with my lightCruiser's stunning speed—so nice to be back at the helm of a fully armed ship, and not some dirty old salvage vessel—it still takes us the best part of one standard earth day before we arrive at Takao.

I place us in orbit around the giant planet and request the connection the Rykkan Chief gave me. While I wait, I take in the magnificent view of Takao's moons. Six of them, two small and four much larger, but all rich in rare earths. And the reason the Jovians despise the Scorpion so much. His restriction on the supply of the rare earths hobbles the Jovian stranglehold on Sector energy trade. I watch three of the picturesque moons flash their multicolored eyes at me, and wonder how Mother Nature has conspired to create such greed in mankind. Or any kind.

On a visit to the ship's bathroom facility, I take in a quick check of my carefully secured purchase: my heart lifts when I find it stowed exactly where it was before Sloper "borrowed" the ship.

In the helmroom, the commPanel lights up with my reply, and we are given docking coordinates for an obscure area in Takao's Resistance-owned region.

The Rykkan Chief watches me tap in the coordinates. "You lucky I have connections on Takao."

I turn to look at him, and smile. "Which is a good thing. But tell me ... why do the Rykkans hate the Scorpion? So much so they will come here as mercenaries and fight for land not their own?"

The Chief's head swivels back and forth, as if he is deciding what to share. "You speak true. We have always had disgust of Scorpion. Do not know why. Maybe to do with trade. Maybe because we are strong"—he points to his squat torso, built for high gravity—"and they little sticks." He shudders, as if the appearance of Takaons is repulsive. "But is good for you and me because we look like another delivery." He grins that red grin.

The irony grows. For all intents and purposes, I'm doing exactly what I was accused of on Rykkamon: delivering a shipload of thugs to Takao. The intention may be different, but the act is the same. I take a deep breath and focus. I'm here for one purpose, and that's to rescue Mitch. But I will have to take care.

On the descent I watch a news holo. The Scorpion has control of more than seventy percent of the planet. The Resistance defends the remainder aggressively, and it is they to whom we deliver our crew. It's easy to see why the Scorpion has amassed such a following. He must be an expert in mass-psychology and social memes, as pithy messages and meme-driven imagery is everywhere I look on the holo.

"Jovians steal our energy, then sell it back to us"
"Talk is cheap. Energy isn't. Jovians out"

"Power to everyone, no more Jovian monopoly"
"Build shields around our moons"
"Takaon truth, not Jovian duplicity"
"Jovian justice is not our justice"
"Take Takao Forward"

We land in the Takaon morning to discover our new "troops" are welcome: there is a mass-rally planned by the Scorpion at five pm, Takao-time. The Resistance are planning a major uprising against the Scorpion's supporters, and this event is to be the crowning glory. The Resistance are relying on their hired Rykkan army to do much of their dirty work.

We meet members of the Resistance, surprised to find a human captain running in a Rykkan crew. They seem glad I am on their side, but the more I hear of the planned altercations, the more I have a sour taste in my mouth. Papa fought for equality and fair treatment, and I feel dirty just being here. Let alone the fact that I have to fight to rescue his son from Sloper's clutches.

While the Chief's men prepare for the upcoming battle, I muse on Sloper's involvement with the Scorpion, and where his payoff lies. Sloper won't lift a finger unless it's for gain of credits. Substantial gain.

I am shaken out of my reverie when the Chief beckons me over to an assembly point. I notice he is out of his restrictive leg brace and arm casts, once again demonstrating the uncanny Rykkan ability to heal—or "self-repair" as they keep calling it.

We camp on the edge of the landing zone, and as far as anyone else would know, we're just another bunch of Rykkans—and token human rebel—preparing to do what we do best: get paid to maim and kill when a fight breaks out.

The Scorpion knows how to stir up trouble and create a crowd. The rally is in the center of the Scorpion's strongest location and the capital of Takao, Hoto. Because it's the capital, it's also the city where the Resistance are free to come and go as they please. "Bring it on," the Scorpion seems to be saying. And bring it, we will.

The rally is to be staged in a massive stadium, capable of holding 500,000 spectators. We are waiting on notification from the Chief's spies as to the exact location of Sloper's lair, but so far the Chief believes we will be able to head into Hoto in the guise of allies of the Resistance. No one will know that we are any different to the Resistance's hired hands. The Scorpion's army will maintain a line beyond which neither protesters, nor their "supporters" can proceed.

But they have not reckoned on a large flanking force of Rykkan mercenaries. From what I can ascertain among the discussions I've overheard, it may well be a bloodbath.

We set off on our march into Hoto. I check my datapad. The salvage ship will arrive in a few hours' time, and I presume Sloper will be right behind them. I set my pad to notify me as soon as the ship is in range, and focus on the task at hand.

The Chief has said very little since landing. I step up beside him, easy in Takao's gravity. He swivels his head. "You are nervous."

"You mistake nerves for apprehensive tension," I say.

He grunts.

"When we approach the building where my brother is held, I plan to be in and out. No fighting. Your job is only to open up access. Do you understand?"

He grunts again, then lets out a suppressed laugh. "You think is simple. Walk in, ask for brother back and walk out, arm with arm."

"Of course not. But I don't plan to make any more trouble than is necessary."

He shrugs. "No trouble. We make sure no fighting by killing

anyone in way."

I stop momentarily, but the Chief continues marching and I stumble to catch up. More Resistance supporters are joining the march, interspersed with Rykkans here and there. "That's your solution to anything? Killing?"

He fixes both bulbous eyes on me. "You think group of Rykkans just walk up to building in Hoto and march in?" He waves a clawed hand at the increasing crowds marching toward the stadium. "Today security is maximum. We find brother quick, otherwise plan to get cruiser not work." He looks ahead for a while, then swivels back to me and grins. "Anyway, we have special codes. I think we get inside."

Slightly reassured, I inhale deeply and double-check my equipment, tucking my laserpistol inside the band of my groundsuit's pants. *I'm coming for you, Mitch. If you're still alive.*

The stadium is in sight ... and earshot. I hear the cheers and screams of a huge, frenzied crowd. They chant for their leader, the Scorpion. "*Sting the Resistance, sting them dead,*" they chant, in an aggressive, devilish rhyme that brings me out in goosebumps.

People on foot crowd the mainways leading in to Hoto. I take a moment to sum up my supposed native comrades. The Chief is right: they are taller than an average earth-descended human, and skinny. They walk with a certain lope from the low gravity, and I try to emulate it. Anything that makes me stand out less. My hair is still in the long, black braid. Better than bright red, but still identifiable. I pull a cap from my backpack, stuff the braid into it and pull it tight to my head. Somehow it feels better.

We turn a corner, jostling shoulders now, and the Chief points out a narrow lane to the right, that runs in between the tall buildings. As prearranged, we peel off into it, one-by-one. The marching crowd beside us is too hungry to beat a path to their chanting enemy to care, though I see we attract a few glances.

As soon as we are well down the laneway, we increase our speed to a brisk jog—easy in the giant planet's low gravity. We race between the tall blocks and around two more corners, then the lead Rykkan dives down a set of stairs, leaping three or four at a time. I follow and soon we are in a complex set of interconnecting subterranean tunnels, dimly lit and festooned with conduits and pipes. The chanting is muffled, but sounds closer. I realize that we are entering the service access tunnels under the stadium.

Loud static from a nearby PA system blasts my ears, then an announcer's voice booms through the tunnel.

"Prepare to salute the Scorpion. Our leader requires your undivided attention. Please be silent as we welcome the Scorpion to the arena."

Silence is not what we hear. Instead a ground-shaking roar erupts that we can feel rumbling through the tunnels. I look up reflexively, as if the roof will crack.

Someone clearly wants workers under the stadium to witness all speeches—then I realize it's probably there to keep tabs on any game commentary; as I understand it, the normal function of the stadium. The loudspeakers are not visible, but they must line every tunnel we run down, because we are forced to be party to the Scorpion's speech.

His voice is electronically distorted to sound mechanical, or computer-generated. I ask the Rykkan jogging next to me why.

"There are death threats to Scorpion"—he flashes his red teeth at me—"good price. So he keep identity secret. No one know the Scorpion."

Helpful. I could come face to face with the man and not know.

I resume my focus as we dodge and weave through the tunnel

system. The Scorpion's speech follows us, as if we are his captive audience. At one point we pass a wall-mounted holo and I steal a brief glimpse of the stadium. Rangy Takaons pack it full, pumping fists into the air. They look toward a massive stage, on which a line-up of tough-looking battle-dress clad officers stand to attention, facing the crowd. An anonymous silhouette broadcasts from a giant holoscreen behind them.

We leave the holo behind, and I glance back to see the camera zoom in and linger on one hard-bitten military face, then we turn, and he is gone.

But the chanting rhetoric continues.

"*Who here is willing to hand our planet on a plate to the Jovians?*"

The audience roars their dissent.

"*Who believes that energy is a law of nature, and not Jovian law?*"

"*WE DO!*" thunders the response.

"*Who believes we must protect our moons and our hard-won wealth from the Jovian energy plunderers?*"

The roar builds.

"*Who believes we must protect our planet and our people from the inevitable Jovian rule, if we simply acquiesce to their advances?*"

The responses crash through the PA system, overwhelming it into an unintelligible cacophony.

My hypnotic jogging rhythm and the low gravity allows me to focus on the speech with a strange clarity. I find it hard to fault the logic: who *would* want the Jovians dominating our sector? Or worse, restricting supply of key energy and key trade routes just to make a profit.

I catch up to the Chief as we weave through more tunnels. He thinks I want to know how much further, but I wave his response away. "Yes, I see we are nearly there. Tell me, is the Resistance supported by the Jovians? Do they provide arms and finance?"

He shakes his head—or swivels in that odd Rykkan manner. "I do not think so."

"Then why do they resist? What's in it for them? I mean ... the Jovians aren't exactly the Sector's friends."

"They fear this Scorpion. His power has swept the world quickly, and Takao was peaceful colony. Too much power anywhere never good idea."

I regard the Chief with new understanding. I thought of him as a thug with no philosophical bent whatsoever. Even alien crooks can surprise you, it seems. Then again, to everyone on this planet, I am also an alien crook. And planning a surprise.

We come to a halt in front of a double-door and security system panel. "You have the special codes?" I say, still slightly breathless, even with the ease of the pace.

The Chief grins. "Yes." He nods to one of his men, who steps forward and attaches several small flat plastisteel pucks around the door's perimeter. He waits for the Chief, who motions us all back several meters and around the last corner, following us in. Then we see the remaining Rykkan run back around. His speed in the low gravity has to be seen to be believed. No wonder they pay the mercenaries good money—

There is an ear-shattering explosion, and I am left reeling. Dust and smoke blows around the corner. Even the Rykkans stagger a little. I hear the thug who set the charges yell at the Chief. It sounds like an apology.

The Chief steps up to me and speaks. It sounds like he is speaking under water. "Our special codes too strong." He grins again. "Perhaps Scorpion will think he has new fans banging big drum." He beckons me and turns.

My ears are still ringing as we make our way into the building.

These corridors are well lit, and I see from the signs this must be a government building. They look the same no matter the planet. The Chief seems to know which direction to head, and I follow, rubbing my ears as if it will improve my hearing.

In the background I hear the Scorpion continuing, but can barely understand what he is saying. Something about launching a tactical military initiative beyond the moons, but more than that, I cannot pick up.

We round a corner and come face-to-face with three security guards. My Rykkan gang does not even stop, but barrel through the tall, slim human-descended Takaons as if they were reeds lining a lake. They shoot all three with a neurostunner as we pass. I flinch a little, knowing full well the agony of neuroweaponry. We leave them writhing on the floor behind us, enter a stairwell and leap down several flights.

The Chief's head swivels, and he calls back over his non-existent shoulder. "We are there in two more levels."

My hearing is returning. I hear the Scorpion winding up his speech with a call to arms. The anonymous, electronic nature of his voice makes him sound even uglier than I imagine him to be.

"*Takao will not lay down.*"

<cheer>

"*Takao will protect its own!*"

<roar>

"*Takao will defend the Sector against domination!*"

<thunderous applause>

We emerge from the stairwell, and my thoughts about the Scorpion vanish. Advancing toward us is a column of guards, weapons raised and already shooting. We fall back into the stairwell, forced to leave one of the Chief's men wounded in the corridor.

The Chief barks out a stream of commands, and two huge

Rykkans take position either side of the stairwell doorway. The guy who laid the charges squats down low, inches forward to the opening. In his left claw is a handful of the small explosive pucks. He extends the arm carefully through the opening. The other two loose an intimidating stream of plasma fire down the corridor. The Rykkan on the floor uses his powerful arm swing and the low gravity to launch the pucks along the corridor's surface, and down to the right.

Except for the plasma rifle shooters, we all pull back, and this time I cover my ears. I still hear the explosion, and feel the rush of hot air and debris rush past us. Some of the shrapnel scratches my cheeks as it blasts by.

I am grabbed by the Chief and dragged out into the corridor. "Fast," he shouts. "We get brother, then fight our way out."

Fight our way out? With approximately half a million angry Takaons only meters above us? I ignore my nagging doubts and rush down the smoking corridor, now littered with body parts and glistening with light-red blood. I have to leap over the carnage to avoid skating along the slippery remains.

I tense my stomach to stop its protests and I yell out for my brother periodically as we advance. Resistance spies told me he's being held in a room on this level.

There is no reply, but we rifle-blast open each door, only to find empty rooms.

Only one door remains, facing us at the end of the corridor. My heart is racing and I gallop up to it, but the Chief beats me. He holds up one hand in a universal gesture. Wait.

We all crouch either side of the door. One Rykkan swings around and virtually empties his plasma rifle's charge to leave a hissing mess of melted plastisteel, and we jump through it. On the other side of the door, Takaon soldiers are trying to pick themselves off the ground, but the Chief's goons mow them down. Beyond the twitching, dying fighters is a plastisteel-barred cage.

A man gets to his feet just outside the cage.

Sloper.

CHAPTER FORTY-ONE

BEHIND THE BARS, A FAMILIAR figure sprawls, tied to a chair. Also in the cage, and holding a laserpistol to his captive's head is another familiar shape. Darpesh.

Everything slows down. We all point weapons at Sloper, including myself. How did he beat me to Takao?

He grins at me through the smoky trails. "Indy. I had a feeling it was you. Brotherly love and all that. But unfortunately it is all for nothing. The rest of my men will be here soon, and unless this is a suicide mission for you and your brother, I suggest you tell your moronic spinhead army—"

He does not finish, as the Chief simultaneously erupts in a piecing war cry and splits Darpesh's head in two with a precise crack of a laserRifle. He swivels to train his weapon on Sloper, and I throw myself in front of him, hoping I'm not too late.

"CHIEF, STOP!" I hold one hand up, staring at the Chief, and at the same time I flick my laserpistol behind me and let off a low power burst at Sloper's ankles. I hear a scream of pain and Sloper hits the floor, though not as hard as I would like.

I glare at the Chief, the blood rising in my face. "We have a deal. But to get my brother out of here, and you to the Constellation, we might need some bargaining power."

Sloper's voice is weak, but clear. "So you do have the Constellation. Taking this gang of thieving spinheads to it would be a Sector-sized mistake." He grunts when another Rykkan kicks him. They may not understand Galactic, but they can still recognize the word spinhead.

I do not look back, but wait for the Chief to calm down. "Where is Jordi?" I call over my shoulder.

Sloper laughs. "He escaped. He predicted you would try to come here before me. After I'd dangled a few credits in front of him as an incentive for his opinion. The coward knew he'd either have to face me or you, so he chose to save his own skin."

I nod. Jordi sold us out to save himself. Probably the only time I'll ever agree with Sloper.

The Chief is breathing heavily. I advance toward him and out of the corner of my eye, I see his men edge in to protect him. We both ignore them. This close, I tower over the Rykkan and look down. "Darpesh is dead. You've had your revenge. But you nearly didn't get the prize. My brother could have died—"

"But he did not. I am perfect shooter." The Chief does not grin this time. "I am entitled to extinguish debt owed to my men killed by this one," he points to the headless Darpesh bleeding out on the ground next to my brother.

"That may be true, but we have a deal, and Sloper is my debt, not yours. Unless you have a magic wand, he is also our pass out of here. Are we agreed? If not, we fight here and now, and you lose the Constellation."

"It's real, then?" The voice is weak, but it's one I've known for years. I whip around to see Mitch raising a smile at me.

I'm happy to see him alive and talking, but cannot help myself. I mimic his voice. "Hi, Sis. Thanks so much for rescuing me from an almost impossible situation. I owe you one."

He manages to laugh, then coughs up more blood trying to talk. I wince and wait for him to speak. Eventually he does. "We're not out yet. But can someone get me out of here? My companion has lost his head."

I motion to Sloper, then kick him when he doesn't move. He

reaches up to a doorpad, taps in a code, and the bars slide up. I walk in and plant a soft kiss on Mitch's forehead. "Glad you're still here."

He glances up. "We have a lot to talk about. Assuming we make it that far."

"Don't worry," I say, cutting the metran-fiber-ropes free with Darpesh's laserdagger. "I brought backup. Unfortunately Sloper beat them—and us—here, which wasn't part of the plan."

Mitch staggers to his feet, then falls against me. Luckily the planet's delicate clutch makes me almost as superhuman as the Rykkans, and I hold him easily. We step out of the cage with me supporting him until we reach Sloper. I kick him again. "On your feet. You want to see the Constellation, you need to come with us."

The Rykkan Chief starts to protest, but I hold up my hand. "We have a deal. It wasn't discussed who I would need to help me honor it. Now you need to get us off the planet." I jerk my head at the blasted doorway. "Preferably as easily as you got us in here."

The Chief's eyes pulse momentarily, then he turns, shouts orders to his men, and they lope off. I follow, almost carrying Mitch, not quite as fast as the group ahead. I figure they can do all the shooting. Sloper limps behind, prodded by a Rykkan bringing up the rear.

The crowd noise has lessened and I no longer hear the Scorpion's digitized voice. I assume the rally is over. Hopefully that means our exit will be under the cover of a moving crowd. Did the predicted violence occur? I have no way of knowing.

We turn into the stairwell and make our way up. I thank the universe for the lessened pull of gravity, or Mitch and I would never make the relentless climb.

We pass the level we entered from and continue to climb

further. I call up to the Chief. "Where are we going?"

"To the roof. You signal for pickup."

"Me? But won't the Scorpion be unimpressed with a group of Rykkans trying to pick up a skyride?" I cannot understand the Chief's plan, but he does not answer. I check my suitcomm is live, and tap a short signal to my own ship, which will then autorelay my coordinates to the salvage ship. If it is here.

I almost bump into the Rykkan Chief, who has hold of Sloper and waits for me at the entry to the roof. "You tell me he is ticket out of here. I think a lot about this. Skyride will see Sloper and you and pick up, no trouble. Then you persuade driver to wait"—he points at my laser rifle—"and I come too."

I incline my head at the others. "Your men?"

He grins. "They fight way out. Not noticed among Resistance. You make pickup of them with other ship. We all meet at battlecruiser. Is perfect plan, yes?"

Mitch is tugging at my arm, and I see Sloper, though pale, is following the conversation intently. I ignore them both. "Yes. Maybe not perfect. But a plan." I leave Mitch to support himself against the stairwell wall, and I stride out—skipfloat out—onto the roof. I pull Sloper behind me, putting up with his wounded scream. He's lucky to be alive. I hail one of the many skyrides hovering over the stadium to transport the more wealthy Takaons, and one drops to us immediately. The doorpad slips back and I get in, motioning to Sloper and further back, to my brother, to follow suit. I lean forward to the pilot and shove a laserpistol barrel in his ear. "Say nothing about your passengers, or you'll never say anything again. I'll pay double credits for your trouble." He nods and says nothing, staring forward.

The Chief is the last to enter the passenger cabin, and I realize we could not have fitted more. Close up, both Mitch and Sloper look worse for wear. I need Sloper alive for now, but my brother will be my priority. I instruct the pilot to take us to the spaceport, no delay, and we whip off, bringing a groan from my brother and a wince from Sloper. I keep my pistol in the pilot's view, pointing at him.

The skyride takes only minutes, but is enough for me to see ugly crowds on the streets, held at bay by Takaon authorities. The predicted bloodbath hasn't eventuated, but even from this height I sense the status quo is on a knife edge.

Despite the brewing tension below us, the Chief's timing and our plan work perfectly. We touch down next to the Slingshot, and I help Mitch out. He needs stims as soon as possible, then proper care, though I am unsure exactly where I will obtain this. We all enter my ship, and I proceed to the medroom, jab stimpacks into Mitch and breathe a sigh of relief.

I turn back to the door, but I am forced back in to the medroom by three large Rykkans, who rip my weaponry from me and push me against the bunk Mitch is lying on. They hold me down—there's no way I can resist Rykkan power. I curse loudly.

The Chief comes in to the small room, filling the confined space.

"What are you doing?" I say. "We had a deal."

"Still same deal. Now with insurance. I keep your brother, you take me to battlecruiser. You give me battlecruiser, I give you brother back." He exposes his red teeth in a grimace. "Maybe I give you Sloper, too."

He turns to leave, then stops, swiveling his head to look back at me. "No battlecruiser. No brother."

CHAPTER FORTY-TWO

I STAY CONSTRAINED AT THE hands of the Chief's men for a while, then get up to move. They push me back. I shake off a strong arm. "Let me go, you fools. How else are we going to get to the Constellation? My ship won't fly itself."

They let me go and I storm out of the room, resisting the urge to look back at Mitch.

I make my way up to the helmroom and shove the Rykkan sitting in the captain's chair out of the way. I glare at the Rykkan Chief, who just grins at me. I turn to my helmpad, set the coordinates for our first hyperDrive hop, and we launch. The cruiser's effortless drive power presses us momentarily back into our seats, though Takao's gravity is an easier escape than Rykkamon. We are soon out of orbit and at the first hop launch point. I tap the pad to engage a preset hyperDrive sequence to where my calculations predict the Constellation will be.

"We'll be there in under twenty-three hours."

"And your friends?" The Chief grins again.

"We'll meet them there. With the rest of your men. But they follow my orders. Our deal stands. Now do you mind if I tend to my brother?" I hear a weak voice in the rear of the helmroom.

"Since you insisted on saving me from execution, perhaps you might see your way to giving me some help here?" It's Sloper. I'd totally forgotten about him. He was my insurance policy for leaving Takao, and now I don't really need him. Though a part of me argues that fact. I'm responsible for him being here, and I'm directly responsible for his injury. I will help the man I once set out to kill. After he gives up information. And after I've treated Mitch.

"Sure thing, Sloper. You'll get your turn." I push up into the air, and float down the passageway to the medbay. I order the Rykkan guards out of the room, and when they don't respond, I slap the commPanel. "Chief, tell your goons they can wait outside the medbay. Some privacy while I treat my brother would be appreciated."

He barks a command over the comm, and the three bulky Rykkans leave. The door slides closed behind them.

Mitch props himself up on his elbows. "What the hell, Indy? You're just going to hand the Constellation over on a silver platter to this guy?"

"Oh ye of no faith." I smile at Mitch. "Let me work you over first. We can talk while I get you fixed up."

I pull the medscanner from the panel next to the bunk and push Mitch gently back down on the bed. I set the scanner to start, and the curved alloy sensor hovers down to Mitch's feet and begins a slow scan up his body.

"How did you find it?" he says.

"Sloper hired me."

"What the—?"

I wave his questions away. "Not important. Not now. But it has no drive. It's just a hulk running on emergency power, with a giant hole of nothingness where its drive should be."

Mitch's eyes light up. "So that's what Errikson was crowing about."

I take my eyes away from the scanner's screen output and look at Mitch. "You knew he had the drive?"

He grunts as the scanner makes its way over his abdomen. "Makes two of us, by the sound of it."

"What happened on Ganymede?"

"I tracked down where Papa's laserSword came from on Mars, and it led me to Ganymede. I found information that some people weren't happy about sharing and had to leave in a hurry. That's when I ran into a trap set by your friend and mine."

"What information?" I have to wait while the scanner passes Mitch's face, then begins the downward scan.

"You first. Why did you agree to take these guys to the Constellation? In the wrong hands ..." he trails off and looks at me. Confusion flickers across his face.

"It's protected. It has a self-defense system that destroys any ship that approaches or tries to board. Whoever is behind the evacuation did a thorough job. There's no sign of so much as a fight on board."

He narrows his eyes. "You've been on board? I thought you said it has a defense system."

The scanner is almost finished, and I wait for it to come to a stop at Mitch's feet. I look at the data on the screen and tap a button to bring it up on the holo for Mitch to see. "You have some serious abdominal injuries. Blood loss. Nothing broken though. We can fix the blood loss, but the injuries need rest and repair. You'll have to take it easy for a while."

He tries to sit up, but even the zero-gee makes him groan and he lies back down, relying on the bunk's autostabilizing straps to hold him gently in place. "Yeah, I have my vacation all planned, so no worries there. But you didn't answer my question. How did you get on board? How does the defense system work—did you hack in?"

I smile. "No need. The ship's Captain can override it."

He chokes briefly. "You found the Constellation's Captain?"

I feel my smile broaden. "I *am* the Constellation's Captain. But don't tell the Chief."

For once, Mitch is lost for words and just stares at me.

CHAPTER FORTY-THREE

I FINISH JABBING A STIMPACK into Sloper. I've already placed a medpatch over his leg wound, but when I looked at the injury before covering it over, I saw the first signs of sepsis. If he doesn't die, he will almost certainly lose the leg. The stims start to take effect. Sloper opens his eyes and looks at me, his face still tight from pain.

"You set out to kill me. Then you save me from summary execution. Next you attempt to shoot off my leg. And now you supply medical assistance. Why?" He grimaces as I cover up the medpatch with skintape.

I sit opposite the man who became my enemy after he killed my father. "Things have changed." I shrug. "I figure you'll tell me exactly what happened. How you led Papa to his death."

"After which you'll kill me anyway?"

"I've had enough of death." I feel the cruiser shimmy slightly as we go through a hyperjump transition. Sloper looks at me strangely.

"Then why did you agree to take this one"—he indicates the Chief, over in a helmchair and listening in to our conversation—"to the Constellation? Putting the galaxy's best weapon in the hands of a brutal gang of pirates hardly seems like a smart idea"—he pauses, and the look on his face intensifies—"if you've had enough of death."

"My brother just escaped his death thanks to me, and no thanks to you. I'm not going to rescue him just to send him straight to his death at the hand of a gang. But I didn't ask for your opinion, or your advice. What I want is to know the truth."

Sloper sneers at me. "Supposing I refuse?"

I lean over and savagely twist his leg under the skintape—and Sloper screams. "Don't think that having had enough of death makes me in any way incapable of causing pain. Or of refusing to administer ongoing treatment. Now talk."

He screws his face up and breathes heavily for a few moments, letting the last breath out slowly before looking me in the eye. I see he is trying to bring his pain under control and I let go.

I wave my hand for him to continue. He shoots a glance at the Chief, then back at me, as if unsure if the Chief should overhear. But I want the Chief to overhear, so I motion for Sloper to continue.

"Jackson hired me to protect him."

"From?" I see this will be like pulling teeth.

"From everyone. As far as I understand, he had stumbled across some discovery everyone and their spacedog wanted. Still wants. No way he'd tell me what that was. But he was scared if someone knew what he knew, his life would be in danger."

"Then he was right."

Sloper shrugs. "There is that. But it was more than just his own life. He was afraid of something falling into the wrong hands." He smiles at me. Not a nice smile. "Same as you. Maybe you want to hire me too—"

He screams again when I twist his leg. I wait for him to breathe through it. "When you did such a good job the last time? You'd be the last on my list. Now continue with the facts. Papa had you protecting him. Then who found him, and what happened?"

Sloper pauses, as if he is considering what to say next. "Both the Jovians and the Scorpion got wind of a discovery. I guess the

Jovians got to him first—"

"He lies." The Rykkan Chief's head swivels back to me. I give him a nod of thanks, though I've already come to the same conclusion.

Sloper's face shows panic. He thinks I'm going to hurt him again. He's correct, but not right now. I carry on my questioning. "So you sold out to the Scorpion, and you set up my father for capture. But when he was exposed, instead of the Scorpion capturing him, the Jovians did."

He curls his lip. "If you know all the answers, why do you need to ask the questions?"

I reach over to put my hand on his leg again, but he holds up a hand. "Alright, alright. Yes. The Scorpion paid me. It's how life works. Everyone has their price." He regards me with a baleful eye. "Even you are old enough to have discovered that."

"Where did the Jovians take him? How did he die?"

"That's the thing. They didn't. They never reached him. He blew his own ship up."

This time I squeeze his leg hard. "You bastard. He paid you to protect him, but he still knew you would sell him out." I let go and sit back, watching the man writhe in agony. The man who deliberately set my father up to die. "The Scorpion was pissed, wasn't he?"

Sloper nods. "The Scorpion thought a friend or family member might offer clues. But I'd heard of you. I knew you were trying to track me down."

"Is that why you hired me to salvage the Constellation? Did the Scorpion force you to?"

He snorts. "Credit me with some intelligence, Madam Captain." He forces the last two words out like an insult. "No, I wanted to find the Constellation to free me from my debt to the Scorpion. In return for helping him take over the Sector and demolish the Jovians, he'd forgive my debt, and give me a remote planet to rule."

I look at the Rykkan Chief and raise my eyebrows.

"He speaks true. But he holds back."

I turn back to Sloper. "And?"

He coughs and a speck of blood flies out of his mouth onto his chin. He wipes it away. "Errikson told the Jovians he suspected you or your brother had access to the Constellation's drive unit. I don't know how he knew, or if it's true, but I knew he'd pursue you. If I had both you and your brother, and the Constellation, then I'd have all the cards."

"Maybe you did. But you played the wrong hand." I push up from my position and float over to the captain's chair. I tap the helmpad and see we still have another fifteen hours before we emerge from our last hyperspace jump. Time enough for a plan. I fake a yawn. "All this scintillating conversation has made me sleepy. I'm taking a couple of hours' rest in my cabin."

I hope Aktip's training has worked, and that sleep is all the Chief thinks I'm doing.

CHAPTER FORTY-FOUR

IN THE END, I MANAGE to grab around five hours sleep, and awake feeling more rested than ever. I'll need my wits about me if I'm to guard the Constellation from desperate hands.

I shower and make my way to the helmroom. Sloper is asleep, but some color has returned to his face. His leg will need someone more experienced than me if he is to save it. The Chief is in the nav chair and swivels to me. "You have energy. Is good."

I ignore him and slide into my captain's chair, tapping the helmpad. Approximately two more hours. Which pass quickly. The cruiser emerges into deep space, a few klicks from where I estimate the Constellation to be.

"We have arrived?" The Rykkan Chief peers at the nav screen.

"Almost. If we exit hyperspace too close, we'll trigger the Constellation's defenses with no time to disable them."

He looks at me closely, and I balance my nerves for what is coming. "You know how to disable this defense?"

"Of course," I lie, remembering to breathe. "How do you think we boarded the last time?"

He scrutinizes me as if to fathom the veracity of my statement. He appears to come to a conclusion. "You have confidence to do this again."

I nod, even though it wasn't a question. "I guarantee passage. I want my brother to live." This time I do not lie, and the Chief is convinced.

"When do others arrive?"

I glance down at the helmpad. "Now, actually." The commPanel is already signaling. I answer and confirm our location. "Salvage vessel, prepare to dock." Plexi acknowledges receipt.

"Why they dock?" The Rykkan Chief is instantly suspicious, though he needn't be.

"I will escort you aboard the Constellation. I require a crew to remain here, as I am sure you require the rest of your men to join you and keep guard over my brother."

"And this one?" He jerks a claw toward Sloper.

"He's not going anywhere. He'll be lucky to live." I look down at my helmpad. "Now if you'll excuse me, I have to plot our course to our destination, dock with the other ship, and hack into the Constellation's systems."

He grunts, then moves out of his chair to head down into the cruiser. Just before he heads off, he holds my gaze. "I make ready with my team. You remember brother."

Don't you worry about that.

CHAPTER FORTY-FIVE

DANIELLI, PLEXI, AKTIP AND ALL but two of the Chief's men board my cruiser, leaving Herg, Zhang and Ortiz on the salvage ship. Seeing Danielli again, my face heats slightly and I quickly look at Aktip. "How are your injuries healing?"

"I am completely repaired, Madam Captain," Aktip replies.

I raise an eyebrow and turn back to Danielli, all thoughts of Ganymede forgotten.

He must recognize the bemused expression on my face and answers my unasked question. "Ma'am, I have learned that the capacity for Rykkan self-repair runs much deeper than I understood. Some process that was initiated on Rykkamon, using Rykkan materials, has enabled our friend to heal completely." He glances at Sloper, who is stirring. "Looks like this one could do with a good dose of the same."

Aktip's head swivels to Danielli. "It will not work on humans."

Danielli lifts his hand. "I know, I know. Just a figure of speech, Aktip."

It's good to see my team playing out some friendship.

"I've located the Constellation," I say. "Exactly where we predicted. Now we're close enough, I'll hack in and disable its defenses." I hold up my finger to my lips. Plexi and Danielli catch on quickly and nod. I see Aktip is a little confused, but stays silent.

I tap the helmpad and place my hand flat, at the same time

using the commPanel to mute all comms. I login to the Constellation and open up entry and access, using "all personnel" for general clearance. To most areas.

The Chief reappears in the helmroom. He handles the zero-gee with quick, but strong movements, unlike Aktip, who is still adjusting how much less energy her powerful muscles need to use.

He acknowledges my crew with a flick of a hand and looks over at me. "We are ready?"

I nod. "These two"—I point to Plexi and Aktip—"will remain at the helm here with full comms to us all. Danielli and I will lead you and your men on board. Once you are satisfied you have the Constellation as your vessel, we will leave on my cruiser. You may take the salvage ship. My men there—Zhang, Ortiz and Herg—will handover on my orders. You may need it for access to and fro. I will show you how to disable the Constellation's defense system once you release my brother. This will be the conclusion of our deal."

In the corner of my eye I am aware of Sloper following intently, his eyes widening when I outline handing over control of the galaxy's most desirable object. I ignore him.

The Chief says nothing, but heads off to the airlock, briefly glancing at me, then Danielli. We follow.

This time we use my cruiser's minishuttle, which only just fits Danielli, me, the Chief and eight of his men once we are all suited up. I retract the bench seats and it's standing room only. Except for me, the pilot. I take us in to the Constellation. Seeing the battlecruiser's sheer size with the naked eye the second time around is no less impressive, and I fly us around, studiously avoiding any sight of the gaping hole in the drive section on our holoscreens. The Chief's men are visibly and audibly excited and he barks out orders. They fall silent, but still gesticulate to each other, pointing through the plexibubbles at the Constellation's impressively armed exterior.

I take us into an airlock I believe allows direct side access to one of the massive hangars. I punch some buttons on the shuttle's helmpad, and we sail in, revealing the interior of a huge, empty hangar.

The Rykkan Chief swivels to look at me and bares his teeth in a grin. "Impressive. Now you take me to helm. Hack in system."

I nod and swipe open the shuttle's double doors. This time we have no podPlates, instead we're using personal jets on our backunits. I lead the way, followed by Danielli. We ascend deck after deck, until we emerge in one of the wide passageways leading into the helm's outer hub. I take us up to the outer bulkhead door and slap my hand on the door, which opens to reveal the inner ring. I motion everyone through.

I see the Rykkans still looking around in disbelief at the sheer scale and technology on the battlecruiser. But the Chief is anxious. He looks at me through his helmet. "You open helmroom now."

I shrug. "So far, we haven't been able to gain access." I place my hand on the doorpad, and the red light flashes a warning.

<<Insufficient Clearance>>

I glance at the Chief. "I may be a good hacker, but this is the Sector's flagship. It may take time; it may be impossible."

He glares at me, then realizes I am telling the truth. Well, partially. He pushes everyone back, then stands at the helm entry with a lasercannon and lets a massive blast hit the metalloy panels.

When the glow fades, we see the door is unaffected. The Chief throws the cannon to the deck, where it bounces off in the zero-gee. One of his men catches it. He swivels back to me. "You trick me."

I am careful in my response. "I have never been able to access the helmroom, and I never promised you this. But we can access all other areas. The Constellation is still yours, including all its weaponry. Helm access or not, it's still in your power."

His bulbous Rykkan eyes gleam behind his faceplate. "Then we use their weapons to enter the helmroom. Or did you not think of that?" He kicks past me and calls into his suit's comms. "We proceed to the armory."

I push off to follow the Chief and show him the way.

CHAPTER FORTY-SIX

ARMORY FOUR IS EMPTY APART from a few laserpistols. The Chief looks frustrated and orders me to open up Armory Five. I sense Danielli edge up to me as I approach the doorpad. I slap it open and motion everyone in to the dark space, deliberately flashing my headbeam on the racks and racks of glistening weapons-tech. The Chief's men raise a chant of success and propel themselves over to the weapon mounts to pull down their new toys. The Chief yells an order in Rykkan and two of his men peel off, heading for a large plasmacannon anchored to some fixtures further down the long room.

The overhead explodes in a shower of sparks and all the Rykkans turn, but too late, as descending SIMs catch them short, firing at all angles.

Except for Danielli, the Chief and me. At the moment of explosion, I grab the Rykkan and hurl him out of the room. Danielli kicks out behind me and throws an EMP grenade in behind him, just as I slap the door closed.

I see the room's interior flash brightly on the doorpad screen, but I am pulled around by the Chief, his eyes hard behind his faceplate. "What is this?"

I say nothing, just tap the doorpad. The lock opens and drifting smoke confronts us. The Chief moves to enter, but I hold him back. "Wait." I motion to Danielli, who slides in to one side and disappears in the murky air. There is a brief flash of laser, then he reappears.

"All clear, Ma'am."

We venture back in to the room. The SIMs have cut the Rykkans to pieces. But the EMP grenade fried the SIMs.

The Chief stops and confronts me. "You knew this trap."

"We only suspected it from what we experienced last time," I correct him, but he knows I am telling the truth.

His brow protuberance rises up and down, then finally he speaks again. "Then why did you not leave me to be killed? And take back this?" He gestures to the ship.

A voice crackles over our suit helmets. It is Aktip. "Because Madam Captain wanted to save your life. Under binding Rykkan custom, you have lifelong debt to repay."

Now it is my turn to grin at the Chief.

CHAPTER FORTY-SEVEN

I TAKE US IN THE minishuttle back to my lightCruiser. The shuttle is empty compared to the outward journey, and I feel a little guilty at the deliberate deaths, especially after my previous declaration.

Sometimes there is a greater need.

We dock and I call a meeting for all crew in the helmroom, including Zhang, Ortiz and Herg by comms. I tell the Chief to bring his two remaining Rykkans up to speed. He assures me they will follow his lead.

After a brief update for those not present on the Constellation, I throw open the floor for comments.

Plexi shrugs. "We have to secure the Constellation fully this time. Perhaps you can use your—"

"My hacking abilities?" I quickly interrupt, looking at Plexi and briefly flicking my eyes at the Rykkan Chief. I'd prefer any knowledge of my status as the Constellation's Captain remain secret. For now.

"Yes." Plexi, always quick, gets the message.

I look around. "Unfortunately, I'm in as far as we can go." Actually the truth, for once.

"Can we move the Constellation to a safe haven?" Mitch has made it to the helmroom, and sucks on a liquipak.

I shake my head. "No power. All we can do is what we did before, and that was risky."

Mitch raises his eyes.

"We backed up the salvage vessel and jammed it in a hangar bay. Then fired up the fDrive."

Mitch chokes on his pak.

"Plexi's plan. Once we had momentum, we blew ourselves out of there."

"Okay, so we don't want to do that again."

I sigh. "Not if we can help it. We're back to square one. Except we have my lightCruiser back"—I look up at Mitch—"and you." I scratch my head. "But we can't let the Jovians anywhere near the Constellation. Besides, they have the drive." Which they don't seem to want, but I keep quiet about that for now. "Ideally, we should tow it to somewhere well defended. Somewhere the Jovians won't dare attempt a confrontation."

The commPanel flashes, and an electronically synthesized voice comes over the all-ship PA system.

"*I can help with that.*"

The Scorpion.

I'm just about to hit the helmpad and boost us away when I feel the lightCruiser shudder. A tractor beam. Instead I tap a private comms channel to the salvage ship. "Zhang?"

"*Under tractor submission, Ma'am. No controls available.*"

Crap.

"What now?" Danielli says. I see sweat forming on his brow and remember his mention of a "previous mission."

"We wait."

The Rykkan Chief squirms in the navchair. "Then we kill him."

"Then we listen," I correct. Though I'm not sure exactly where listening to a dictator of the Scorpion's narcissistic bent will get us.

The holopanel springs up and I see a large warship approaching—or rather, we're approaching it. It might be substantial, but it's dwarfed by the Constellation looming in the background. The spacelock opens and the tractor beam pulls us in. Gantry-cranes connect and secure us. I see the salvage vessel float in next to us. We wait for our fate.

"*Air pressure at 100%. You may disembark. All parties proceed to the debriefing suite by following the appointed officer. Captain Jackson please come to the helm boardroom—you will be escorted. No arms are permitted.*"

I tap the commPanel to reply. "I need assurance of safe passage for my crew. No recriminations for any prior employment."

"*If you mean your mercenaries, then your request is noted.*"

The Scorpion seems well informed, but I sense Danielli's relief. But I'm not finished.

"What about the Rykkans and our prisoner?"

"*Sloper? Bring him with the others The Rykkans will be held separately, with the exception of their leader and your communications officer, who will proceed with your crew.*"

Sloper can barely stand up, let alone walk, so I have Danielli and the Chief maneuver him out of our airlock, where two of the Scorpion's men take him away. Two other officers stand aside, in between our two ships, clearly waiting for me. I engage my magboots and walk across.

"Captain Jackson reporting as requested. What will you do with my crew?" But they remain silent, and one of them indicates that I should follow him. The other falls in line behind me.

We ascend several decks, enter artificial gravity, and just outside what I assume is the helmroom entry, a door in the side bulkhead slides open. I am escorted into a spacious room, big enough to sit twenty around a sleek, alloy, oval boardroom table. A control center sits at one end of the table, slightly raised. Standing behind the control panel is a middle-aged woman, in uniform. She smiles at me and gestures for me to sit. I deliberately sit at the other end. If the Scorpion is going to try to intimidate me, I'll play his game. With my rules.

The officers leave and the door slides closed. I look around while I wait. There is nothing to show this is the war-room of a ruthless dictator. No maps, pictures, declarations. Just sheer, austere gray alloy walls.

I look back at the woman, who looks back at me.

I smile. She smiles.

I look around more, then back at the woman.

"Seems like the Scorpion likes to keep his captives waiting," I say coolly.

"The Scorpion," the woman answers assertively, "always waits for her captives to relax before offering sustenance."

My jaw drops. The woman nods. "Yes." She taps a pad on her arm and I detect a subtle change in the soundscape. "I am the Scorpion," she continues, only now, her voice is electronically synthesized—and male. She taps the pad again. "Satisfied?" she says in her normal voice. "Or do you need more proof?"

I shake my head dumbly.

She steps away from the control panel and walks over to stand next to me. I notice she limps slightly. She wears a fawn uniform, with short, neck-length dark brown hair. A slightly hard—maybe weary—face, but with smile lines. She holds out her hand. "Congratulations. You found the Sector's biggest mystery, took on the Jovians and rescued your brother from underneath my nose."

I shake her hand. It is warm. "You didn't know Sloper had taken Mitch to Takao?" A rather obvious question I think, but I don't know what else to say.

She shakes her head and draws up the chair next to me. She regards me for a while before continuing. "Nor did I know Sloper had purchased the Constellation's coordinates."

"Then how did you find us?"

She smiles and her eyes crinkle. "When a human arrives on Takao with a bunch of Rykkans who are not mercenaries, it gets my attention. Sloper isn't as smart as he thinks he is; after that it was easy. I had him implanted with a skinbeacon." She leans forward. "And here we are. Now ... what shall we do with this useless wreck of a battlecruiser? I gather you could use some help."

But I am not that easily won over. "I want my crew brought up here. I won't make any move when it comes to the Constellation without their full support. I won't give up my hacks to the Constellation's defenses until we all agree." I look hard into her eyes.

She throws up her hands. "Of course, Captain. I wouldn't have it any other way. I'll have them brought up." She taps the pad on her arm, gives instructions, then looks back at me. "*Now* would you like some refreshments?"

CHAPTER FORTY-EIGHT

WHILE I WAIT FOR THE rest of my crew—and one prisoner—to arrive, I partake of the energy drink the Scorpion provided and fire a few questions of my own.

"What do you want with the Constellation?"

She looks at me with amusement. "For it not to fall into the hands of the Jovians. Next?"

I try another tack. "Why do you disguise your identity? And who else knows?"

She shrugs. "Only two of my direct reports. As far as the crew on this ship, they know me as a senior commanding officer in the Scorpion's Marine Corps. As to why, any study of dictators throughout history will show you it's not possible to carry out what I wish to see happen as a woman. So I remain an enigma. A silhouette. Convenient for inducing fear, don't you think?"

I'm beginning to recover, maybe thanks to the energy drink. "Inducing fear. Tell me more. Why do all this? Why the elaborate setup?"

The Scorpion leans back in her chair and sips from her own fruit juice. "When I was twelve, the Blood Empire invaded and the first Sector War started. I may have escaped, but my planet was not so lucky."

I gesture for her to go on.

She waves her hand noncommittally. "Vaporized. Unfortunately, so were my parents and four older brothers." She regards me with sad eyes. "I see the Jovian rise to power; their growing control of our energy supplies, and the possibility they will take the Sector by force. I can't allow that to happen again."

I feel my brow furrow. "But why all the drama? Why not just lead and persuade? Why the cartoon-style memes and the dumbed-down sloganizing?"

She snorts. "You've obviously not studied the same leaders of history I have. It's populist messages and unseen threats that mobilize the masses. Not informed strategy and reasoned voting. Sad to say." She takes a breath. "If I'm to get the majority of Takao behind me, I have to speak in a way they understand. That they *feel*." She taps her chest.

The door slides back and my crew file in, brought up at the rear by Sloper, carried by the same two goons. They dump him in the nearest seat and leave, tapping the door closed. I nod my head at Danielli, Aktip and the rest, and they take seats around us.

"We waiting for this Scorpion?" Plexi says, looking around the room, bright-eyed. "Like to tell him to his face how dumbsnark those rallies are." She looks at me, embarrassed. "Watched them on the holo on the way in to Takao, Ma'am."

"You can tell him to her face right now," I jerk my thumb at the Scorpion sitting next to me, displaying an amused smile.

Plexi stands up. "No shit?!" Her hand flies to her mouth. "Oops. Beg my pardon, Ma'am." She sits down.

The Scorpion leans forward, looks around at my crew, and at Sloper, whose eyes are wide. He obviously didn't know either.

She has a serious expression. "I'm not what you think, and I need your help. I've already taken a significant risk disclosing my identity to you."

"Why would we help you?" Mitch asks. Clearly brighter, he still looks the worse for wear. "You and your scum over there nearly got me killed."

"And I thought Sloper rescued you from Errikson? Isn't that right, Sloper?"

Sloper says nothing. He looks to be in overload. The Scorpion smiles at Mitch. "But I see you harbor resentment. Should I dispose of him for you?" She reaches down and draws up a laserpistol, aims it directly at Sloper, but before she has a chance to do anything else, I slam her arm to the table. She looks back at me. "Oh. Sorry." She hands me the laserpistol. "You want to do the honors."

I push the pistol away, across the table. "No executions. Not even him. There are bigger problems to solve." I look around the room, slowly taking in my team. "The Scorpion is on our side. Her goal is to prevent the Jovians using the Constellation to dominate the Sector. My question is, why take the Constellation anywhere? If Errikson and the Jovians have the drive, the ship is no threat. It can't be used against Takao."

I see the nods of agreement and I turn to face the Scorpion. "So if you are serious about protecting the Constellation and dismissing the Jovian threat, you need to prove to us you can be trusted."

Confusion flickers across her face. "How? State your request."

I point along the table to the Rykkan Chief. "Meet your new trading partner."

The Chief seems almost as startled as the Scorpion. Almost. Then he breaks out into an enormous red grin.

CHAPTER FORTY-NINE

ALL EYES ARE NOW ON me, and I wait for the hubbub to diminish until I speak again.

"Here's how it will work. Sloper's power resides in his control over the trade routes he runs for you."

The Scorpion—I wish I had another name for her, but that can wait—waves her finger for me to continue. I do. "So we don't need to kill him; just remove his power. Or rather, give it to someone else." I flick my eyes to the Rykkan Chief, who has not lost his grin.

Sloper however, protests. The Scorpion shuts him up with her palm and looks at me. She seems fascinated.

I take this as a positive. "You have a problem on your planet, yes?"

She nods.

"So here's what I suggest, and what you will agree to. You assign all of Sloper's trade deals and treaties to the Rykkans."

"You can't—" Sloper forgets he is badly injured and tries to jump up. He only succeeds in crying out in pain, slowly sinking back into his seat and glaring at me.

I continue. "My friend, the Chief here, will look after the entire operation—"

I have to hold up both hands to stop everyone chiming in. I wait for silence.

"The Chief owes me a lifetime debt." I look at the Rykkan. "This cannot be undone. True?"

"True," he says. His grin is fading a little. I look at Aktip and raise my eyes.

"Ma'am Captain, I cannot tell if he speaks the truth unless he drops his block."

The Chief looks over to Aktip and spreads his hand and claw. "Is truth now, yes?"

Aktip looks at me. "Madam Captain, he is telling the truth, but ..."

"But?"

"He is correct to be concerned. You are still considered a criminal on Rykkamon." She looks confused for a moment. "As am I."

The Rykkan Chief waves a claw. "Can all be fixed with story for politician-father of injured boy. And a special gift from Takao I think." He eyes the Scorpion. I forced the Chief into his lifelong debt, but that doesn't stop him from being wily. I'd almost forgotten that somewhere, thanks to me, there is a young Rykkan minus one arm.

I hold the Scorpion's gaze and carry on. "I will personally vouch for the Chief's trading skills, and rather surprisingly for his general philosophical understanding of what needs to happen. And since I didn't finish, before, I will add that Sloper's operation includes the official trade"—I pause for effect—"and the unofficial trade. Which the Chief is particularly well qualified to oversee."

"Presumably at some point, you'll tell me what is supposed to be in this for me?" The Scorpion has played into my hands.

"The Chief and his men will, with your announced amnesty, seek to redeploy all the Rykkan mercenaries as trade ambassadors engaged in the execution of the new trade operation." Again I hold up my hand as everyone wants to speak. But the Scorpion just waits.

"You will also agree to almost all the demands from the Resistance, in return for their agreement to work together for a peaceful solution." Not that they'll have much choice without their paid mercenaries, but I leave this for the Scorpion to piece together. "Their supporters will be glad of your peace offering, when you could have just crushed them. Your own followers will praise your ending of the bloody violence. You will control Takao, secure your trade routes; have brought peace and be ready to repel any Jovian offensives."

Now no one speaks. Danielli and Plexi look at me with admiration, the Rykkan Chief still has a slight smile, and Sloper looks haggard and beaten. Herg, Zhang and Ortiz watch the Scorpion intently.

The Scorpion's mouth turns up a little at one end. "Touché, Madam Captain. I have one condition."

I incline my head. "Let me guess. None of this can be negotiated over hyper-relay, so we need to bring the Constellation to Takao, and you and I will travel ahead in our other ships to make the new arrangements."

Her face breaks out into a broad smile. "I like you. Even more so that you're on my side, and not the Jovians'."

I smile back. "Then we have a deal. Now ... apparently you have a way to transport a battlecruiser?"

CHAPTER FIFTY

I STAND AT THE WARSHIP'S panoramic viewport and watch two giant hyperDrive units being maneuvered out of the warship's cargo hold and slowly propelled to the Constellation with tugdrones. The Scorpion tells me it will take two to three days and an entire team of twelve engineers to complete the task of attaching the drives. I tell myself she seems all too well prepared, but what other choice do I have? I've not told anyone except my own close crew and Mitch that I am the Constellation's Captain. I intend to keep that close to my chest.

I sense a presence at my side. Danielli. He nods to me and watches the operation. I sometimes wonder about Danielli. The strong silent type ... yet he clearly enjoyed that kiss. He catches me looking at him. "Yes, Ma'am?"

"You're not on duty, Danielli. Indy is my name."

He shifts uncomfortably. "Yes, Ms. Jackson."

I smile. "That will have to do, I guess. But you came to ask me something."

"Am I that obvious?" He studies me for a while. "Do you think our new Rykkan ambassador can pull it off?"

I suck in air through my teeth before I reply. "Yes. Yes, I believe so. There's something stoic about the Rykkans. They are both forthright in their integrity and their corruption. It had me puzzled for a while."

Danielli tilts his head. "And?"

"I realized their sensing ability and the harsh climate must have built a resolve to cope no matter what. It's not a place for hiding anything. Or if you do, everyone knows. Our friend is no idiot—and he is beholden to his debt to me. He'll make it work." Though I may have to lend a helping hand. If I ever get the chance.

It's my turn to study Danielli, who has turned to watch the activity outside, and I give him a long look before continuing. "What do you make of this?"—I gesture to the viewport—"Have you seen anything like it on your travels?"

He shakes his head, continuing to stare out at the oversized cosmic ballet unfolding in front of us. Or below us. Or above us. Directions are not important. Until you need to go somewhere.

"No, Miss. Uh, Indy. I've never seen it before. Though I have heard of such portable drives used to move large constructions across the Sector. Never a battlecruiser though."

"There's only one Constellation, eh?" I smile at him. "Presumably no one was expecting to have to do this with it."

He twists his head and looks at me sharply. "Someone must have, Ma'am."

"Do expand, Danielli." I watch the huge hyperDrive units get maneuvered to either side of the massive battlecruiser, and we lose sight of one of them as it "orbits" the mothership's circumference.

"The ship's original drive was removed with surgical precision. Now this Scorpion turns up with a salvage solution that just happens to work with two of the Constellation's hangar bays."

I see the tiny figures below us busy themselves around the bristling hull of the battlecruiser, connecting data cables and powertrains. Occasionally bright lights reflect off the impervious alloy of the ship's weapons turrets, caught in the transitory sweep of some engineer's headbeam. Small pod-units accompany the mechanical engineering team. If I look carefully, I think I see tiny laserwelder flashes.

"Ma'am?"

I drag myself from my reverie. "Thinking, Danielli. About what you just said. But I have no answer. Except to say you may be right." I look him in the eye. "You don't trust the Scorpion?"

He hesitates. "I'm not a politician, Ms. Jackson, I'm a soldier. But I do know you don't get to a position of power such as she commands by being wholly trustworthy."

"Hmm. And when you're actually a woman in disguise."

"That I wouldn't know, Ms. Jackson. She took a big risk confiding in us. We need to take care she doesn't continue to keep her identity a secret by disposing of us."

I tap my finger on my lip and survey the scene. "Very true. But call me Indy. Please." And with that, I pirouette around to the walkway behind us, and head down to the medbay, leaving Danielli watching the slow motion space theater against a silky-black backdrop.

CHAPTER FIFTY-ONE

MITCH IS ON A MEDBUNK again, a tangle of tubes draped around him.

One condition I added to the Scorpion's list was that I would not disable my "hacked defense" of the Constellation until I was happy that Mitch was receiving the warship's best treatment. Takao's medical science enjoys a reputation for its high standards, and I figured that the Scorpion's warship would naturally be at the forefront of technology.

For good measure, I suggested she send Sloper along for a renovation job too. I had an idea he could still be useful to us.

I smile at my brother, who now looks the picture of health. "Hey, Michelangelo. S'up?"

He curls his lip at me. "You know I hate that name."

"It's the one your parents gave you. You should be thankful."

"What—that I had parents, or that they were historical art nerds?"

There's that word, "were," again.

"I don't know that Papa was anything other than a pure spacemath geek. Mama was the arty one as far as I know. He just liked her cute vocabulary. But hey, small talk can wait."

He looks at me with a baleful expression. "What kind of world do we live in, when talk of your dead parents is considered 'small talk'?"

I change the subject. "You said you stumbled across information. On Ganymede. Must have been important if you had to leave in a hurry. Care to share?"

"And I thought you were here to check on my health."

"Shall I remind you that you are alive because someone who cares about you wouldn't be told what to do?" I raise an eyebrow.

He grunts. "Fair enough. But I'm not sure you're going to like what I discovered."

I wait.

Mitch shifts on the medbunk to look at me square on. "The Jovians are rumored to be developing an energy source that will make 3He redundant."

I've almost forgotten my past life. I groan. "Great. So even if we get out of this mess, there's nothing to go back to except an energy market ruled by the Jovians."

My brother nods. "I was right."

"About what?"

"That you wouldn't like it."

"You're lucky you're already badly injured. Means there's no need for me to beat you up." I sigh. "Not that it matters anymore. Energy trade, I mean. Not your injury. Strange as it sounds, we might have bigger problems than the Jovian's energy trade schemes. Danielli seems to think someone expected to be able to refit the Constellation's drive."

Mitch sits up, bringing a web of tubing with him. "Really? But from what you showed me, it's a clean-cut extraction. No terminations, no obvious reconnection points. Anyway, moot point I guess. Who would want to refit it—we'd only end up with the Sector's greatest liability, with no Captain and no General Garnek to make sense of it all." He looks at me. "Sorry. But you're no battle—"

I place my finger on his lips. "That conversation can wait. But you're right. The fact that someone went to a great deal of trouble to remove the drive, and leave the Constellation drifting seems to imply we are better off with it hobbled."

He laughs. "Yeah. Just imagine the Jovians and the Scorpion teaming up; putting the Constellation back together and ..." he trails off and stops laughing.

I look at him. "Exactly."

CHAPTER FIFTY-TWO

I LEAVE MITCH ALONE WITH his thoughts and meet with Danielli, Plexi and Aktip back on my own lightCruiser, now out of the warship's hangar and docked to its side.

"Aktip, as far as anyone else knows, I've managed to get you limited access to the Constellation's comms and unsecured databanks. I told them it was a hack I engineered so you could help coordinate activity while I'm on my way to Takao, but in reality you have the Captain's comms authority level. Make sure you keep it hidden. Use Ortiz and Zhang if you need help. Herg will be on hand if you want someone to create a diversion."

I want Aktip to be across all comms. She'll send an encrypted hyper-relay if she senses any foul play with the massive battlecruiser. Or if, for some non-nefarious reason, the twin hyperDrive operation goes belly up. It shouldn't, as the engineers have assured us the slow hops they've programmed are less than twenty percent of the power levels that both the hyperDrives and the Constellation could easily tolerate.

But we are better to be completely paranoid, and the Scorpion agrees.

She and I will head off to Takao separately. She in her scoutcruiser, me with my limited crew and Mitch in my lightCruiser. We will arrive first by a small margin; the Slingshot being one of Errikson's finest, trumping even Takao's superb tech. I argued for the two ships, purely for redundancy, or if one of us needs to make an emergency errand.

Aktip nods and heads off to the warship's commsroom.

I look at Danielli and Plexi, who seem to be expecting me to say something.

"Right now I don't have the slightest idea how all this will turn out, nor what we should or shouldn't do with the Constellation and its drive. As far as I can see, it's a giant mess that everyone wants a piece of."

Plexi turns up the corner of her mouth, her pixie eyes sparkling. "Then our mission is to make sure they don't, is that right, Ma'am?"

I grin. Plexi is always on it. "Yes, Plexi. At the very least, we will make sure things don't get worse."

But they will, of course.

CHAPTER FIFTY-THREE

MY LIGHTCRUISER IS ONLY A couple of hours adrift of our final leg back to Takao when the hyper-relay flashes on my commPanel. I accept the message and Aktip appears on the holo for everyone in the helmroom to see. She, of course, cannot see us. Hyper-relays are one way only, and the message might have a delay of days or weeks. But I see from Aktip's code at the bottom of the holo that not only is the message encrypted and flagged as emergency status, but she has waited until the delay between us will only be around thirty minutes.

Enough time for everyone to act, and still send replies to Aktip if needed.

And before we reach Takao.

My heart pounds. Has someone stolen the Constellation from under our noses?

My Rykkan friend's face comes to life, and she begins to speak. "Madam Captain, please excuse my intrusion. To reduce any immediate concerns, I must inform you that the Constellation's journey proceeds as planned. We will arrive at Takao exactly as predicted. The engineers' plans have performed as they suggested they would"—this is Aktip's code for letting me know she has picked up no lies or deceit with her senses—"and the hyperDrives are functioning well." She pauses. I sense the "but" coming.

"You also allocated me a task. I must now report that something unexpected has been discovered. Please to be accepting the transmitted file. I will assume you take approximately three minutes to comprehend the communication."

A small orange icon flashes at me from the holo. A file—also encrypted. It's unlike Aktip to beat around the bush, and I sense she is deliberately withholding information. Is she concerned about being overheard?

The file opens. It is a video file, with dataslides and Aktip's voice-over.

"Madam Captain, while investigating the comms history of the Constellation as you requested, I encountered an unusual quarantined section for transmissions. Since I am unable to use full Captain's access, I attempted to gain unauthorized entry."

I wonder why transmissions have caught Aktip's attention enough to provoke an emergency. After four years lost in space and cut adrift, any transmissions will be well beyond their use-by-date.

Aktip looks uncomfortable—probably because she's having to use my old hacking tricks to "gain unauthorized entry."

The dataslides move to the next view and I am watching a close up metatag of an incoming data packet. Aktip continues. "Please to see the datestamp." I peer in while she talks. I suck in a breath involuntarily and then zoom the holo in to confirm. I hear Danielli and Plexi next to me both let out a low whistle.

The date is yesterday's, shown in galactic standard notation. Around nineteen hours ago in fact. But who is transmitting from the ship? Then the next slide switches into view and I see the datapacket was inbound. Inbound? Who knew the Constellation's location, and how to send data back to base? Who knew the hobbled ship would even receive the data?

"As you see, this is incoming information. I do not think anyone else can intercept or read this data, it was encrypted to

Captain's level, but not requiring the secondary authority. Now to please assimilate the accompanying data." She switches the screen across and sets it to scroll.

DS DRONE FIFTEEN: SECTOR TWENTY-FIVE OH NINE

ACTIVITY THRESHOLD TRIGGERED: LEVEL 4, FOR IMMEDIATE TRANSMISSION

ACTIVITY DETAILS: LARGE MASS, POWERED SPACEFLIGHT VEHICLES, MEDIUM TO LARGE SIZE

WEAPON FINGERPRINT: CONFIRMED TO LEVEL SIX

DIRECTION OF TRAVEL: TO SECTOR FRINGE

CURRENT ACTIVITY: STATIONARY IN MILITARY FORMATION

IDENTITY OF VEHICLES: UNKNOWN. DATA EXTRAPOLATION INDICATES 87% LIKELIHOOD BLOOD EMPIRE.

The screen flicks back to Aktip. "Madam Captain, please advise if action required."

The holo switches off.

I can feel my neck and shoulders tense and try to roll them looser. It doesn't work. "First impressions?" I look to Danielli and Plexi.

Danielli speaks first. "Let's look at what we know, Ma'am. Someone, or some group has dispatched up to fifteen or more drones to monitor outposts. The data has been sent back to what they presumably knew was a disabled ship, where only the Captain"—he shoots me a knowing look—"would be in a position to receive the reports. They—and their drones—were also able to track the Constellation's position in space. All of which is interesting—"

"Until you get to the part about the Blood Empire assembling forces at the Sector's fringe."

"Indeed. Assuming all this is true."

"Who would fabricate such a thing? That's some elaborate hoax."

"We really need access to that helmroom," Plexi says.

"You think we'd know more?"

"Sure," she says. "Otherwise why restrict access? Maybe we should ask the Scorpion for help? Seems like she has some pretty serious tech at her disposal."

I mull that over for a while. No doubt the Scorpion could help ... but someone has gone to a lot of trouble to keep this under wraps. "I trust the Scorpion on this, but it's not like we go back a long way. It's all new ground, and not something I'd want to make a Sector-sized error with."

Danielli frowns. "Surely it's in all our interests to be warned of a Blood Empire play on the Sector?"

I purse my lips. "You'd think so. But then why quarantine the drone's data back to the Constellation? Why not broadcast it to all regions?"

Plexi looks excited. "Because whoever set it up wanted it to only fall into one person's hands."

"Who?" I am perplexed.

Danielli looks at me strangely. "Ma'am, if you haven't worked that out yet, I'm beginning to wonder if we have the right 'Captain.'"

It sinks in. "Oh," I say. "Oh."

CHAPTER FIFTY-FOUR

MY ENTRY INTO TAKAO FOR the second time is considerably different. The Scorpion's scoutcruiser arrives into orbit hours after mine, but I'm already cleared for descent; the Scorpion is obviously relaying orders ahead of us.

Our ships descend out of orbit together, to a private complex of military landing pads. A bulbous, low-slung and blacked-out shuttlepod exits a sleek alloy-clad building nearby. The pod first locks onto the Scorpion's ship, then disengages and hovers over to collect us. A medhover docks at my cruiser and transfers Mitch separately.

"Amazing that she has kept this under cover for so long," Danielli observes while we wait.

"I'm sure it's on the penalty of death if anyone finds out," I say, casting Danielli a meaningful look. He responds with a wry smile.

Soon we are in the pod and transported into the building. The Scorpion falls in with a nondescript crew: just another security detail on their way about the gleaming corridors. We ascend to the top floor and enter a massive war room. On one side there is a panoramic window overlooking the pads. I see my ship next to the Scorpion's and several other powerful-looking fightships, armed, and by the look of the officials milling around, on standby.

A huge circular table with a hollow center, sufficient to sit thirty, dominates the war room. I count eighteen high-ranking officials already seated, all of whom look at me as I lead my ragtag crew to some empty seats. I can't help but hear a few unkind words muttered about Rykkans.

I'm relieved I've maintained my dyed black hair and braid. No point in advertising myself indelibly. Someone might connect some dots that should remain unattached.

We take our seats, and it is at that point I realize the Scorpion has not followed us in. From the table's center, a holo springs to life, and I now see the male silhouette of "the Scorpion" and hear the familiar digitally generated voice announce his presence.

"Good afternoon. Let me introduce Captain India Jackson and some of her crew. Captain Jackson is the owner of the lightCruiser Slingshot and the salvage operator who discovered the location of the Constellation. The Captain has also proved to be a helpful collaborator and now partner in our initiatives against the Jovians and the prevention of the Jovian domination of energy trade. She was able to hack into the Constellation and disable defenses left onboard that no other salvage operator has successfully bypassed. I am also disappointed to inform you that our trading partner Sloper, has been double-crossing us, and is now under imprisonment. Sloper kidnapped Captain Jackson's brother and held him on Takao without my knowledge, and was trying to blackmail Captain Jackson to deliver the Constellation to him."

The silhouette pauses, and I catch Danielli surreptitiously scrutinizing one of the Scorpion's senior uniformed advisers across the table. I'm sure I've seen his face before. I make a mental note to ask Danielli about it after the meeting.

The Scorpion resumes.

"I have already briefed you all on this on my return to Takao, and repeat myself here for the benefit of the Captain and her crew. More important is that Captain Jackson has agreed for

Takao to be the safe haven for the anchoring of the Constellation. In return for some trade agreements."

Everyone stirs at the latter announcement. Except the man Danielli was checking out, who instead regards me with a hard expression. I realize where I've seen him before: on the stadium's large holoscreen. Is he one of Sloper's allies?

"These trade agreements will be made public shortly, and need not concern you strategically, except for the fact that Captain Jackson has been instrumental in securing the support of Rykkamon, and the removal of all Rykkan mercenaries from Takao."

Now I have everyone's attention.

"Meaning we are now in a superior position of defense against the Jovians. For tactical discussion, I will handover to Admiral Simpson to brief us on our revised plans." The silhouette in the center dims in anticipation.

Admiral Simpson turns out to be the man with the hard face. Of course. He clears his throat. "Ladies and gentlemen." He acknowledges me and Plexi as he says the words. "We find the balance of power is now shifted. You are all aware that Captain Jackson has also located the Constellation's stolen drive in the possession of the Jovians."

"Errikson, strictly speaking," I correct him, which doesn't appear to amuse the man. "And we don't know that the drive was technically stolen, at least not initially."

The lean-faced Admiral eyes me. "Do elaborate."

I muse on how much to share and catch Danielli's eye. His expression seems to suggest, "proceed with caution." Good advice, I think. "The Constellation's drive, as I'm sure you already know from your leader's advance reports, was removed with a technical precision unknown to us. According to Errikson, he obtained the mechanism and plans for this operation from an unnamed party, and built oversized lasercutters for this single purpose. The drive may not have been stolen at all. Though I will agree, its possession by the Jovians is as good as if it were stolen. Perhaps whoever encouraged Errikson to remove the drive didn't expect him to shack up with the Jovian mafia. They've never made good bedmates in the past."

The Admiral nods slowly. "And why do you think the Jovians want the drive?"

I smile at him. "Isn't that obvious? Between you and the Jovians, there is the potential to refit the ship and own the most powerful battlecruiser known to mankind—and Rykkankind."

I glance sideways at the Chief with sudden realization that aside from my crew, the only person here I am willing to trust is the Rykkan Chief. My life seems ruled by irony. "I imagine they'll be keen to get their hands on the Constellation once they know it's moored at Takao." But since Errikson showed no desire to capture the ship itself, I know full well that what the mafia is really after resides in the drive.

"Then we should preempt their interest and make our own crystal clear." The Admiral looks around the table. "Any objections, or are we all in agreement our ultimate tactical plan is to strike at the Jovians and recover the drive?"

Seventeen hands go up and seventeen "Aye"s make the answer obvious.

"Then we reconvene in one hour. I will discuss our timeframe and resources with the Scorpion. On your return, please advise current deployment, and your proposed tactics for recovering the drive." He looks at me. "Thank you for your time, Captain Jackson. My men will assist you in completing the trade treaty. You are free to travel around Takao as you see fit." He smiles, but his eyes do not. "I will ensure the safety of your crew. Take in the sights before you leave."

And I am dismissed. Just like that.

We depart with everyone else and soon find ourselves in a hospitality area, awaiting our escort. I head over to the Rykkan Chief, who has one hand and claw on the metal barrier under the plexiglass viewing window and is looking out over the landing pads. Surveying his new domain perhaps.

I get his attention. "Who was telling the truth?"

The Chief looks at me and bares his red grin. "No one. Not even you."

CHAPTER FIFTY-FIVE

OUR ESCORT ARRIVES—TWO LESS-THAN communicative soldiers—and to my shock, Danielli asks them to take us to the best local eatery in Hoto. He notices me looking at him and when he sees the two soldiers are not paying any attention, he gives his head a micro shake, asking me not to question his decision. I acknowledge his gesture by rubbing my stomach. "Nice idea. It's been a while since I've eaten something that wasn't dried last century, or quenched my thirst with a liquid of questionable recycled origin."

One of our escorts interjects. "Sorry Ma'am. This one"—he points to the Chief—"won't be welcome in the restaurant."

I stop and confront the guy. "Then I suggest you request the Scorpion calls ahead and makes his request known. Rykkans are about to become Takao's new ally. Maybe this can be the beginning of a beautiful new friendship, and what better place to strut it than where it will be noticed. Understand?"

The soldier swallows. "Yes, Captain." He jerks his head to his companion, who moves off to a nearby commPanel.

I start walking again and take Danielli by the elbow. "Danielli. You seem to have some knowledge of Takaon cuisine. I'm sure we can squeeze in a gourmet experience or two before we leave."

He laughs and we walk on, sweeping in Plexi and leaving an obviously confused Rykkan Chief in our wake. He'll have difficulty sensing who is telling any truths right now.

Twenty minutes later, our arrival causes quite a stir, and the maître d' quickly shepherds us to a private suite in the back. I was banking on it, and judging by the relief on the Chief's face, he was too. Street-smart though he is, he probably doesn't want to have to justify all the bad deeds committed by his race against the very people eating in the restaurant. It still doesn't stop all of us pausing mid-forkful when we hear a loud argument break out in the main restaurant. We hear the word "spinhead" clearly mentioned more than a few times. News travels fast, no matter the planet.

Our escorts left, presumably ordered to leave us alone during dinner, though I'm certain they'll reappear to make sure we "sight-see" appropriately. But that's not in my game plan. For now, I'm curious as to what Danielli's intent is, and I use a natural break in the serving of the garish blue and purple, but delicious food, to beckon Danielli closer.

All four of us lean in across the table.

"Admiral Simpson is General Garnek," Danielli says softly.

Danielli's bombshell stuns us all into silence. Even Plexi has nothing. This time it's me who is first to respond, albeit with a stupid question. I'm still in shock.

"Are you sure? It's not just a coincidental resemblance?"

Danielli shakes his head. "I'd know him anywhere. Small scar here." He points just behind his right ear.

"Does he know you?"

"No. I never saw him in person. Only in speeches."

"Wait. You worked for the Sector Marines?"

He hints at a smile, then it drops away. "Long story. Almost served on the Constellation."

Plexi's eyebrows shoot up. Evidently he kept that one close to his chest.

"It explains why the Scorpion was so well-informed about the Constellation's design—but if he gets wind I have ... a certain status, then we could find ourselves"—I want to say myself, but cannot avoid dragging my crew into this—"in more trouble. Now we really can't afford for them to possess the drive. With control of that and my access ..."

I leave the rest unsaid. The Scorpion might find a way to force me to run the Constellation, and use Garnek's treason to force the Sector to its knees. I stand up abruptly, forgetting the low gravity, and inadvertently leap to the ceiling and back. "Mitch! We have to get him back to our ship before the Scorpion uses him as leverage." My poor brother, reduced yet again to a pawn in an intra-galactic power play.

Danielli nods. "Agreed. But what will you do about their plan? Go AWOL? With no, ah ... person of authorized status available to them, they'll find it hard to do anything."

"But perhaps not impossible. No, what we need to do is to join them, and help them get the drive from the Jovians."

Plexi groans. "I was afraid you were going to say that. But how will we do that?"

I feel my jaw tighten. "I'll tell the Scorpion exactly why the Jovians want the drive ... and me."

Plexi's eyes narrow. "Which is?"

"You'll have to wait while I make up a plausible answer," I say.

CHAPTER FIFTY-SIX

I LEAD US OUT OF the restaurant, ignoring the "spinhead" commentary coming from tables filled with tall, lean Takaons. I stand outside. And wait.

I don't have to wait long. Our two escorts draw in from their observation positions.

"Ready to board ship, Ma'am?" the lead uniform says.

"Take me to the Scorpion. Captain's orders. Immediately." I stand with my arms crossed.

The grunt doesn't compute at first. "I ... sorry, Ma'am, my orders are to—hey!" Danielli is behind him with the kid's head in an armlock. I smile. The unfolding action momentarily stumps the other escort, but he doesn't even get his weapon raised before Plexi has liberated it from his hands and stands next to him, the laserpistol aimed at his groin.

"You have your orders, soldier," I say. "Besides. When the Scorpion and Admiral Simpson hear what I have to say, you might even earn a little bonus. I mean, didn't we tell you the nature of our confidential business and you insisted on taking us back to HQ? If you get my drift."

The soldier nods in Danielli's armlock, and Danielli eases off. Plexi pushes the other forward, and he holds out his hand to receive his weapon back. Plexi just gives him her pixie grin and motions with his own weapon for him to start walking to the nearest hoverstop.

In minutes we are in front of a commPanel at the base's

security hut, and in discussion with the Scorpion's silhouette. After a few veiled references to make my case, the silhouette directs us to meet back in the war room.

This time the Scorpion is present in the flesh with only the Admiral by her side. We move in to sit alongside them at the massive round table, stark in its emptiness. I look at the Scorpion and flick my eyes at Simpson.

She nods. "He knows. One of the two. You may speak plainly here. You said you have classified information. Why did you not reveal this earlier?"

"A good strategist never plays all her cards when only one is needed," I say.

"So what's changed?"

I look around the empty room. "I don't see my brother here yet?"

The Scorpion smiles. "Fair enough." She reaches forward and taps an icon on the table's holo. "Bring the boy in."

The door slides open and Mitch enters. He wears an archetypal yellow Takaon robe; is freshly shaved, and looking in the best of health. He looks at me. "Sis. Needed the big gun here?"

I laugh. "You look more like a guru from SpiritCity. But you need to hear this, too. We're all involved, whether we like it or not." I want to add, "And you started it when you stole back Papa's laserSword," but I don't.

"When do you intend to let us in on your secret?" Simpson looks put out. Good.

I lean forward on the table. "We need to get the drive from the Jovians."

Simpson says nothing. Just stares.

"You're stating the obvious," the Scorpion says, but she has that slight trace of a smile. Meaning, "I believe you have something here."

"You are prepared to take it by force. With or without my help."

"Please," Simpson says. "This is not military school. State your point."

I engage him with a smile. "Suppose I tell you they don't want the drive. They might even give it to you if you ask nicely."

"Pah!" Admiral Simpson is not a patient man, but the Scorpion lays her hand on his arm.

"Wait, John. This kid is not stupid. She single-handedly resolved our Resistance problem. She hacked the Constellation, and she allowed me to bring it here. She knows the Jovians are dangerous. Hear her out."

I smile briefly at her and continue. "Here's what I know. The Jovians want access to what is in the drive. Not the drive itself. From what I can tell, Errikson was about ready to discard it after he'd retrieved its data. And there's only one reason anyone would give up a chance of ownership of the Constellation."

"If the alternative was even more powerful." Simpson looks thoughtful. My opinion of the man is in flux. He's complex, and I must be careful.

"Yes. What do the Jovian mafia worship the most?"

"Control of the Sector energy markets. That one's easy. We've been at the sharp end of that for decades." The Scorpion runs a finger over her lips absently. "So Errikson has been employed to mine the drive for the data, which presumably gives them some leverage over energy supply."

I nod. "That's my deduction. I saw it with my own eyes at Ganymede's stations. Errikson was almost blasé about the drive."

Her brow creases. She looks at Simpson, who shrugs, folds his arms and says, "If the Jovians gain control over the Sector's energy supplies, we may as well surrender now. Not only that, the Sector will fall into civil chaos—"

"And if Oberon learns of it, we'll be sitting ducks." The Scorpion's face is grim.

I've never heard the term before, but the meaning is obvious. What is more telling is the look Simpson gives me when the Scorpion mentions Oberon. Does he know more than he's letting on? Danielli's intense concentration on the Admiral is palpable.

"Wait." The Scorpion is still thinking, and has her finger in the air. "If the information in the drive is more important to the Jovians than the drive itself, and clearly Errikson hasn't given it to them yet, what's stopping him?"

I take a deep breath. "He can't access it. Can't even hack into it."

She studies me closely. "Are you telling me what I think you are telling me?"

"That's right. He needs me. Or, as it turns out"—I shoot a glance at my brother—"me or Mitch." I see him startle momentarily. "Which is why I'm going to help you steal it back."

CHAPTER FIFTY-SEVEN

WE ARE BACK IN MY lightCruiser, and we assemble informally in the mess. Simpson and the Scorpion agreed to put my plan to the rest of the war committee. All we can do is wait. The Scorpion offered me the use of the base's hospitality area, but I declined, pleading the need for a familiar space.

What I really want is a meeting in private with my crew.

"The Constellation will be here in a few hours." Danielli looks up from the navpanel.

"At the moment, all I need from the ship is Aktip and the rest of our crew," I say.

"I miss Herg," Plexi says in mock mourning. I smile to myself at our attempt to make light of things. A very human trait, as Aktip might observe. Plexi looks over at Mitch. "You'll like Herg. He has a way with words."

"The ones he remembers." Danielli stands up. "Sorry, Ma'am. I hate waiting. There's a job for us to do and only politics in the way."

"Welcome to our new world. So let's use the time to our advantage." Which is what I need: for Danielli and his team to be tightly focused. I need to lead with conviction for my plan to work.

"I've been thinking."

Plexi looks up. "Seems to me that's one of our assets."

"Don't speak too soon. You might not like my next thought."

"Which is?" Danielli raises an eyebrow. He is more casual

now. I've earned his respect, and he trusts me as a peer, dropping his official veneer.

"The last time Oberon was defeated, there was only one reason for our win."

"Even I know that," Mitch says, giving me a look. "The Constellation and General Garnek. That's what won that war. So what are you saying? That now we need the Constellation and Captain India Jackson?"

"You catch on quick. Despite your old age."

He rolls his eyes. "So now you're going to tell us that your next thought is to refit the Constellation and go kick Oberon's ass."

I smile. "I'm so glad you're on my team. When we all think the same way—"

"Wait—you're serious?" Plexi is passing a look between us. "This is not some sis-bro teasing?"

Mitch looks over at Plexi and sits back on the edge of the mess's table. "Sadly, no. She's always had a lust for power."

I kick Mitch and the Takaon gravity nudges him away from the table. He scowls.

"Seriously now. The last time the Blood Empire took on the Sector, the Constellation was our last line of defense. We need that drive."

"So does everyone else, apparently." Mitch is still mad.

I shake my head. "No. Actually the Jovians don't want it."

"But even if we just pick it up from the Jovians, hide it from the Scorpion, sneak the drive back into the ship without anyone noticing, and apply the magic glue, where does that leave us?"

"Equipped to defend our sector," Danielli says softly. "The Captain is correct. Someone suspected that the Blood Empire would be back to try again, someone smart enough to dispatch spotter drones and to have them report back to a shipwreck."

"Why was the ship hobbled, though? If they were so smart,

what's the big deal?" Mitch says, his annoyance subsiding.

I shrug. "Maybe whoever it was knew about the Sector's internal trade issues and wanted to disrupt them."

Mitch holds my gaze. "They knew about you, too."

I look at my feet, then back up again. "That one I can't explain. But you're right, there's a missing piece of the puzzle."

"A drive-sized one," Plexi says.

I frown. "Someone must know something."

Danielli's head jerks up. "Right. So why not ask him?"

We all stare at Danielli, then it dawns on me. "Simpson. Or rather, Garnek. You want to question Garnek."

"Not me, Ma'am, with all due respect. You. You're the only one who can get to him."

CHAPTER FIFTY-EIGHT

I AM ESCORTED INTO SIMPSON'S empty office without question. I decided to come alone. I figure a young woman on her own might not threaten him.

His office is sparse. No pictures of family, no awards, trophies or medals. Just a plain alloy desk, two holopanels and controls recessed into the desk. His one token gesture of comfort is a microcoffee machine; a retro fad among the educated.

Which makes me I realize I know nothing about Simpson/Garnek's education. I am in the middle of deciding where to begin when a gruff voice behind me speaks. "When you have inspected the room sufficiently, please sit."

Simpson comes from behind me, walks around his desk and sits. His hands are steepled together and he waits for me to take my seat.

"Where did you train, Admiral Simpson?" I think I can pump him for information more easily if I show interest.

"I'm not here for small talk, Ms. Jackson. State your request."

I grit my teeth. "That would be Captain Jackson, to you, Admiral. And I want to know your opinion of the Constellation."

His face flickers. Stress maybe? I can't tell. I have to remember that whether he really is Garnek or not, he's still dangerous. No one gets to that level of rank without a degree of ruthlessness.

"I think it's impressive, but useless. A symbol of times past. Now are we done?" He half rises out of his seat, but I stop him.

"I'm not here to trade blows, sir. I located the Constellation and hacked it with no help from anyone, and so far, no thanks. I think I'm entitled to collect as much information as I can." My cards are on the table.

"What makes you think I know anything?" Again that brief look.

I hold my hands out in front of me, palm up. "I don't. I'm betting that a man of your stature never makes a decision without all available information at his fingertips. No matter the source of the information. So let me ask you, why do you think the Constellation was abandoned? Why was the drive removed? And why with such precision?"

He taps his fingers against each other. "If I did know this information, why would I give it to you?"

I can't help roll my eyes. "Admiral, this is not a pissing contest. I'm meant to be on your side."

"Not the imagery I'd anticipated, Captain. But I'll be straight with you. I have no idea why the Constellation's drive was taken, nor how it can be refitted. But I do know we are in a highly flammable scenario with the Jovians, and I will not permit an inexperienced—and young—female pirate captain determine our agenda." He stands. "I'm prepared to assist you because my superior insists. But the moment my interests diverge from yours ..." He shrugs. Then walks around and stands next to me.

He seems to be inspecting me, as if committing my face to memory. I'm grateful for my laziness: my hair is still black and in a braid. I don't know if Garnek knew of my father, but I'd rather he didn't put two and two together. Then I realize my stupidity: he has my name, and Mitch's. He's only one holo-swipe away from knowing everything about us.

He motions to the coffee machine. "Help yourself. I believe old-school coffee is popular among the youngsters these days." He strides out, leaving me no better off.

Except for one thing. He only admitted he didn't know why the drive was taken. Which means he must know why the ship was abandoned.

CHAPTER FIFTY-NINE

I SEND A BRIEF ENCRYPTED message to Pedro through his underground channel on Ganymede, and am halfway back to my ship when I encounter my crew coming toward me on the opposite hoverTrack. I step off and wait. I'm becoming used to the low gravity and so I jog on the spot while I wait to reengage my muscles. My laziness has extended past my hair. Probably the fact that since we landed, my brain has been spinning.

I smooth down my groundsuit. My body feels good actually. Lithe, tense, ready for action. Mitch grins when he gets up close. "You look like you're about to go on a date."

"Pfft. Where are you all going, anyway? I'm not aware I authorized leave."

"War room." Danielli nods to the building behind me. "Your date is ready for you, apparently. We've been summoned. I left the Chief back on the ship."

I hop lightly over to their hoverTrack. "Is the Constellation here now?"

Plexi nods. "Twenty-five minutes ago. In outer orbit. Aktip, Herg and the others are on their way down by shuttle."

"Then send a request they join us in the war room."

Plexi grins. "Two steps ahead of you, Madam Captain."

I look up at the building we approach. I wonder if I'll see it again, and I question how my friends will react to my plan. I look at Mitch, and he catches me looking. He acknowledges the contact with a brief lifting of his eyebrows, as if he is complicit in my plot.

Which, if it is to work, he has to be.

We reach the building, and guards escort us into the packed war room, now filled with people seated around the table. Extra seats are in place behind each VIP, more than one in some cases. The room hums with activity, and I see the faint silhouette of the Scorpion superimposed in the table's center.

I look around for a seat at the table. There are none. I catch an aide's eye as he passes. He points to the other side of the table where two rows of chairs line up against the wall. In the dark, and well away from the main action.

Danielli leans in and whispers. "One wonders why we were summoned, Ma'am. They do not intend to ask for any contribution from us."

I turn my head to him and smile. "And when has that ever stopped me?"

He grins and follows me to our demoted destination.

I take a seat and motion Danielli next to me, but then I spy Aktip enter the room on the other side, causing a ripple of conversation, and I stand again, waving so Aktip notices me. Several aides and some of the table's occupants frown at me. I don't care. They need me and the Rykkans now. No matter where they seat me.

Aktip spots us and heads across. I notice she deliberately limits the range of her movements, showing caution in adjusting to Takao's gravity. I move Danielli so that Aktip is between us. "Any more data?" I say softly. Aktip shakes her head, which in a Rykkan is more like a swivel. But clear enough.

The room falls silent and I see Simpson is standing. He outlines the situation so far. He ignores me completely; this is his show now. He makes a point of calling up holos depicting how their fleet will disperse, how many ships are involved, and that he expects the mission to be tough, but not beyond Takao's military capability. Well within it, if the man is to be believed.

His lean face, emotionless expression, hard eyes, and deliberate manner of speech leaves no one in doubt who is in charge.

The central holo brightens. "Thank you, Admiral Simpson," grates the electronic silhouette. "If I may summarize our intent. We will recover the Constellation's drive. Under no circumstances will the Jovians be allowed to retain it."

The Scorpion emphasizes "under no circumstances" as if underlining the words. Judging by the somber looks of the battle-ready men around the table, this means we fight to the death. If required.

"The Admiral believes this mission to be easily within the capacity of our fleet. But I will not have this left to chance. You must choose your best men. Fill them with the fear of a Jovian-led Sector. Promise them recognition for heroic tasks. It may be within our capability, but I do not expect any of you to hold back. You are authorized to proceed with maximum force."

The men at the table exchange glances while their aides furiously tap into datapads.

Which means almost none of them notice that I have stood and walked into the spotlit area. None of them except Simpson, who watched me the whole way. I now stand at the table in between two seated ranking officers.

"Actually no," I say, shocking the table into frozen silence. Apparently you don't contradict the Scorpion. "The last thing you need to do is risk your talented men in an unnecessary display of maximum force."

And I tell them my real plan. Even my crew look stunned, but I couldn't bring myself to brief them before the meeting. They'd never let me do it.

Mitch just stares at me.

Oddly, the first person to second it at the Scorpion's request is none other than Admiral Simpson.

Have I been played?

CHAPTER SIXTY

THE SLINGSHOT SLIPS OUT OF hyperspace virtually on Ganymede's doorstep. Jupiter's muted marbled surface dwarfs the backdrop and for a moment I am taken by the gas giant's sheer beauty and rustic-banded might.

The slight pull of gravity against the plasticuffs around my wrists remind me of my plight. The commPanel is already flashing its urgent red presence, and the Rykkan Chief, seated in the captain's chair, leans across the navpanel to answer.

"LightCruiser Slingshot." The Chief never wastes words. I look back at Mitch and Sloper, both of whom are also cuffed and tied down to their seats.

"Ganymede Customs. State your clearance and docking destination."

"Anywhere I talk to big chiefs."

The commPanel goes quiet. A new voice takes over. "What is your intention, lightCruiser? You do not have clearance to dock."

"I tell you. I talk to big chiefs. Top Jovian head man."

I think the Chief is enjoying himself. I struggle against my cuffs, then give up.

"Permission denied. Please state your intention, or be forced to surrender control."

The Chief cackles. "Maybe you try this force. You not succeed against my ship."

There is a long gap in communication.

"What was your origin at launch, lightCruiser?"

"Takao."

Another silence. The Chief taps the panel. "Anyone still home?"

The disembodied voice responds. "Ganymede cannot grant clearance. You must leave the region within five minutes or be considered a viable enemy target."

"Tell Jovian big chiefs I have present for them. They pay much money." He grins a toothy red cavern.

The voice is starting to sound frustrated. "Please provide proof of your trading authority."

The Chief punches up the holo, then reverses the view, so it mirrors our interior. He adjusts the cam sliders until the screen shows me—now back in full flaming red hair—Mitch, and Sloper. I scowl at the cam and the Chief just laughs. "I think you see authority now."

Another voice breaks in, this one authoritative. "Advance to spaceport G4. You will be met and your merchandise inspected."

The bulky Rykkan taps the commPanel closed, looks at each of us without saying a word, then swivels back to concentrate on taking us in.

Which does not take long.

The authorities board my ship, and I find myself face-to-face with a midlevel Jovian official. He looks me up and down, then moves to Mitch and Sloper, who he greets with a smile. "A pleasure to see you indisposed." Sloper does not respond.

The official moves back to me. "India Jackson. Spacewhore. And her dim brother. Welcome back to Ganymede. Your colleague Errikson is waiting for you."

I say nothing. I'll only encourage him, so instead I look away.

He tells us to stand and await our escort, and the official orders the Rykkan Chief to wait.

"Why I wait? You pay now. You have merchandise. Now I

take big ship drive. Big Jovian already agree on hyper-relay." The Chief breaks out in a line of Rykkan sweat on his brow protuberance.

The official leans in to the Rykkan, one corner of his mouth turned up in a smile. "Big Jovian change mind. So you wait. Unless you want to leave without the drive?"

The Chief doesn't answer. He just lowers himself into the captain's chair. *My* captain's chair. He watches as they lead us away, maneuvering awkwardly with our tied wrists in the nearly zero-gee.

We enter a sleek-looking inter-satellite speedster. A guard takes Sloper elsewhere, but I barely register his expression as we race away from the port.

"Where are we going?" I ask, casually, not really expecting an honest answer.

The official looks at me. "The yards. A little test. Make sure the merchandise is not fake." He gives me a flat smile.

Mitch leans across and whispers. "Was this in your plan?"

CHAPTER SIXTY-ONE

THE SPEEDSTER TAKES US TO the hangar Plexi rescued us from previously. Errikson is standing waiting for us when we emerge from the speedster. He sports a broad grin and watches as a guard cuts us free from our plasticuffs. "Excellent. Both possibilities in the one place. Now please accompany me for the last test. No suits needed this time. You'll understand the Jovians never settle a trade until they verify the goods."

I shrug. "You only need a palm scan for that. Why bring us here? The deal is done as soon as you get the scan."

Errikson's grin widens further. "The scanning device we will be using to test is not quite as portable as the ones you might be used to." He spins in the low gravity and kicks off. I feel a prod in my back and turn to see one of Errikson's men shoving me. I push his weapon away, showing my distaste on my face, and propel myself off to follow Errikson.

We float through several passageways until we break out into a smaller hangar. At the end of the empty space there is an area ringed by powerful spotlights, all trained on an apparently hastily rigged airlock.

The lock is open, revealing an expandable bridge which connects to another, closed lock. Temporary sensors swathe the far airlock's bulkhead. Men and women work on remote datapads, adjusting controls and exchanging readings. Inset into the far lock is a smaller door, on its right-hand side a controlpanel.

Underneath the panel is a small stenciled sign.

It reads: "WARNING. DANGEROUS EQUIPMENT INSIDE. UNAUTHORIZED ENTRY IS HAZARDOUS."

And underneath that, another, smaller text sign. "AUTHORIZED CONSTELLATION PERSONNEL ONLY"

The drive.

CHAPTER SIXTY-TWO

ERRIKSON ORDERS ALL HIS MEN to retreat. He motions Mitch and me to follow him to the drive's entry door. He points to the controlpanel. "Your fingerscan test. Of sorts. As you can see, we are unable to open access to the drive. As soon as you verify you have access, I will confirm with General Marius that the Rykkan will be given the drive." He looks at me strangely. "Once we have finished with it."

I sigh. "Let's get it over with." I step up to the controlpanel and slap my hand on the plate. A circle of red spots race around the perimeter of my hand, speeding up ... then they freeze and turn green. A message appears on the screen.

<<ENTRY ACCESS CONFIRMED>>

But the door remains closed. I look to Errikson for guidance. He scowls. "Try again."

I do, with the same result.

"Let the boy try."

Mitch steps up and completes the same task. The red spots race around his hand, again they freeze and turn to green ... and we see the same message.

Errikson curses.

I smile at him. "Voice control perhaps?"

He jerks his head at the panel, and I run through the procedure again. This time, after the message appears, I speak. "Captain Jackson of the Constellation requesting access."

Errikson's head twists around to stare at me, then he slowly breaks out into a smile. He looks back at the entry, which remains closed.

But a new message appears.

<<PLEASE ENTER SECONDARY AUTHORIZATION>>

I look from Mitch to Errikson. "Well?"

A new voice calls from behind us. A deep, authoritative male voice. "The boy tries now." I turn to see a thickset, swarthy man, his face set without humor.

"Yes, General," Errikson responds quickly and gestures to Mitch. My brother comes forward and places his hand on the panel again. When the green light appears, the door slides away to reveal a dark entry, to what appears to be an endless, unlit cavern.

Errikson can't wipe the smile off his face.

A shout arises from within the hangar behind us. Someone is calling the General. "General Marius!" The man pushes over to us and comes to a clumsy halt, saluting the Jovian General at the same time as gaining a handhold.

"Speak."

"Sir, you are requested in the command center. The Scorpion has assembled his fleet on the far side of Jupiter."

I shoot a glance at Mitch. He looks worried. This is not an agreed part of our plan—and worse, it could mean all bets are off when it comes to leaving with the drive. Or our lives.

The General glares at us both. "Explain."

I square him off. This is not the time for my normal flippant response. I decide to go with the truth.

"General Marius, I know nothing of this. My deal with the Scorpion was to come here and retrieve the drive. The Rykkan Chief's presumed taking of us as hostage was a ruse, no more. I know as much as you do about this." My mind is racing for options, but I find none.

Marius regards me for a moment, then turns to the aide. "Tell General Karalis to mobilize our defense and launch response fighters. I will attend the command center shortly." The man salutes and launches off, already tapping into his datapad and talking.

The General looks back at Errikson. "We have little time. I suggest you use it wisely. Bring me the information you promised." He gestures to the open doorway.

Errikson pushes me and Mitch forward. I step into the darkness—and lighting flickers on. Mitch follows, and I hear him gasp.

CHAPTER SIXTY-THREE

THE INTERIOR OF THE DRIVE is vast. And not at all what I expected. Instead of hundreds of meters of tubing, wiring and electronic interfaces, I am confronted by a colossal, impervious black box-like unit. It almost fills the cavernous space. There is no obvious control point or access.

Errikson can hardly contain himself. "What do you see?"

"Why would I tell you?" I throw back at him, "when you can come in and see for yourself."

"I think you will tell me everything you know about this drive, and your status." He grins.

I turn around and look past Mitch at Errikson standing beyond the open doorway. "What are you playing at? The Scorpion is about to attack, General Marius is impatient to get what we have agreed to give him—there's nothing more to know."

Errikson leers at me. "Except what I know about your father."

Now Mitch turns around, and I can see the tension in his body from behind. "Tell me now, or this guy"—he indicates the Jovian General, who is observing us with an increasing dark expression—"might get impatient with our very slow progress."

General Marius raises his hand. "Enough. Errikson, deliver what I have requested. Report back in twenty minutes." He spins around, pushes off the bulkhead and floats over to the hangar exit.

Errikson's gleeful face drops. He kicks off and enters the

drive's doorway, glaring at me all the way.

Until a battery of lasers hidden in the drive's open airlock seals slice him to ribbons. I hear a brief shout of pain, then his mangled body continues—slowly—to the deck. I look away from the spreading cloud of blood droplets.

I can hear a commotion from the other end of the hangar. The General had obviously heard Errikson's dying cry and is heading back to us at full speed. He expertly arrests his flight on the temporary airlock bridge. He looks at us, then down at Errikson's smoking remains, then back at us.

I turn up my palms. "I—we—had nothing to do with it."

"That is the second time you claim this." The Jovian's voice cuts through us. "Why should I believe you?"

"Because of this." Mitch steps through the doorway, and I let out a shriek. But he emerges untouched. No laser attack. He beckons behind him for me to do the same. I follow through, my entire body screaming in tense protest, but nothing happens.

Mitch looks at the General. "Did you see us disable anything? Watch again." He retreats through the doorway, studiously avoiding the ugly mess on one side, and I follow him. Nothing happens.

The General flicks his hand and three soldiers appear at his side. He points to one of them. "Join them." The soldier looks terrified, but braces himself and launches through the opening.

The lasers slice him into pieces. So fast, he has no time to make a sound. His jerking body parts continue their arc, spurting fluids and gradually becoming separate chunks of flesh and bone drifting in space. I push my stomach down and try to look away, but the General is ordering us to return. This time I am grateful to leave the two ugly deaths behind me.

Marius displays nothing, except an air of curiosity. A thinking general. He looks between us and appears to come to a decision.

"Take them away. A holding cell. We will return to this later."

I try to argue. "How? Errikson is dead. No one else can manipulate the data like he could."

The General's face is impassive. "Errikson is no longer of any importance. Alive or dead. I have what I need." Then he dismisses us and leaves.

Several men crowd around us, and though my body has become numb, I feel my wrists plasticuffed, then they manhandle us through the spaceyard's labyrinth passageways and shove us into a bare, windowless cell.

The door slides closed.

Mitch eyes me. "That went well."

But all I can think about is with Errikson dead, I'll never know what he threatened to tell me about Papa.

CHAPTER SIXTY-FOUR

IN THE DEPTHS OF THE spaceyard it's hard to know how the Scorpion's attack is faring. Explosions can't be heard from space. But I know what the Scorpion's ultimate target is. And I have to stop her taking it.

I look over at Mitch, who is sitting, staring at the dull alloy deck. "Worried?" I say.

He casts a grim look my way. "We're screwed. Doesn't matter who wins. Whether the Jovians get the drive or the Scorpion, doesn't much matter. Neither of them have the Sector's interest at heart."

"Have you forgotten the small matter of the Circle of Seven's fleet?"

He shrugs. "Why does that make any difference? Whoever controls the Constellation or its drive's secrets, controls us. Jovians, the Scorpion, Oberon—we're screwed by all of them."

I think for a moment. "Why didn't General Marius send us into the drive again?"

"I guess he was more concerned with an impending attack."

"But Errikson insisted that the data was key for them. It's as if it doesn't matter anymore." I try to get comfortable, but zero-gee makes your body do strange things when you try to lie down. I give up and float a little, steadying myself to keep looking at Mitch.

He screws his face up. "Dunno what they'd get from that black thing, but I suppose once they saw only we had access, they knew they could take their time."

I straighten my body out with a jolt as a thought comes to me. I accidentally kick against the bulkhead and have to wait until I touch the other side to stop myself. "Genius! That's it."

Mitch looks interested, his eyes bright. "You've worked out a way to get us out of here, make the Jovians and the Scorpion best friends and defeat the Blood Empire?"

"Cynic. But no, it's worse than that. What do the Jovians rely on to maintain their stranglehold over the Sector?"

"Easy. Energy supply. Elementary economics. What's your point? ... Wait. You think the drive has information about energy that is important to them?"

I shake my head. "No. If it was important to them, we'd be in there now, extracting information."

Mitch looks puzzled. "I don't get it."

"Then let me spell it out for you. Remember you told me you heard the Jovians were developing something to make 3He redundant? The Jovians only wanted the data so they could stop anyone else from getting their hands on it. That's why they fed Errikson the line about making sure he got the drive and access to it—"

"And?"

"Let me finish. Whatever it is in that drive, they know that if that information was widely available, it would wipe out their hold over energy prices and trade. They'd have no power ... literally. The Jovians aren't interested in developing anything new. They want to do the opposite. They want to destroy it."

"Now you're just guessing."

"Maybe. But if it was that important to Marius, why are we still sitting in this cell?"

A dawning realization sweeps over Mitch's face. "Because we might be the only two people in the Galaxy who can unlock what is in the Constellation's drive."

I nod. "And the best way to prevent anyone else knowing or gaining access is—"

"To throw away the key."

"Precisely. This is a death row cell."

CHAPTER SIXTY-FIVE

I AM ABOUT TO SPEAK when the entire structure around us shudders. I hear muted thumps. Explosions in space have no sound, but I'm not in space.

Mitch stares at me. "The Scorpion."

"We gotta get out of here."

He nods. "Or die trying."

"Probably that," I say, and kick myself down to the only door. There are no controls, no small crevices, no handy panel I could unscrew—even if I had a multitool—not even a commPanel to yell for help.

Not that anyone would come.

I pat my suit pants with my cuffed hands, as if I've somehow managed to pack a handy pocket lasercutter.

I bang on the door, but all that does is push me away and up to the overhead. I push back off, noting that the overhead is the same smooth, seamless alloy as the rest of the cell.

Mitch is now inspecting the door. He puts his head next to the edge where the door would open first. "Hey! Let us out! We can help fight! We know about the Scorpion's weapons!" He looks back at me, frustration written all over his face. "Any ideas?"

I think as calmly as possible—not so easy when the thumps are coming more frequently, and louder too. I can smell the distinctive odor of fried electrics. I look at Mitch, then kick over to him. I hug my brother.

"No ideas. I think this is it. I love you, Mitch. I hope we meet Papa soon."

He says nothing, and hugs me back. Tight.

The smell of destroyed circuitry is strong now, yet the explosive sounds are still distant. The analytical part of me tries to separate out the facts: we are not under direct attack at the cell, yet something is frying the electronics close to us. I look at the door—then push my brother away. "Mitch! The door!"

We both look at the cell's entrance. Part of the door and bulkhead is glowing. I push to the back of the cell and brace myself. I hope my death is not painful—maybe quick, like Errikson. I hug myself tight and switch my attention to Mitch. I'd like my final moment to be a vision of my brother, not the flash of a laser.

I am fortunate I averted my gaze from the door, as a sun-bright flash turns everything white, and for a moment, I am snowblind.

Then the light fades away, all I can smell is the acrid circuitry, and standing amid the smoke, a lasercutter in one hand and a laserSword in the other, is a figure in a spacesuit.

Mitch is blinking and looking around. He can't see yet. I lower myself, pushing carefully down the bulkhead, taking advantage of the fact that I am at the rear of the smoke-filled cell. Then I twist until my feet are flat against the rear bulkhead and push off as hard as I can.

I hit the figure in the knees and we both fly across the passageway. I am trying to grab the laserSword, knowing it is my last hope for freedom. As soon as the Scorpion's men "rescue" us, as soon as they realize the power Mitch and I have over the drive and the Constellation, our lives are forfeit, enslaved forever. I bury the thought and I wrestle for control of the weapon.

Finally my opponent wrenches a hand free, throws the

lasercutter spinning down the passageway, and rips his helmet off.

"Indy! I know you love me, but honestly, we can save this for later."

It's Jordi.

CHAPTER SIXTY-SIX

MITCH FLIES OUT OF THE cell and grabs Jordi around the neck with his cuffed hands. "You bastard betrayer. You sold us out to Sloper. I'm gonna kill you."

Jordi can barely speak. "Sloper is dead." He chokes. "Let go. Some guy called Pedro told me you were here, but we don't have time for this."

More thumps—now causing the entire structure to reverberate—underline Jordi's point.

I pull Mitch away and look at Jordi. "Where to?"

"My ship. Well, technically not mine. Yet." He points to two objects in the passageway. Personal drivepacks, used in zero-gee for low speed maneuvers. Usually outside a spacecraft, but I'm not complaining. A simple compressed-air unit, they will speed up our exit. Now I see Jordi also wears one.

Sounds of battle echo down the passageway, and I feel my heart pounding. Jordi cuts our cuffs away, and Mitch and I strap on the packs. I'm thankful Pedro had his network well primed for news of us, and I'm impressed with his lateral thinking response to my message.

We fly behind Jordi, twisting and turning down the passageways. We encounter no one, but when we finally emerge into a large hangar, I see why. Hundreds of Jovians engage a stream of Takaons in battle, attacking them from the other end of the hangar. A Takaon cutting ship has pierced the closed bulkhead airlock, lodging itself in place, and sealing the breach with its own hull. The ship is still disgorging soldiers, who shoot as soon as they disembark.

We pass close to the bulkheads lining the hangar's far side, removed from the fighting. The combatants completely ignore us. Jordi halts at a smaller, human sized airlock and punches it open. I see a flexiconnection to another ship beyond. Jordi removes his drivepack and we do the same. He pushes off through the small space, then Mitch. I am about to follow when a shadow passes behind me and I glance back to see an armored figure approaching fast. I yell ahead. "Jordi!" I twist around to defend myself.

My bare hands are no match for my assailant's laserdagger, and he plunges it into my side.

The searing pain cuts deep, strangely ice-cold, and I feel my body crumple into the fetal position, shutting down. I try to speak, but the icy spread of death in my side strikes me dumb. I try to hold myself with one hand, but my arm will not function, and I look at it as if in slow motion, willing it to move.

The unnamed attacker in front of me is about to strike again, when I see through blurry vision a bright red stream of liquid shoot out from his chest, and he flies away from us, his arms and legs flailing slowly until they stop. I cannot move, and I watch him float away, inert.

My vision shifts abruptly, and I sense I am being pulled along. My head is tight. My body is ice. I am paralyzed. I cannot speak.

And now I cannot breathe.

Gone.

CHAPTER SIXTY-SEVEN

A FACE SWIMS INTO MY vision. Indistinct, but familiar. Papa when he was young. I try to reach up to embrace him, but I am stuck somewhere. I cannot move my mouth. I lose him again into the black.

It's Papa again—this time he speaks. "Indy. Don't go. Stay with us. Be strong."

It's not Papa at all. It's Mitch.

"Mitch," I say weakly.

He shushes me. "I've given you stims. You're badly hurt, so don't try to move. Just breathe and stay focused and I'll get you to a medbay."

I give him a weak smile and try to breathe as he asks. Pain rips through me and I wince. The black is inviting me again, but a nagging sensation inside me makes me believe I have something important to do, and I push it away.

I hear Mitch talking to someone. About me and going somewhere quickly.

The black returns and this time I succumb.

I wake with a start and my eyes flick open. I can see a ship's overhead above me. I am lying down. Strapped in. I try to move, but my body gives me a reminder of the pain of a laserdagger slicing into my side.

"You're stronger than I thought." Jordi looks down at me,

grinning. "I think it's the depth of your love for me. It kept you going."

"How bad ..." I cannot finish the croaking sentence.

Mitch appears into view. "Not good at all. It should have killed you. I can only imagine that the one time you needed the luck of the devil, he showed up and gave it to you. He must have missed all the vital organs."

"Didn't know I had non-vital ones," I manage to whisper. "But they hurt just the same."

"You lost a lot of blood. I reckon a busted rib or two, plenty of muscles sliced up. Maybe a lung problem."

That explains the difficulty breathing.

"Where going?" I croak.

"Nearest medbay. But the Jovians have declared war on Takao. Your double-crossing boyfriend here tells me that the Scorpion sent a splinter squad to attack the spaceyard. He thinks they already have the drive, but the mayhem underway right now could mean anyone gets hold of it. And this ship is only a tug."

A spacetug. No hyperDrive. Minimal facilities and unarmed.

"Where medbay?" I am fading. I don't know if I can make it.

My brother's face darkens. "We're requesting help. It's the best I can do, Indy. Your life is more important."

What he means is: we can send out an SOS and request a medteam, but we will be prisoners of war.

If a Jovian medteam gets to us first, our prisoner of war status will mean little.

What's the point?

I slip into unconsciousness.

I can't have been out for long, as Mitch is still hovering over me. He has a stim injector in one hand. "We've found a medteam." But the look on his face tells me there is something else.

"What?"

He hesitates. "It's the Scorpion. She knows you're injured. She's proposing a deal."

"Don't take it."

He reaches over and pulls a holopad across. "Not that simple. She wants to talk to you directly." He taps the icon, and the holo appears over my bed. The Scorpion's image springs into view. The woman herself, not some digitized fiction.

"Ah, Captain Jackson. I am sorry to hear of your wounds."

"No you're not. You want something." I wonder how the conversation would proceed if she knew which ship I really captain.

The woman smiles. Showing no emotion in her eyes. "Always to the point. So let me get to it for you. Your brother and his friend tell me you have hours to live unless you get help."

I flick my gaze to Mitch. His face is white, and he wipes something from his eye.

I look back at the holo. Right now all I can move on the bed is my head, my eyes and my mouth. I assume Mitch—or Jordi—have deliberately anesthetized the rest of my body so I am not permitted to feel the truth the Scorpion is revealing: I am facing death.

"What of it? Are you saying you suddenly care about me?"

"We can enjoy a mutually beneficial exchange. I give you your life."

"And I give you the Constellation and the drive. How did I guess."

The Scorpion smiles again. "There's more. In return for helping me restore the drive—oh yes, I know the Jovians discovered you have access to it—I will grant you and your comrades senior positions in my command. If nothing else, you've proved to be a highly resourceful asset. One I'd rather have on my side."

"I bet you would. But you went back on our deal. You attacked the Jovians, you started a war we don't need, and even if you give us so-called positions, I know one day I'll still end up stabbed in the side. An experience I'm keen not to repeat. My answer is no."

Her mouth tightens. "I suspected so. A decision you'll no doubt regret."

The holo goes blank and Mitch pushes it away. It floats to the bulkhead and bounces off, slowly.

He looks at me with sadness on his face. "You just signed your death warrant. No one else will come to our rescue. But you had to trade your own life for your principles. Why, Indy?"

I manage a small smile. "You think she really wants me dead?"

His face brightens. "Good point." Then his expression drops again. "The result's still the same: she captures us, you get fixed up, we have to submit to her threats."

I try to shrug, but my shoulders don't listen. "But it's our move. Not hers."

He stares at me. "And that's important? I don't see how."

I smile weakly. "Nor me. But I'll think of something."

CHAPTER SIXTY-EIGHT

I DON'T THINK FOR LONG, as sirens and red warning lights swamp our small spacetug. I sense movement—slight disturbances in gravity, or more accurately, shifting mass—as Jordi takes evasive action. We are under attack. Jordi is one of the best pilots I know, but a spacetug with a great pilot can be trumped by the freshest of recruits behind a starfighter's sophisticated weapon's system.

An explosion rocks the rear of our ship, and debris streams through the cabin. The tug really has only one main area, I am located aft on a pull-down bunk, intended for sleep. Not medical treatment.

Mitch pushes over to me, his face haggard. He carries a medisuit and helmet and proceeds to unstrap me and manhandle me into the suit.

"Don't bother, Mitch. I'm dead anyway. At least the Scorpion won't realize her main prize was taken out by some idiot fighter. One of her own." I try to fight him, but my body is paralyzed, and anyway, it's getting harder to breathe.

Mitch ignores me, closes my helmet and dons his own suit. I cannot see Jordi at the helm upfront. Instead, I imagine him frantically tapping away at the helmpad. My head still senses movement, and though Jordi or Mitch have silenced the sirens, the red warnings continue to flash.

In seconds we'll be spacedust, blown to pieces by superior weaponry.

The Jovians and the Scorpion can go to hell.

I'm going to Papa.

Mitch heads over to somewhere out of my sight. I am moving—fast now—and I see the cabin flying past me, then it's gone as I shoot out into space.

My last vision from the inside was of Jordi, strapped into his seat, wrestling at the controls of the laboring tug, trying to make it respond like a lightCruiser.

He is fighting a losing battle.

The tug vanishes into the distance, and as I float out into space, I realize Jordi wasn't wearing a suit.

Mitch floats up beside me. He has used a drivepack to navigate to my side. I am confused. Dying in space; dying on the ship; dying in some medbay—what's the difference?

We cannot communicate. We just float. The spacetug has long gone. Mitch presses his faceplate to mine. His eyes search mine, anxious. I blink back at him.

I am still alive.

Mitch's head jerks up from mine. I see a reflection in his faceplate. Lights, then gleaming alloy. I feel myself grabbed and pulled.

Into a familiar airlock.

My airlock.

My lightCruiser. Slingshot.

I sense the airlock close, and someone peers down at me. It's the Rykkan Chief. He grins first, then speaks. I can hear him through my helmet. "You not die yet. Still have debt." Then he pushes me to the ship's medbay—far more sophisticated than the tug's.

The tug. I look around for Mitch. He is at my other side, taking off his helmet and reaching down for mine. I wait until mine is off.

"Jordi?"

Mitch knows what I'm asking and shakes his head with a glum expression. "He didn't make it. He used the tug as a decoy to save us. Told me he wanted to make things right."

I feel numb. No matter how big the scale, war is always personal.

CHAPTER SIXTY-NINE

WE EMERGE FROM HYPERSPACE. I don't know where we are, but I do know I feel a whole lot better. I can actually feel my body, so I try to sit up.

Big mistake.

After the lancing pain in my side subsides, I lie back on the bunk in the medbay. I realize it was probably the exit from hyperspace that woke me—that odd internal sensation in your organs that never quite stops being disconcerting.

After a short while, I discover I can move my right arm without too much disturbance to my left side. I reach for the holo and tap the comms open.

"Mitch? Anyone?"

A gruff voice responds. "He sleep. Captain feeling better now." It's not a question, and I smile inside at the idea of being around Rykkans again.

"Yes. Still pain, but I'm not dead. Thanks to you. How did you know where to find us?"

The disembodied voice replies from the holo's speaker. "Use Rykkan senses. Jovian hospitality not good, then Scorpion come and I sense you hurt. Maybe very bad. So I kill some Jovians and take your cruiser. Look for you with sense and track you in tug. But dangerous with other fighter."

I nod, even though he cannot see me. "What happened?"

There is a pause. "I make communication with tug pilot. He say pick up two spacewalkers. He say he draw fighter away." The

Rykkan stops talking. I feel a strange sense. As if a tiny spider is crawling inside my head. Not unpleasant. "He was friend."

"In the end, yes. Where do we head now?"

"NewSwiss12. I find journey in your navigation panel."

Of course. From Aktip's injury, which seems long ago now. I wonder what has become of Aktip. Our original plan had her remain on Takao. At least she is safe there. For now. A wave of shock floods over me—no doubt a delayed reaction to my own serious injury—and I feel a tear escape at the thought of so many lives depending on me. Lives lost because of me.

Papa, did you bring this on?

He does not answer, of course.

So many things wrong: my father's killer dead, but not at my hands as I imagined; the Sector plunging into civil war, and what remains of my family and friends risking their lives for me.

Yet I feel powerless to act.

I try to distract myself. "When do we land on NewSwiss12?" There is no answer.

"Chief?"

No response. I look around for help, but there is no way I can move. It's too painful. I try again.

"Chief? Captain to the bridge, is anyone there?"

"Sorry, Indy," Mitch replies. "The Chief needed me in the helmroom." He sounds bleary from sleep. "Incoming signal. Encrypted. The Chief didn't know how to answer."

"Encrypted? Do we know who and where from yet?"

"No. I've just requested that. I'll buzz you as soon as I know."

Surely no one followed us from Ganymede? I make the mistake of taking a deep breath, and wince and scream simultaneously.

"Indy? Are you okay?"

"Yes. No. Wondering when this will all stop."

Silence. I imagine Mitch is dealing with the comms.

I hear the helm chatter as Mitch opens up the channel to me. The icon flashes orange to show "private" and his face appears on the holo. He looks surprised and confused at the same time.

"Who is it?" I ask.

Mitch hesitates a moment. "Admiral Simpson. At the helm of a stealthfighter."

I suck in a breath and flinch at the pain. I can't seem to cut myself—or my friends—a break. "Oh crap. Can we run?"

Mitch shakes his head. "That's the thing. He said we can if we want. Then he said if the Constellation's Captain Jackson is willing to meet with General Garnek, our Papa would be proud."

I stare at Mitch in the holo. "Bring me to the helmroom."

The Constellation's *Captain* Jackson.

He knew all along.

CHAPTER SEVENTY

Mitch and the Rykkan Chief detach my bunk into a makeshift gurney and bring me and my bed to the helmroom. Mitch flattens two of the passenger seats with a tap of a button, and they arrange me so I can see the holoscreen.

On which is Simpson. Garnek. He inclines his head to me. He has a serious look on his face. "I understand you are injured."

"What is it to you? Why should I trust anything you say?"

He says nothing, but reaches forward out of my view and adjusts the zoom. The field of view pulls back and I see sitting next to Garnek ... Aktip. I start to sit up—then remember my wound and manage to stop myself. "Aktip! Are you okay? Has Simpson hurt you?"

Simpson—or Garnek—interrupts. "Please call me General Garnek. Admiral Simpson is no more. Your friend is unhurt and is here of her own free will."

I am a little lost. "Then I am the one missing all the information."

"He speaks true," Aktip says. "But you should not be speaking at all. You need medical help. Self-repair."

I smile. "Humans don't self-repair in the same way as Rykkans, Aktip. I thought you knew that. But I'm glad to see you are unhurt. Will someone tell me what is going on?"

Garnek speaks. "I will share everything in person. Let me give you enough to let you know I can be trusted, but we will need to go to Takao as soon as practicable. There I can assure you of the best treatment."

I frown. "At the hands of the Scorpion? I think not. No matter how much you can be trusted."

"Then listen. The Scorpion has taken the drive. I offered to have it transported to Takao while she continues the fight against the Jovians. She's wanted to dismantle them for decades, so she is completely obsessed. She trusts me ... but once she knows you and I are on Takao, along with the drive, it won't take her long to piece together what has happened."

"And what has happened, exactly?" I regard him coolly.

"I have always been on your side. Your father's side. I'll explain later. In fact, it was your resemblance to your father that first caught me when I saw you on the Scorpion's holo. Once I found out your name, the rest was easy. Now your hair is no longer black, I see quite plainly the little girl I once met."

I remember to breathe.

"I took some time to come around to the fact that you weren't just a petty space pirate, and that Jackson's daughter hadn't betrayed her father's values. I realized you'd almost certainly have full Captain status. You were smart to hold that fact back from the Scorpion. But I admit I didn't have full confidence in what you would do with it, so I maintained my deceit and watched." He pauses for a moment as if to evaluate me before moving on. "After you proposed your ... bold plan, I was convinced of your intent. When chaos erupted with the Jovians, I knew I had to get to you before she did, without you mistaking my intentions. That's where your friend here came in."

Aktip's head does that little shimmy. "The General came to me in secret, Madam Captain. He told me who he was, not knowing I already knew. He said he had to find you and work together. If humans have been well-trained, they can sometimes confuse Rykkans, but not for truth this deep. I told him your plan, and he said you are in grave danger. I have debt, so I come with him."

My mind is in a whirl. "Okay." I look back to Garnek. His countenance is softer.

He nods. "I know your Papa worked on the drive. Some new physics, a breakthrough he said. The rest I'll tell you—"

"On Takao. What other choice do I have? Flash us the hyperDrive hop coordinates. I'm sure you already know the fastest route."

Garnek looks relieved. "Yes, Captain."

CHAPTER SEVENTY-ONE

I'M IN THE MEDBAY ON Takao. My position is reversed from before: now it's me who is lying on the bed, adorned with tubes, and with Mitch standing over me.

"How is it?" he asks.

I move both arms freely, tubes swinging with me as I do so. "I couldn't do this a few hours ago. The docs say a few more hours and I'll be able to move without all this." I gesture at the tubing. "But I won't be winning any races."

Thankfully, I'm on Takao and not Rykkamon. I wouldn't have lasted in Rykkamon's gravity, but Takao's, while tough compared to zero-gee, is bearable. Not only that, their medteams seem to be able to pull off what no one else can. Though not quite up to the Rykkan self-repair biology.

I look up at Mitch. "Status?" He knows what I'm asking.

"Aktip is on the Constellation checking. Also Simpson"—he is careful to use Garnek's Takaon identity in case of prying local ears—"is bringing the drive across. No word on the Jovian battle. I left the Chief on the cruiser monitoring chatter."

Some figures appear at the doorway and Mitch waves them in. Danielli, Plexi and Herg. Followed by Zhang and Ortiz.

"Where've you been hiding out?" I ask Danielli.

"After you and the Chief left, the Scorpion put out an alert for us. But Herg knew a bartender in Hoto. He put us up in the backroom and we waited to hear news from Ganymede. When we heard you'd been captured, Plexi tracked down Aktip.

Simpson conveniently 'granted' us amnesty and we've been on the Constellation since then."

I raise my brow. Danielli gets what I'm asking. "No, Ma'am. No one can work out if it can be refitted."

Which is three sides of a credit, I think. On one hand, if the Constellation remains an unusable hulk, the Scorpion won't have the firepower to take on the Sector. On the other hand, the Jovians will be free to continue their dominance over the Sector's energy trade.

But the real issue is that the Blood Empire will wipe the floor with us.

Garnek enters, with Aktip. This is turning out to be a party. I see that Garnek and Aktip are wearing very sober expressions. They make their way to stand next to me.

"Ma'am." Garnek nods his head. "Good to see your health is recovering."

"But you have bad news."

Aktip looks at me as if she is wondering if I too, can sense human thoughts.

Garnek nods again. He gestures to Aktip who thrusts a portable holo in front of me and taps play.

The holo springs up with a starry backdrop I do not recognize.

"Sector fringe," the General explains, when he sees the look on my face. Danielli, Plexi, and the others crowd around, and we all watch as a swarm of insects cross into view.

Except they are not insects.

I watch as thousands upon thousands of battlefighters move past the drone's viewcam. Sufficiently far away to remain undetected, but close enough to reveal the horror of what Oberon has planned for the Circle of Seven's return. I turn my head to Aktip. "When?"

"It is perhaps from twenty to thirty hours ago. But they are weeks away from the Sector."

I look at Garnek. "Admiral Simpson, how long before the Scorpion returns?"

He knows what I imply and grimaces. "Several hours. Less, if she has eyes here." He is circumspect, but we all get the message. Sooner rather than later, the Scorpion will realize that "Simpson" has double-crossed her. Whether she knows Simpson is Garnek, or that I am the Constellation's Captain is unknown, but it won't matter. She'll lock the planet down.

"Papa ordered the evacuation of the Constellation, didn't he?" I hold General Garnek's gaze.

He barely reacts. "Yes."

"Why?"

He shrugs. "No one knew, but it happened fast. As soon as we defeated Oberon, your father took the ship into deep space. Apparently there was supposed to have been an issue with the drive. From what I can gather since, he was making modifications to the drive's functionality. He couldn't make them mid-battle I guess."

Why did I never know about Papa's past? I look at Mitch, but he looks as lost as I am. Papa went to great length to show us the blackmarket trading ropes, and to insist we do our best to continue his illicit work. Then he left, and the next I knew was that Sloper had killed him. Mom was long gone by then, so we had no one to ask. One more reason Mitch and I are close.

I shake myself back into the present and look around at my friends. I am about to request their input for our next move when the base's security alarm erupts.

"The Scorpion is here." Garnek gives me a grim look and races out of the room.

I leap out of bed, ignoring the bruising pain in my side, and I rip out the tubes. Danielli tries to tell me I still need hours more healing, but I won't have it.

I look at Plexi. "Can you get us to the Constellation?"

"Yes." Her eyes glisten brightly.

I turn to Danielli and Aktip. "Will we get access to it?"

They both say, "Yes," in unison.

"Good. I have an idea."

CHAPTER SEVENTY-TWO

WE PICK UP THE CHIEF from my lightCruiser, and we're on our way to the Constellation in the shuttle when Garnek calls through on a private line. He is careful not to name names.

"The alarm was for you. We're to be on the lookout for the lightCruiser. She hasn't yet put two and two together—probably because she has her hands tied with the war she triggered—and hasn't placed me in the picture. But knowing her, it won't be long. In the meantime, I can divert attention here, then join you at the last minute."

"Don't leave it too late," I say. "I think I'm going to need you."

"If I hear in your voice what I think I'm hearing, you'll have trouble stopping me. Over and out."

Danielli says with a smile, "Now that's the General Garnek I knew."

I am less optimistic. "We still have to get into the Constellation. Even though we've docked the lightCruiser under a fake name, it won't take long to trace it back. From there, it's a quick enough deduction to connect a tall red-head under Garnek's wing to a major double-cross. We need to work quickly."

"Well, you're the one with all the ideas," Mitch says.

I hold his gaze and lift my chin. "It's not the ideas I'm worried about."

He looks at me inquisitively.

"It's whether they'll work."

"In the timeframe? We can always play for delaying tactics,"

Danielli says.

"No. I'm worried they'll work at all."

"Ah." Danielli looks at me with narrowed eyes.

CHAPTER SEVENTY-THREE

WE MAKE IT TO THE spaceport in outer orbit where the Constellation hangs in space. Even though this port is well away from Takao—for good reason—the battlecruiser makes an ominous man-made moon for the giant planet. I watch through the shuttle's observation port as the silvery-gray alloy hull dwarfs everything else in our vision, and wonder what conversations the vessel is stimulating among the highly opinionated Takaons.

Our approach takes us around where the ship's drive would normally be and my heart jumps a beat when I see the massive physical drive floating in space next to the main ship. As if waiting to come home.

We dock at a makeshift gantry and airlock entry to the ship. We disembark and don our suits for when we are inside. An official requests our ID, and I show the fake ones Garnek holo'd to us before we left the planet's surface. We're engineers, dispatched to investigate the cruiser's life support and gravitational systems and ready them for use when power is restored. We pass off our two Rykkans as engineering specialists, invited along as a token of the new alliance. I hold my breath, hoping that the official isn't familiar with the rumors of the red-headed captive.

He glances at me and looks me up and down, running his eyes over my shiny flightSuit. I do my best to look suggestive and put on my "flirty face." The one that Mitch always says makes me look as if I'm desperate to use the bathroom. Maybe that's why

I've never been lucky with men.

But this time it works, and the official gives me an appreciative glance as he waves us through.

One small hurdle passed.

All the big ones left.

We close our helmet's faceplates, pressurize suits, exit the airlock and enter the ship. We requisition podPlates, and make our way through the massive battlecruiser. I glance at Plexi and nod to her podPlate's screen. She grins and punches up the schematic. Somehow I knew she'd be ready.

Both Aktip and the Chief have trouble with their hovering podPlates. Being used to 1.9 gee might make you all-powerful on many other planets, but when it comes to the subtlety required to pilot a plate in null gravity, they are both lacking, despite the Chief's normal prowess in zero-gee. They start and stop like a Martian taxi-cab. Their oversized suits only exaggerate the incongruity. If the stakes weren't so high, I'd laugh.

Plexi threads us through dark passageways and up and down between decks, occasionally stopping to check her schematic. I ask her to steer us away from any other working groups where possible, just in case.

We only see one other team on the far side of a massive empty hangar, working on the damaged z-wing. They ignore us when we pass through.

We eventually reach the outer helmroom unchallenged, and after we dismount our podPlates, I slap the doorpad to take us through into the circular passageway that encloses the helm.

Now it's do or die. If this doesn't work, my only option is to surrender to the Scorpion and agree to her deal.

I place my gloved hand on the doorpad. The red lights circle, then come to a halt and turn green. I drop my hand and speak.

"Captain Jackson requesting access to the helm."

<<**Acknowledged and confirmed. Please enter secondary authorization.**>>

I hesitate a moment.

Then I turn to my brother and indicate the panel. "Mitch. Your turn."

He looks around him in surprise. As if there was another "Mitch" on board. He moves forward to the panel and places his hand on it. The lights circle red, then switch to green.

<<**DNA and biometrics confirmed. Please state your name for voice comparison**.>>

"Mitch Jackson."

<<**Welcome to the Constellation, Lieutenant Commander Jackson.**>>

The helmdoors slide apart.

CHAPTER SEVENTY-FOUR

THE SIGHT TAKES MY BREATH away. Even with emergency-only power, the Constellation's helm is beautiful. It's the size of a circular warehouse and staggering in scale.

A massive, round black-onyx platform table, presumably supported by a hidden central pillar, occupies the center of the dome-like space. Hover chairs and commPanels populate the meeting table, which also features a central holo. Raised up on a circular mezzanine, and surrounding the table are banks of what are presumably navigation, comms, weapons, engineering and various systems workpods—all set up to face the table.

I struggle to make out precise details in the barely lit room, but on the opposite side to our entry point is the Captain's, Pilot's and Chief Officer's raised dais, with red-cushclad high-backed chairs. A purpose-built control stalk and holo extends from each.

I look up and realize that what I thought was a domed overhead is a giant holoscreen.

I drop my gaze and look around the room. A few minimal lights blink here and there, but mostly, it's as if someone just turned off the lights and went home.

"This was your big idea?" Mitch's voice comes into my helmet.

I turn so I can see him directly through his faceplate. "What do you mean?"

"That I'm the secondary authorization. Any idiot could see that."

I snort. "Obviously, since you worked it out. But no, that's not my big idea. However, I still need the help of an idiot or two to make it work. So if you don't mind?" I gesture to the Captain's chair across the room, push Mitch out of my way and kick myself around the perimeter of the helmroom. I ignore the flash of pain in my side and let adrenaline takeover.

Close up, the detail is impressive. I run my gloved fingers over the hand-finished metalloy surfaces, the rubbed-cushclad hover chairs, I admire the sleek, ergonomic layout—this ship was someone's baby. An expensive one.

My small team streams into the room, awaiting my instructions. I see Plexi almost salivating over the controls, but Danielli and Herg remain impassive. Aktip and the Chief just look awkward and out of place, their innate bulk and strength, and Aktip's lack of experience, are a disadvantage in zero-gee. Ortiz and Zhang immediately float themselves into nearby workpods and start investigating the controls.

"Just tell me what you see," I say to them as I make my way past, making sure they get my meaning. "I don't want to trigger any more incidents."

I reach the Captain's chair and slide in, motioning Mitch into the Pilot's seat beside me. I meet Plexi's eyes across the room, bright inside her helmet, and flick my thumb at the Chief Officer's seat next to me. She doesn't wait for a second invitation, but kicks up in a graceful flight straight across the gleaming black table, touches her hands down on the far edge to somersault around, and lands feet first into the chair.

"Aktip, find a useful comms port access and a place for the Chief. Danielli, you're on weapons. Herg—you take engineering. You'll need trial and error to find the best terminal, but Aktip, I'm guessing you'll be able to guide us." I have no idea if Herg's mechanical prowess means he can cope with engineering, but at this stage it doesn't matter.

I look at Plexi. "Can we remotely access the dronetugs ferrying the drive?"

She grins. "Looks like this place can access anything."

I smile. "Here's the plan. While you bring the drive close by, Mitch, Aktip, and I are going searching."

"What for?" Mitch gives me an odd look.

"I don't know, since I've never seen it before." I hesitate, thinking my idea will sound even more stupid when said out loud, but it's all I have. "Did anyone notice that this ship has no signs of damage, other than the removal of the drive?"

Danielli sounds thoughtful over the suitcomm. "Indeed, Ma'am. As you have pointed out before. No remains, no mess, no battle scars."

"Not just that." I wave my hand around. "Everything still looks like new. Yet the Constellation defeated the greatest threat to the Sector ever. Why is there no sign of this anywhere? No wear and tear? Even this seat looks like it was installed yesterday."

My words cause everyone to glance around, as if the answer were in front of us. Which, in a way, I think it is.

The Chief gives me a Rykkan shrug. "Why important now? I prefer dirty ship that works to useless shiny metal coffin."

Plexi straightens. "I'm into the dronetugs." Then her face falls, and she looks at me. "And I'm out again. Looks like we need authority from Takao to work those mothers."

"Can't you hack in?" Mitch says.

Plexi shakes her head. "That's what I did. But the security booted me out again."

Mitch looks at me. "Indy? Captain override?"

"And give us away? There's no guarantee my authorization will work, but it will definitely raise a giant red flag to the Scorpion."

Herg looks up from his panel. He'd been buried in it since we took our places. "Captain Jackson, I know those dronetug designs. We had them back in the old yards. They all have a manual override on the exterior." He reddens. "We used to sit on 'em after a few slammers. Race them around the shipyards."

"Me too, Captain. Herg's not the only one with a history." Ortiz looks sheepish.

Danielli floats up and spins around to look between me and Herg. "Then with your permission, Ma'am, I suggest Herg, Ortiz and I exit to the dronetugs and take them over. I am presuming your plan is to maneuver the drive back into place?"

I nod. "Anyone in possession of both the ship and the drive would be planning it. Working out if it's even possible. Understanding how everything has to connect together. But there's a big difference between weeks of planning, analysis and committee-based decision-making, and our need. Which is somewhat more urgent."

Then there's my idea.

Manually piloting the tugs to bring a skyscraper-sized battlecruiser-drive into place is fraught with danger. One slip, and a man might be crushed, or flung away into space. I know what Danielli is risking, and it's not a request I can make.

I hesitate. "So, yes. It is my plan. But not my order to you and your men. I'm the ship's captain, not your direct superior. I can't order you to do that."

"But I can." General Garnek floats through the open helmdoor, and I belatedly realize it would have been smart to close that. "Excellent suggestion, Danielli. Take Herg and get into position."

"No." The Rykkan Chief stands stiff and proud. "Take me. Not the weak ones." He points to Herg and Ortiz.

Danielli smiles. "I'll take you all. The more dronetugs we can run at once, the faster we'll get the drive in."

"You'll need to be better than fast," Garnek says. The anxious look in his eyes behind his faceplate belies his calm manner. "The Scorpion is only an hour away from her return. And she's presumably worked out that something isn't right, because what remains of her fleet is launching from planetside. If we don't get the Constellation operational in the next thirty minutes, we're all dead."

I like it when there's no pressure.

CHAPTER SEVENTY-FIVE

"Can we get more power in here?" I ask Zhang, who has stationed himself at a mezzanine workpod to my left. "Maybe redirect what is used elsewhere on the ship? I'd like to light this helmroom up." Secretly I am worried that my audacious plan might require more power than we have on hand. I figure if I ask Zhang to investigate what is on tap without panicking anyone, that will help our mood. Then I can panic for everyone.

Zhang works on the controlpanel in front of him, then looks up at me. "All power available was already being used when we entered, Captain. I'm picking up messages from other engineering crews on deck saying that their energy supplies are shut down. They are leaving the ship."

"Leaving?" I furrow my brow.

Aktip answers. "They have been ordered, Madam Captain. I monitored the comms." She speaks in her normal flat tone, but I see the beginnings of a nervous swivel inside her suit.

"Which will also mean a party of soldiers will board to investigate," Garnek adds. "Won't be long before they discover what has happened and who is here."

"Then we seal the helmroom. With all the trouble we had with access, we'll be hard to dig out." I get busy on my own panel, and the helmroom doors slide closed. I'm also painfully aware that I'm locking Danielli, the Chief, Herg and Ortiz out. A faint blue glow circles the holodome above. I presume this indicates some type of battlesafe mode.

Garnek points up and around. "The helmroom was deliberately constructed as a sphere, buried in the top third of the ship. Hard to penetrate. In theory it's self-sustaining. Never tested though." He looks at me from inside his helmet and says nothing.

I nod. I'm thinking of Danielli and the others, who aren't protected by our spherical cocoon. I tap open our closed comms. "Danielli, status?"

"Exiting locks to the dronetugs, Ma'am. The ship was deserted—any ideas why?"

"All work crews ordered to leave. We may have shown our hand too early. It's all on you now. Expect company. We'll do what we can from here to prevent access. Make haste, as soon as you are in position begin operations. Don't wait for my order."

"Aye, Ma'am." Danielli's confidence is reassuring.

"Indy, we can lock down the ship," Mitch says, looking into his own commPanel. "There's a special mode. Want me to do it?"

I look at Garnek.

He shrugs. "Smart thinking. I never had call for it. No one ever got this close."

"Then do it," I say to Mitch. I mentally cross my fingers for sufficient power, now that the work crews have gone.

"Needs us both to authorize." He places his hand on his chair's holopanel and I do the same on mine. "Lieutenant Commander Jackson requests lock down mode."

<<**Lock down mode pending activation. Captain override required.**>>

"Captain Jackson authorizes override," I say, and hold my breath.

<<**Lock down mode engaged.**>>

All lights dim, but the blue glow around the lower edge of the holodome shifts to red.

Danielli's voice comes through the comms. "Dronetugs under manual control and maneuvering Constellation's drive into position."

"Acknowledged." I try to sound calm. Mitch, Garnek, Aktip and Plexi are all looking at me.

A siren erupts, startling us all. Plexi taps her navpanel, then looks at me with wide eyes. "Warships. Advancing on us."

There is nothing we can do. I hear an echo of the Scorpion's strange prophetic metaphor in my head: "We'll be sitting ducks, unable to move."

Only this time, she is not part of the "we."

CHAPTER SEVENTY-SIX

I SLAP MY COMMPANEL. "DANIELLI. We have company. How long?"

I hear a grunt in my helmet comm in reply. "Sorry Ma'am. We're having to jump from drone to drone to up the speed. The Rykkan's idea. It's tricky,"—I hear another grunt and imagine him pushing off one tug—"if we miss a target there's no coming back. I estimate three minutes for the drive to enter the ship."

"We'll try to draw fire, Danielli."

Plexi looks at me in alarm. "How?"

I point to Garnek. "My guess is that the General here didn't take a shuttle up to us. He would have looked for the fastest, most capable ship that was available."

Plexi sucks in a breath, audible behind her faceplate. "The Slingshot."

Garnek nods confirmation. "I don't see how that helps."

I grin. "Then watch." I tap into my commPanel and activate a private hack channel into the stolen cruiser. Errikson built these things with a few extras. He assumed that no one knew about them, but pirates have a habit of finding out. The smart ones.

I punch up a display and direct a small holo to the center table below us. A schematic of my ship appears. It's docked to the side of the Constellation. I power up and impel it slowly away—but fast enough to alert anyone monitoring movement. The ship is several hundred meters from us when Plexi reports a splinter group of warships moving away from the main group heading our way.

I smile. Exactly what I would do: use part of my force to track down and capture a rogue ship. Spread out and wait.

They'll be expecting the lightCruiser to flee. Instead, I steer it to face the main incoming force.

They won't be expecting a suicide mission.

Especially one carrying a powerful cargo.

I launch the fDrive.

The holo shows the ship dwindle to a dot, and I activate autozoom. We track the ship as I turn it back toward the main cluster of advancing ships. The Scorpion's captains are no fools, however, and their primary formation shifts instantly, as if constructing an open-ended spherical net around the lightCruiser.

The cruiser speeds into the net, which closes behind me, and I register alerts from the ship's sensors showing armed weaponry trained on it. Its shields are up, and I wonder what they are waiting for—then I realize that the Scorpion expects me to be aboard. She wants me alive.

I play her game and bring the cruiser to a halt. In a standoff, encircled by a slowly closing group of warships.

The cruiser's comm blares. "Jackson and crew. Surrender and you will be given safe passage. Shut down all power except life-support and prepare for boarding."

I hold my finger over an unusual icon on my holopad. Out of the corner of my eye, I notice Plexi peering at me, but I keep my gaze trained on the holo above the table. The circle is tightening, the gap has closed. I wait until the inevitable—the sphere to form completely and close around my ship.

"Jackson, acknowledge."

I cannot stall much longer, but I don't know how close Danielli is. "Captain Jackson acknowledging comms. How will you guarantee safe passage? From where I sit, it doesn't look safe."

Another voice comes through the comms. Private channel to the cruiser. A female voice. "No games, Jackson. You'll be safe. My personal guarantee."

The Scorpion knows I'm important. But I sense she is still missing some vital information.

"Then send your personal escort. I will shut down systems as requested."

"You have it. Stand by." I hear the Scorpion's victorious smile escaping through her tone.

I shut down the cruiser's drives and watch the holo intently. A tiny object detaches from a ship in the sphere and makes its way to my trapped cruiser.

My finger hovers.

The object is close—only a few hundred meters from the cruiser.

I tap my finger.

The entire holo flashes brilliant white, and gradually fades, leaving us all blinking to restore vision.

My ship is still encircled.

But the Constellation's sensors tell me that every single warship in that sphere no longer has power.

Thousands of vessels, dead in space. Including mine. A pang of regret crosses my thoughts. I liked my cruiser. Maybe I'll get it back one day.

"What the—?" Mitch is staring at the holo.

I give my crew a rueful smile. "I didn't kill anyone. As long as they have a rescue operation, they'll have enough oxygen to last until they're picked up. Though they might get a little cold while they wait."

"Ma'am, I am unable to understand," Aktip says.

Garnek clears his throat. "Let me hypothesize. Captain

Jackson here just used a highly illegal—and massively powerful by the look of it—EMP hull-penetrating device to fry the main operational systems of over a thousand ships." He narrows his eyes at me. "A device outlawed at the end of the last Sector War. All state bodies agreed ownership created too great a risk. Small enough to transport unnoticed and too powerful to fall into the wrong hands. Every instance was dumped into a remote red dwarf."

I shrug. "Every instance except one."

"Where did you get it?" Plexi's face flushes, even through her faceplate, which is now fogging up. There's no doubting Plexi has a thing for weaponry.

"Rykkamon. Paid a lot of money for it. I hid it in the cruiser. I wasn't expecting to use it. I was hoping to trade it for information about Papa's death."

"I think you just did. You're a lot smarter than I gave you credit. However"—the Scorpion's voice hardens—"I can no longer guarantee safe passage."

I immediately cut the comms channel to my defunct lightCruiser. With no power to her vessel, I have no idea how the Scorpion has kept the channel open.

Zhang looks up at me from his workpod, panic in his eyes. "Captain. The Scorpion is in the group of splinter ships. They're reforming and coming around on Sergeant Danielli and the others right now."

Shit. Shit, shit, shit.

CHAPTER SEVENTY-SEVEN

"*DRIVE IS ENTERING THE SHIP.*"

"Danielli, you'll have company very soon. Abandon project." I can't place my friends in danger. We've done enough.

"*I'm sorry, Ma'am. Comms breaking up. One minute and we should be able to let the drive run accurately on inertia. As long as you can stop it.*"

As long as you can stop it. That's what I want to know as well. I turn to Mitch. "You wanted to know my big idea?" He says nothing, just looks. "I thought I'd better share. You know ... in case."

"Get on with it, Sis."

I feel the tension in my jaw. "The Constellation has a self-repair system. It's why we never see any damage. I'm guessing that the reason for the drive's surgically precise extraction is that it could be put back together using the ship's own system."

I hear Mitch exhale and watch his faceplate cloud over. "You're *guessing*?"

I nod. "I watched Aktip get 'self-repaired' on Rykkamon. You had the same experience as me on Takao, when we were badly wounded. If flesh and blood can be encouraged to accelerate self-repair, why not an inert object?"

"An asteroid-sized hole and a do-it-yourself engine installation? Seems like a long shot. Not so much a guess as a lottery bet."

"If you have a better idea, now's the time to share." I hold his gaze.

Garnek regards me with a look of curiosity. "I'd bet on Frederic's daughter. Seems to me one of his little secrets has just been revealed."

I don't have any idea what he is on about, but now is not the time to question why Mitch and I know so little about Papa's secret life.

"Sorry to interrupt the chit-chat. Drive entering under inertia. Abandoning drones and—" Danielli's comm goes dead.

I ignore Mitch and turn my attention to my holopanel. I locate the ship's maintenance systems and tap through the commands.

The Rykkan Chief's voice bursts into my comms. *"Captain, open locks! We cannot enter!"*

I stay focused on my panel, frantically punching settings and yell at my comm-mike. "Mitch, disable lock down. Let them in."

"You're the Constellation's Captain. Now I understand." The Scorpion's voice enters my earpiece. She speaks softly. *"I have your friends in my weapon range. Right now they are outside starboard minilock 138. Open the locks and you save your friends. But your defense will disappear, and I will force your surrender. Or keep your defense and lose your friends. Your choice."* Her voice clicks off. I have no way of knowing if she is telling the truth, but I will not abandon my friends. I locate her channel and block all comms.

"Let them in, Mitch."

"Already done, as ordered, Captain."

<<**Self-repair system activated. Drive mechanism reinstallation detected. Do you wish to install drive?**>>

Really? You have to ask? "Confirm drive installation. Proceed at maximum speed."

I see Garnek's eyes widen as the holodome above us springs to life, showing an interior view of the massive drive descending into the bowels of the battlecruiser. I have no idea how severed connections, pipes, cables and bulkheads become reattached to the drive's enigmatic interior, but this time I do more than mentally cross my fingers.

<<**Power depletion at 100% in 44 minutes.**>>

"What does that mean?" I look at Plexi and Aktip in panic.

"I dunno. You're the Captain," Plexi says, looking down at her panel. "But I think we're running down the battery to start the engine."

Trust Plexi to sum it up so simply.

"*We are in. Close locks.*" It's Herg. He sounds hurt.

"Madam Captain. Lock down mode is unavailable." Aktip's head swivels inside her helmet.

"Constellation, this is Captain Jackson. Engage lock down mode."

<<**Lock down mode unavailable during self-repair.**>>

I take a deep breath and look up at the holodome. The drive is almost in place. The Constellation's system had done what I expected: converted the drive's inertia to energy and slowed it down, as well as provide more juice for the self-repair. Whoever modified it was a genius.

"I heard rumors of top-to-bottom mods—after we'd been ordered off." Garnek is also looking at the holodome. "But nothing of this magnitude. Then again"—he looks directly at me—"your father was much like you. Ambitious to the point of defiance."

Papa did this? Mitch and I exchange glances.

"*Are you closing the locks or not?*"

Herg. I look to Mitch and the General. "Sorry, Herg. Operation not possible. Can you make it back to the helmroom?"

And where is Danielli? My heart sinks.

"*Negative. Preparing to engage enemy. Good luck with the drive.*"

My friends are dying. Or dead. I draw myself up to leave. I will not let the Scorpion get the better of me.

Garnek is watching me. "Let me go to them. I'm no use to you here."

"No use?" I look at the dome then back to Garnek. "You're the only one of us who has commanded this ship in battle."

He shrugs. "You two have full authorization. You only need me as an adviser." He pushes over to the exit lock. "And that I can do over the comms. Let me out. Maybe I can save them."

My mouth tightens and I nod to Zhang to open the helmdoors.

The General is barely out of sight and the doors closing when the dome's red glow intensifies and an insistent buzzer sounds in my ear. I whip my head around to Aktip and Plexi.

But it's Mitch who answers. "Proximity alarm. Sensors say around two thousand Jovian fighters just appeared in local space. Got any more EMP bombs?"

CHAPTER SEVENTY-EIGHT

"Where in hell were they hiding?" My brain asks my rhetorical question out loud.

"*We'd always suspected the Jovians had a contingency plan.*" Garnek answers over the comm, breathing heavily. I envisage him pushing through the passageways, twisting and turning to reach Danielli, Herg, Ortiz and the Chief before the inevitable. "*My guess is they'd gathered a strong base somewhere off Galantria, or close by, waiting on a hyper-relay, or local spies.*"

"Local spies, given the time frame." I look up at the dome, and as if anticipating my next question, the ship responds.

<<**Self-repair 76% complete. Power depletion in 18 minutes.**>>

"What does *that* mean?" I almost spit out the words.

<<**Interpreted answer with 67% probability of accuracy: Self-repair will complete with less than two minutes of power available.**>>

Sixteen minutes.

I look at Plexi. "How long until the Jovians are within range?"

She doesn't need to look at her panel to tell me. "Twelve minutes, max, Captain." She looks at me, waiting for instruction. Instead, I check in with Garnek.

"General Garnek, have you reached them yet?"

"*Yes. Danielli is badly hurt, unconscious. Herg also hurt, bleeding. The Chief and Ortiz are okay. I'm dragging them away* with the Chief's help. He wanted to stay and fight, but there's no point."

I hear him hesitate.

"*May I speak plainly?*"

"General, I'm upset you have to ask. I'm not exactly an experienced battleship captain."

"*We may argue about that—but quickly: I have loyal followers in the Scorpion's fleet.*"

"I imagine so. And?"

"*Can you patch me into them?*"

Garnek's intent dawns on me, and I furrow my brow. "Maybe. If you're thinking what I'm thinking, it's worth a try. Better stand by for an all-ships broadcast. I'll do my best. Admiral."

"*Roger that.*" I hear his grin.

But I'm not smiling. I can only hope my battlecruiser will let me have enough power to hack the Scorpion's comms. And that I have the smarts to pull off the greatest hack of all Sector-time.

I swipe into the holo and drill down into the comms code. "Allow full programmatic access." I hear the tightness in my voice. I reach the root comms and scan for the Scorpion's chatter ... and find it.

"Open Channels 557.1 to 7468. Full broadcast power. Source transmission"—I glance at my commPanel to check Garnek's suit ID—"Suit Comm ID 22834, located at minilock 138."

<<Confirm action for systems conflict. Operation will deplete power allocated to self-repair operation.>>

"Impact on self-repair completion?"

<<Unknown. Probability of completion ... 82%.>>

Probability of us surviving if the Jovians get to us? Zero percent.

"Confirm instruction. Divert power to broadcast channel as requested." I tap Garnek's private channel. "Better make it quick.

Every second reduces our power. You're on in ten."

"*I'll make my words count.*"

We wait, then the air buzzes. All-comms includes us, apparently. Garnek's authority-laden voice booms through the helmroom and our suitcomms.

"*Admiral Simpson on all-comms. Attention all Commanding Officers. Hostile Jovian enemy fleet is within range and attacking. I order every man and woman still with power to defend Takao to the death. This order supersedes all previous orders, effectively immediately. For our honor! For Takao!*"

I cut the power diversion. I cannot bring myself to watch the screens, only the progress of the self-repair. "Self-repair status?" I say, conscious of my weariness.

<<**Self-repair 91% complete. Awaiting bootup commands.**>>

Bootup commands?

I look at Mitch. He opens his hands wide. Plexi shrugs.

Aktip works away on her own panel, then looks over to me. "Some of the Scorpion's ships are leaving her splinter group. Some left then returned. Approximately twenty-five percent are heading to the Jovians."

"Not enough," I mutter.

"*Enough to keep them busy and off our backs for a little while. Speaking of which, can you close the locks?*"

"Not yet. Apparently I need to issue a bootup command for the self-repair. Any ideas?"

"*Knowing your father, it would be something you and Mitch would both know instinctively.*"

My brother and I exchange glances again. Papa was known for his self-deprecating humor. He used to refer to himself as "the greatest of all time," with his tongue firmly in his cheek. Though if he'd equipped the Constellation with a complete self-repair system, few people would disagree with him. My brother was even named after the artist they called the greatest of all time, Michelangelo, which was Papa's little joke—

"Wait!" I say, "I have it."

Mitch looks at me. "You got me. So go ahead. Take your time. We can wait."

I scowl at him. "Constellation, bootup reinstalled drive. Bootup command: Michelangelo."

Mitch groans over the comms.

Silence.

<<**Self-repair 97% complete. Awaiting bootup commands.**>>

I search my brain. Papa wouldn't have made it that hard. He would have chosen something memorable, something indelible, impossible to forget—

I jerk awake, remembering Pedro's last words to me on NewSwiss12. "Constellation, bootup reinstalled drive. Bootup command: The Divine One."

<<**Bootup sequence initiated.**>>

The ship shudders. A vibration from its depths travels like a wave through all of us. I grab my helmchair's arms in reflex.

The dome light switches to a pulsing green broken-line and begins to circle in an ever increasing velocity, until it becomes a green blur.

A piercing whine makes it impossible to think and we all reach for our comms controls.

"What is it?" Mitch shouts at me, his voice distant over the muted comms.

I shake my head and throw up my arms. Whatever it is, we are at the ship's mercy.

The helmroom springs to life. Every panel dances with lights: the dome's racing pulse stops and dims to a low glow, and a muted off-white light with no observable source bathes the helmroom with a gentle reassurance. The brushed surfaces and onyx table take on a rich, opulent gleam.

All of which I ignore, and spin my holo around, swiping to get to the power status. I speak to the ship at the same time. "Constellation, engage lock down mode. Captain Jackson emergency override. Close all open locks."

<<**Lock down mode engaged. Mini-lock 138 closed.**>>

I breathe a sigh of relief and peer at the holopanel.

And look again.

Mitch and Plexi are doing the same. They both look at me. So do Aktip and Zhang.

"I guess you're seeing what I'm seeing?"

They all nod inside their suits.

I look back down at the holopanel's display. I've chosen the energy status. I need to know if the drive repair has worked. The fastest way to see that on any ship is check the power status. If that shows a reading, then no need to look under the hood, to use an ancient phrase.

My holo is showing the following: **ENERGY STATUS: CALCULATION FAILED. ESTIMATED RESERVES: INFINITE.**

The Divine One indeed.

CHAPTER SEVENTY-NINE

"*ANY CHANCE OF HELPING ME get these guys to medbay?*"

Crap. Garnek. I imagine Danielli in a pool of blood. I push out of my chair, but Mitch holds me back.

He looks me in the eye. "I'll go. You're still healing, right? You and Plexi work out what this means. No energy is infinite, no matter how clever Papa was. If you go, you'll only get upset, and to be completely truthful, I care more about having a well-rested Captain in full control, and at the helm. We have a slight issue with some unfriendly visitors to our party and I have a feeling you and the ship have a special understanding."

I nod, tell Plexi she's now on pilot duty and watch Mitch wait for Zhang to open the helmdoors. This time I order them left open: a ship in full lockdown and with apparently infinite energy supply won't be an easy victim.

Aktip clears her throat. "Madam Captain?"

"Yes, Aktip?" I say, with a voice weary from tension and running on adrenaline.

"Now we have power, may I recommend artificial gravity and pressurization?"

I'm grateful for Aktip's thoughtfulness. "At one-gee?"

"I can manage one-gee, Madam."

"Then I agree." I look to my right. "Plexi—weapons inventory?"

She gives me a huge grin. "Ah ... extensive. And all operational. But our hand weapon armories are limited. As you know."

"I might need more detail than 'extensive,' Plexi," I say with a straight face. "How about this: what do we have in the Constellation's arsenal that will frighten around two thousand Jovian fighters?"

Plexi swipes through her holo. "Plenty for a skirmish with a few hundred. This thing is peppered with cannons like an angry porcupine."

I don't know what an angry porcupine is, but I assume Plexi refers to the Constellation's exterior. "So no starNukes? No plasmaMines?"

She shakes her head.

"Atmosphere restored and artificial gravity booting up," Aktip says. "Safe to remove helmets."

I can't wait to take mine off. Fear and sweat don't make for close friends. I feel the relief when I remove it, though my hair just sticks to my head, reminding me I'm in less than prime condition. As if the constant dull pain in my side isn't enough.

I explore the Constellation's commandPanel. Some functionality seems to have been hastily added; some non-standard screens show basic and clumsy interfaces. A couple jog old memories, but I keep swiping and after a few taps on the pad, I discover what I'm looking for: the holodome. I tap again and it comes to life.

The dome appears transparent; a marvelous illusion, as if we are under a giant plexidome.

In the middle of two thousand Jovian fighters.

Plexi whistles. "Maybe we should run."

I consider her suggestion. Leave the Scorpion and the Jovians to engage in civil war. It wouldn't be pretty, and the victor would still want to track the Constellation down.

Then there would be all the innocent victims—on both Takao and Ganymede and their respective outposts.

No. Papa had set this up. He wouldn't run away. He may not have expected to have been killed so unexpectedly, but he'd planned far enough ahead to have programmed in his successors. His plan B.

"Plexi, set a course for the Jovians."

"But they are coming to us?"

I turn to her and hold eye contact. "Do we have fDrive power?"

She shrinks a little from my stare. "In spades. You saw the levels."

"Then follow my order. Let's take the fight to them. That's Captain Jackson speaking."

She shrinks even more. "Yes, Captain."

I have no idea what Papa equipped the Constellation with, but it defeated Oberon's last army. What could it do against a couple of thousand Jovian ships? What I do know is that I need General Garnek. Papa was smart, but I grew up a space pirate. Street smart maybe, but a battlecruiser's captain in name only. I tap my comm.

"General Garnek."

"*Yes, Ma'am.*"

"Your presence is requested in the helmroom. We have full operational functionality. I believe you have won battles in this ship before. I don't plan to be the first Captain to lose."

CHAPTER EIGHTY

"WHAT IS YOUR PLAN?" GARNEK'S words reach me as he travels back. He sounds as if he is in a metal tube.

"To force a truce. No more killing."

Garnek's next words come in person and he emerges from a sliding panel outside the helmroom's open door. A gravtube exit. Of course—he'd know the ship better than any of us, and with power restored, he'd use the fastest means of transport. "Too far gone for that, Ma'am. Neither side will want to give up their power. Everyone's hand is shown now, and control of the Sector is within reach. And neither side will want the other to have the Constellation."

His words sink in. "You mean they'd both rather see the ship destroyed than fall into enemy hands?"

The General nods. "That's about the size of it." He looks up at the holodome. "But I see we are headed into the hornet's nest. Why is that?"

I purse my lips. "To tell the truth, I'm not sure." I hear Plexi's sharp intake of breath. "Papa seems to have done his best to make the Constellation invincible. Maybe I can't destroy all their ships—not that I want to—but if they see that the Constellation cannot be won with any force, they might lay down arms for parlay."

Garnek looks at me curiously. "Captain, please do not take this as a slight on your actions to date, but I believe you are being naïve. Even if they put down arms, this is the Jovian mafia you are dealing with. And remember, I know the Scorpion better than anyone. She's never going to give up. Not now."

Once again, his words strike home. But this time for a different reason.

"I have an idea."

Plexi groans and Aktip's head swivels to me.

CHAPTER EIGHTY-ONE

WE REACH THE JOVIAN FLEET—or rather, monstrous cloud—of ships and I halt the Constellation in front of them. Aktip tells me the Scorpion's remaining fleet has followed us at a distance, perhaps expecting another EMP bomb. If only.

"Get me the Jovian Commanding Officer on the comm," I tell Aktip.

A giant holo image appears in the dome and lowers so we can all see the image forming. The Constellation's tech is impressive. The holo dissolves to reveal a familiar face. General Marius. A smaller image of me is inset on the bottom right.

"Jackson. You must be here to offer surrender. Which I am prepared to accept. With conditions."

I raise an eyebrow, wondering if a giant eyebrow is simultaneously levitating in midair in Marius's ship. "Presumably that I also surrender the Constellation's energy tech. I have a suspicion you understand its ... unlimited potential to disrupt your Sector power?" Infinite energy—whatever that meant—would put the damper on any energy trade if it got into the hands of the everyman. Or Takaon. Or Rykkan.

Marius laughs. "Then you understand my terms, Jackson."

"*Captain* Jackson," Garnek says. "Captain of the Constellation."

Marius looks genuinely surprised. "That *is* a bonus, Admiral Simpson. Not only do I get both the drive and the ship, but I have its Captain. That would explain why Errikson believed you and your brother would have access to the drive."

I lean forward. "General Marius. Have you heard of General Garnek?"

He furrows his brow. "The man who fought Oberon? Ran away once the war was over, I believe." He guffaws, then stops. "Your point?"

I wave my holopan controls. The small image-in-image pans across to Garnek. "He ran nowhere. Meet General Garnek. The man who will bring you to your knees."

Marius freezes, then peers into the holo. Then laughs again, though he appears less certain this time. "So Simpson is Garnek. Who will singlehandedly defeat thousands of precision Jovian fighters using only his powerful team of"—he looks around in mock amazement—"a couple of Rykkans and some mercenary has-beens."

I pan the holo back and nod. "Sad, but true. Skill and wits can still defeat brawn. And a lack of brains. But you haven't asked for my terms."

He scowls. "I don't need them. Jovian technology exceeds the Constellation's era."

I carry on. "All I ask is that you down arms so I can show you something of personal interest."

He stares at me. "You want what?"

"I thought you'd agree. Plexi, can you call up my suit footage?"

She nods, a confused look on her face. "I need the approximate timestamp though."

I incline my head, all the while keeping my eyes on Marius. "Take it from when we met the Scorpion in person. We were brought into the warship from outside the Constellation, and I was taken to their boardroom. Do you have it?"

"Yes."

"Put it up on the holo."

The holo runs the footage of the Scorpion carrying on conversation with me. I watch the Jovian's face as he takes in who he has been facing off in an intra-Sector war of wills.

"The Scorpion is a woman." He speaks softly.

I wave Plexi to stop the footage. "A powerful one. The Scorpion has beaten your every move. No Jovian attempts on Takao's moons have ever succeeded."

"What of it?" He almost growls the words out.

I smile sweetly. "Right now, I can open an all-comms link to every Jovian ship in the region—oh yes, the Constellation can do that. I just did the same to the Scorpion. Why do you think she waits behind?"

"So?" He narrows his eyes.

"So I will show them that I, a woman—and the Scorpion, another woman—have had the better of General Marius. Many times. Marius is no match for us. He is a weak man. You want me to do that? How quickly will you be overthrown?"

Marius roars. "Enough!" The holo goes black.

"Forward, full speed, Plexi!" I yell. I glance down to the helmpad and shift settings.

Garnek has sat down and regards me with a level eye. "You don't need me at all."

"You bet I do," I say out the corner of my mouth, pushing screens and icons around to find what jogged my memory before. "There!" I swipe the clunky black and gold icon across the pad and it expands into a glittering gold ring—now mirrored around the dome's lower circle.

A large section of the holo switches to a gold and black rectangle. Inside is the text: **MODE: INVINCIBLE**.

I wait for the firepower to come and hold my breath.

CHAPTER EIGHTY-TWO

ON THE REST OF THE holo, I see the massive Jovian fleet coming closer as we approach each other. Seconds pass until we are in plasma range. Hundreds—thousands—of fighters swarm in and bombard the Constellation with plasmacannon fire. I cannot help but flinch.

Garnek doesn't. He remains impassive, watching the holo.

All we see are splashes of white from all around the holodome as the plasma weapons find their target and wash off.

I force our ship further into the Jovian swarm, pushing past the plasma raining down on us, shrugging it off. I stop in the middle and wait.

Minutes pass, as we watch fighter after fighter swarm in and try to hit some vulnerable part. I make no move to retaliate. I just wait for them to tire of their game.

The holo flicks on to reveal a still-angry Marius. "You think you can outwit me forever? I will hunt you down."

I hold my finger over a button. "So I can tell your officers exactly who has you at a disadvantage? A young, untrained woman. A pirate. Answer me this, Marius. Do you want me on your side, or not?"

His face jerks up. "I side with no one."

"Then I will leave you at the mercy of Oberon while I gather my allies." I turn to Aktip and ask her to broadcast the images of the Blood Empire's fleet gathering at the Sector's boundary.

"What is this?" Marius is furious.

I smile. "What you just agreed to. Oberon's forces are amassing. They'll be here in weeks. So far, your own fleet can be defeated by a girl in an old battlecruiser. I think Oberon will be happy to engage battle, until he tires of you. Now, I must bid farewell."

I cut the holo and whip around to Plexi. "Back us out and into the Scorpion's remaining ships. We have no time to lose."

Plexi is on it. Whatever doubt she had has vanished and her fingers fly. I feel the massive battlecruiser shudder slightly, but the only real sensation of speed we have is the blur of Jovian ships racing past the holo above us as we rapidly retreat. I stare at the holo, waiting, waiting. Then they move after us.

Good.

Garnek has folded his arms and watches me. "Your father was an amazing man. Who knew he had a daughter that would surpass even his genius."

"We're not done yet. Anyway, I have another job for you."

"His son's still pretty capable you know." Mitch appears through the doors. "But I have to admit, that was intense. Did you really think he wouldn't want to admit being beaten by a woman?"

Garnek speaks up. "A ruse. The Captain wanted to rile him. Though I will say I entertained at least some possibility we'd be roasted into spacedust." He looks at me. "Where did that 'invincible' trick come from?"

"No trick." I look up at the holo to see we are now being followed, this time by the Jovians. Also keeping their distance. "Papa used to use it on you, Mitch. Remember? 'Invincible mode' he would say, and plant himself, waiting for you to charge at him. When I was flicking through the commandPanel, I saw what looked like a new function added called 'Invincible Mode.' I figured it was another of Papa's modifications and played my hand."

"A guess?" Garnek raises his eyes.

"Calculated. Well ... calculated based on something I deduced regarding the drive's energy reserves."

"Approaching the Scorpion's fleet," Plexi announces.

I keep my eyes on Garnek. "Now we're really going to pull back the curtain. Ready for your miraculous return-to-duty speech, General?"

Garnek nods, and I tap the comms again. I pull up the previous hack into the Scorpion's fleet and point to Garnek. He clears his throat.

"Attention all Takaon commanding officers and men. I am General Garnek, previous Chief Military Space Corps Officer of the battlecruiser Constellation. I must inform you that the person you know as the Scorpion is not who you think he is."

I nod at Plexi, and she runs the footage of the Scorpion from my suit again.

Garnek continues. "This woman has deliberately misled you; manipulated you and deceived you into thinking you had enemies that never existed. I inserted myself into Takao after the Sector war, knowing that someone was responsible for destabilizing our defense against Oberon's might to build their own power base. Over the last four years I infiltrated the Scorpion's ranks, and over that time have become known to you as Admiral Simpson. As you can probably guess, I discovered the true identity of the Scorpion and the person attempting to take over our Sector by stealth. I vowed to prevent this from happening, but was beaten to it by the Constellation's new Captain. I ask you now to question your loyalty: Oberon's forces gather again"—he waves his hand and Plexi switches to the drone footage—"and only a highly organized response from our Sector, led by the Constellation, will see the Blood Empire retreat. The

Jovians have turned down our offer. Perhaps they prefer to fight it out alone with Oberon's Circle of Seven. So be it. But I have served with the Takaons, and I know your honor and caliber: if there was ever a fleet in the Sector worthy of following the Constellation into battle, you are it. You may confirm your allegiance with us by sending the confirmation signal, 'United Sector' to this commchannel."

Garnek wipes his brow and I wait, looking to the holo for evidence our play has worked.

One by one we see the red dots on the holodome turn green as the Constellation's computer receives the confirmation signals and switches the allegiance of the opposition we still fly towards. I take a breath. "Now for the final showdown," I say to myself. I look at Plexi. "Spin us around. We head back to the Jovians."

Plexi looks incredulous, but complies.

"I hope you know what you're doing," Mitch mutters, and taps his helmpad to bring up the Constellation's weapons system.

"You won't need that," I say. I watch the holo and the schematic Aktip has constructed showing the two forces approaching each other. The one not-so-tiny speck in between them is the Constellation.

I hit the commPanel again, this time opening two private channels. The holodome shifts to show Marius and the Scorpion, who quickly realize I have conferenced them in, staring at each other in giant imagery above us.

"Marius knows he cannot destroy the Constellation, and you"—I point to the Scorpion—"no longer enjoy the power you had. But all of our grudges are about to be dwarfed by a new Sector war. If we fight each other, Oberon wins. We cooperate, and together we defeat him. After which I will ensure the Constellation's secrets will change our Sector for the good of everybody."

"What choice do we have," the Scorpion sneers. "You're only replacing either one of us with a new dictator. If you think you can do it better than anyone else, then you're no better than the thousands who have risen—and fallen—before you. Go ahead. Play your holier than thou game. I'll take my chances with Oberon." She appears to sit back, wearing a triumphant look.

I try to maintain my confidence. "General Marius. The Scorpion's men are no longer hers to command. I have their loyalty. Together we can stop the Sector tearing itself apart, and turn to defend ourselves against the real threat."

Marius taps his chin. I think I am getting through to him. He turns behind him and barks an unheard order, then turns back to me. "I gave my answer before, girl. I side with no *man*. As for women ... they are not fit for battle. Only for making soldiers." He cuts communication.

"Charming," Plexi says.

My mouth is still open and I close it slowly. The Scorpion is smiling at me. A capricious smile. I shut the comms down and slump back in my captain's chair, feeling ill-equipped for this role I've been thrust into.

Up on the holo, the two fleets commence firing.

CHAPTER EIGHTY-THREE

THE CONSTELLATION IS STILL IN Invincible Mode, and despite the firepower trained on us, and by each opposing fleet on each other, we remain unaffected.

"This can't be happening. We're weeks away from facing down the Circle of Seven, and these idiots want to play shoot 'em up." I look to Garnek and Mitch, then Plexi and Aktip. Garnek has the hint of a smile on his face. I narrow my gaze at him. "What is it General? Amused that I couldn't measure up?"

He shakes his head slowly. "No. But you've missed the one thing the Constellation is famed for."

I hold my palms out. "It's the Sector's best battlecruiser. It defeated Oberon's Blood Empire four years ago. I know what it's famous for."

He looks me in the eye, all the while a battle rages above us, played out like a movie on our holo. The Constellation is indifferent to the pica-watts of power being expended, both on us, and on the opposing forces.

"Exactly." His eyes bore through me. "You know *what* the ship is famous for." He moves closer. "But you've not once asked *how* we did it."

I feel my face flush. Garnek is right. I'm heading up the Sector's best weapon against Oberon, yet I've no idea how it was previously used. I'm arrogant and stupid, preferring to believe in Papa's deliverance and genius, and my own hype. I stand up to leave the helm. "You're right. I stand down. Please take over, I declare myself incompetent."

He shakes his head again. "Far from it. You've devised solutions based on ingenuity, not brute force. You've exploited weak links; played a layered game of tactics, and let people blossom under your leadership. You are far more a Commanding Officer than I was."

"Than you are," I correct.

"Was. But that's not important now. Your father has gifted you power over your opponents, more than you can imagine. The Constellation's power was kept undisclosed, even after the war ended, for good reason. I was wary of revealing it, not knowing how you would carry such responsibility."

The holo flashes white, then red, then white again as the battle rages in silence. Dots representing ships flare briefly then disappear.

Garnek continues. "You can stop all this now and save lives. Or you can flee and fight your own battle against Oberon."

I jerk my head up. "You know which one I choose. Have chosen."

He nods and stands. "So let's show them what the Constellation did to Oberon."

I hold up my hand. "Not so fast. I won't mass murder just to put an end to one battle. Only to lose the moral war. I won't be like them."

He smiles. "No need. Watch." He walks over to my helmpad and swipes through until he finds a screen I've not seen before. He taps in some codes, then flicks the pad around to me. "It needs your authority. The Captain's authority."

I look down at the screen. It reads: 'Null-E Field Enabled. Authorization requested. Minimum level voice and DNA.'

I place my hand on the pad and wait for it to glow green. "Captain Jackson at the helm." I look at Garnek. "Request authority to deploy Null-E Field."

<<**Authorization accepted. Ready to deploy.**>>

I wait a moment and look Garnek in the eyes. "No death? Guaranteed?"

Garnek shakes his head. "No death."

I take a breath. "Deploy Null-E Field."

The dome brightens and the view zooms out. I see the plasma traces crisscrossing the screen, ships hitting each other; damage reports winking on and off, and in the middle, the Constellation, deflecting fire, oblivious to damage.

A small translucent-orange circle begins to expand from the Constellation, increasing in diameter. I see that it is in fact not a circle, but a sphere. I look at Garnek, but he merely shakes his head briefly and indicates the unfolding picture above us on the holodome.

The orange sphere is now large enough to encompass the ships closer to us. I notice with a start that any plasma traces simply end at the orange sphere. Then I notice the sphere gaining in size with each absorption.

Mitch sucks in a breath. "It's sucking out the energy."

Garnek nods, while looking up at the dome. "Very good observation. Almost exactly what your father intended—only back then we had limited energy supplies. Our reach was restricted, and we had to be strategic in its deployment."

The orange sphere accelerates its growth, until it fills the entire holodome. No plasma traces are visible, only a spattered map of orange dots within the sphere.

"Disabled ships," Garnek says.

An alarm sounds and the orange sphere flashes. The entire helmroom lighting dims.

<<**Range limits reached.**>>

"Seems we have a similar limitation."

Garnek shrugs. "No matter, it's enough for our purposes. Still much more than I ever had at my disposal."

"Will they ... are they?"

"They'll be fine. The field is designed to consume energy, not destroy electronics like an EMP would, but it leaves a maintenance reserve. Not enough to run weapons. Enough for life-support."

"You never fought Oberon. You just crippled him," I say, wide-eyed.

Garnek nods. "And you've just done the same. Despite the Constellation's extraordinary firepower, there was no way I would win against the Circle of Seven in a straight shootout. Luckily, we had a strategic advantage they not only didn't know about, it would never have entered their minds. Back then, the Blood Empire relied on sheer brute force."

"Where does the energy go? Laws of thermodynamics and all that." Plexi peers at her panel as if divining the answer.

Garnek shrugs. "I'm not the scientist. Jackson reckoned he'd used it to restore an imbalance in dark energy, but I never understood the man."

"Maybe that's where we got the infinite energy reading from," I murmur, mesmerized by the display above.

"Not important right now. Time for you to open the comms again. This time they will listen. And if they don't, people below them will. Send the message: the Blood Empire are coming, and we need their help."

CHAPTER EIGHTY-FOUR

I TAKE A FEW MOMENTS to compose myself, then open the all-comms broadcast. Aktip has set up a hyper-relay to nearby Takao, then on to Ganymede, Rykkamon and onward. It may take days, but everyone in the Sector will hear my words.

"This is Captain Jackson of the battlecruiser Constellation. Our Sector is about to face Oberon's Circle of Seven and the Blood Empire for a second time. I have sighted their forces and they are formidable. We must all cooperate and join forces, not bicker and fight. I promise an end to monopolistic trades, and to share the Constellation's energy technology with all who join us. Our universe was never meant to be divided up and hoarded for one man—or woman's—benefit, but to be shared and used with mutual respect.

"Both the Jovian leadership and the Scorpion have ended their opposition at my request. Anyone who opposes joining with us to prevent Oberon's attack will be left to their own devices, but do not expect the Blood Empire to show mercy. The Constellation is our best physical weapon, but the Sector's secret weapon is you. Fight each other, and Oberon wins. Band together, and we all live. Shortly a new command station will be established on Rykkamon's outer orbits. Our enemies within the Sector are no more: now there is only one enemy—and he shall be defeated.

"Those who hold weapons to each other's heads, drop them now; those who hold grudges against races, release them now; those who do not trust their leaders to follow our call, rise up now."

I shut the comms down, exhausted. I reach to the helmpad and hesitate, my finger halted in the air. Though the Constellation is not at risk, my rallying call to action is. There's only one way to find out if my demand to lay down arms was successful, and we have at least a temporary truce.

<<**Null-E Field Disabled.**>>

I feel us all holding our breath together.

Not one ship left with power moves to attack. And not one plasma trace crosses the screen.

I exhale.

CHAPTER EIGHTY-FIVE

I ENTER THE MEDBAY. HERG is up on his feet, limping badly, a massive medpatch surrounding his bulky thigh. He grins when he sees me, then his grin drops when he sees my eyes searching. He flicks his eyes over to a bunk surrounded by drapes. I walk over and swipe them away.

The Rykkan Chief sits next to the medbed. He looks tired and barely acknowledges me when I enter. Herg comes in after me. "He won't leave. Insists that he can sense Danielli's health."

"He's probably right." I bend down to look at the monitor. Danielli's vital signs are weak. He is close to death.

Across his legs is a machine I have not seen before. I look at Herg with inquiring eyes.

"Your brother found it. 'Self-repair,' he kept saying, like he was on a mission. Did we win?"

"Not yet." I look at Danielli, whose face is pallid. An eyelid flutters. I lean down and place my cheek next to his. "Please stay with us. I need you," I whisper into his ear.

He is trying to say something. I place my hand on his chest. "No talking." He won't listen. I put my ear close to his face.

"Iss." His voice is barely audible. His eyes stay closed. I look at the Chief, but he is not paying attention, just staring at Danielli.

I gesture to Herg to come close. He limps over. "What's with him?" I ask, pointing to the Chief.

"Danielli saved his life. Got in the line of fire of a Takaon fighter and pushed the Chief here out of the way. Danielli took a hit. Both legs. Messy. Now the Chief says he owes a lifelong debt. Won't let Danielli die, or he has to die with him. Or something."

Danielli stirs again. I lean in.

"Is."

I strain to hear. "What is it, Danielli? 'Is'? Is what?"

His eyes flutter open and widen when they see me. "Iss," he says, so softly I can barely hear.

The machine next to me starts beeping. Urgently. Danielli twitches, then goes into convulsions on the bunk. I shoot Herg a frantic look. "What's happening?"

He shrugs. "Dunno. Ask your brother, he seems to know what he's doing."

"He's not here!" I look at the machine in desperation. Some of the readings look low to me, but I have no idea. Danielli jerks once more, then stops, inert.

"Danielli!" I scream, but his eyes don't look at me. They just stare up, unblinking.

Mitch rushes in and goes straight to the machine. "Jeez, Indy. He's dying. Quick, move your butt." He pushes me out of the way and straddles Danielli on the bunk. He pulls a massive stimpack from his suit, undoes the wrapper and slams it into Danielli's chest. Danielli jerks upwards, but Mitch holds him down. He looks back at me. "Old fashioned CPR. You do the mouth-to-mouth. I'll do the heart." He pounds Danielli's chest rhythmically, indicating for me to go to Danielli's mouth.

I reach across, maneuvering my body so I can squeeze between Mitch and Danielli's face, then plant my mouth over his.

Strangely, he tastes good. I exhale hard, inflating his lungs, then pull away while Mitch pounds. I put my mouth across again and force air into Danielli, willing him to live.

I pull away again. Danielli's eyes haven't blinked once.

"Keep going," Mitch grunts. "I've seen them come back from worse. Just keep going ... and pray."

Pray?

I put my mouth over Danielli's again. His unshaven chin rasps my cheek, but I keep his mouth apart with my hand pulling on his chin, and each time Mitch tells me, I breathe out as hard as I can until my own lungs are empty.

I hear the tiniest of sounds from Danielli and feel a slight movement of air against my mouth close to his. "Come on, Danielli. You've had worse," I mutter, then place my mouth on his.

This time he responds. Tries to kiss me. I pull away and look at Mitch. "He's alive! He's breathing."

Mitch looks over at the machine and nods. He gets off Danielli, who is clearly now breathing by himself, and checks the monitor's display carefully. "I think he's over the worst. Signs are stronger now." He looks over his shoulder back at me. "He must like you."

"Iss." Danielli is trying to speak again. I lean down, turn my ear to his mouth. "Wanted. To say. Enjoyed kiss. Before die."

"Danielli, you're not going to die." I lean over and kiss him. Properly this time.

"She speaks true," The Rykkan Chief says. I pull away from Danielli and look at the Chief. He bares a big red grin at me.

Mitch coughs. "You're welcome," he says, turning away from the machine, and strides out.

CHAPTER EIGHTY-SIX

I'M WITH MITCH AND GARNEK in the helmroom going through some datafiles we found buried in the Constellation's Captain's filesys, and couldn't open. We're sat around the smooth onyx table, as if we'd known no other home.

"It's an aberration," Mitch says. "Some artifact left over from when Papa encoded my and Indy's statuses. What else could it be?"

I sit back and ponder. We are in orbit around Rykkamon. Where everything started. Where Mitch once raced into some old cruiser I had been trying to fix, brandishing Papa's laserSword.

Now I'm sitting here, Captain of the Sector's most powerful battlecruiser, casually making plans to defend our patch of the Galaxy against some evil overlord.

Most of the Sector has fallen in with us; those who didn't immediately do so were persuaded by people more capable than me, and now we have a senior advisory group bigger than my network of pirate trading buddies from my previous life. Though the Chief tells me it's best if I don't show my face on Rykkamon for a while.

The Scorpion has vanished, and Marius was imprisoned by his direct reports, who quoted some Jovian regulation about not being fit to command.

None of which is important any more. Now we have to regroup and decide how to best repel the Blood Empire. And none of us have any idea how Papa set this all up, or how he ensured that both Mitch and I survived to captain the Constellation. Or why us. Why not Garnek, or someone more experienced? Maybe it was all a question of a convergence of opportunity. Or just pure luck.

I look over at Mitch, in earnest conversation with General Garnek. I remember his excitement at finding Papa's sword. Then I sit up straight.

"Mitch."

He stops mid-sentence. "What?"

"What happened to Papa's laserSword? How did the Jovians get it? You never told me."

He takes a deep breath, recalling what seems to have occurred eons ago. "They found it stashed on some run-down trader's ship. They didn't know it was Papa's, but they knew it was heavily modded."

"Then if they didn't know it was Papa's, how did you know?"

He breaks out into a smile. "Easy. Not many swords like that have EMP slug launchers, and second, Papa had etched his number into the stock. No one else would have any idea what that meant."

I nodded slowly. "Did you say the datafile was protected?"

"Looks like it. Why?"

The helmroom doors slide apart, and my face lights up to see Danielli. He's in a medbay hover chair, accompanied by none other than the Chief and Aktip. I frown at his legs, but he brushes my concern aside. "All healing as expected, Ma'am."

"Ma'am?" I tease, enjoying his discomfort.

"Yes, Ma'am. Ah, Indy. Is there some kind of meeting here, or can we join?"

"Ha. As if any of you have to ask. We found a datapacket, maybe put there by my father. It's protected, but I think I just worked out the code."

Mitch rolls his eyes. "Here we go again. Alright, I'll humor you. Yes, it's a magic file, left by our dead father, just waiting for his brilliant daughter to crack the code ..."

He trails off when he sees my cold expression. "Okay, okay. Let's try to open it. What's the code then?"

He looks at me expectantly.

I smile. "1508."

Mitch's face drops and he pales. He knows I'm right. Papa's lucky number. The one he'd etched on his weapon. Only known as something special to us—and Mom, presumably, since it was the old Earth year some painter dude started some famous painting. Somewhere. Who knew? But anyone else would just think it a random number.

He calls up the file and punches in the code. The holodome springs to life, and we are all taken aback to see an animation of a datafile unpacking, ending with a huge caricature of a cherub. Papa's humor is all over it.

The image expands, and an immense male face fills the dome's holo. I tap my commandPanel, and the image resizes and leaps down to hover over the center of our circular table.

The man has a flock of glossy dark hair, a strong nose, high cheekbones and keen eyes. Garnek turns his head to me and we acknowledge a shared history. Of all of us, he's the only one outside Mitch and me that would remember Papa's handsome face.

I look at my father's visage, back from the dead. Strangely, he doesn't quite look at me, a quirk of the camera angle. I shift to make eye contact with the image and brush against Danielli, who squeezes my hand.

My father speaks and we all become silent. His voice is as deep as I remember. I choke back tears.

"This recording is only being accessed if one of either my son or daughter is at the controls of the Constellation. For which I am grateful." He sighs and wipes his hand through his hair. I get a brief glimpse of an out-of-focus and unrecognizable scene behind him. Outside somewhere. Verdant plant-life. People moving maybe?

"I put some moves into play I'm not sure I should have. Our discoveries have the potential to change all life in our galaxy, yet"—he looks away, as if in thought, then comes back—"in the wrong hands, will cause mayhem. Somehow, Oberon knows what I—now you—have. He won't rest until he, too, has it within his possession. Most of it is still in here"—he taps his head—"but smart scientists will reverse engineer the drive. I just happened to find the answers first. Led the way. But for now, I thought it better I escape. I know that made it hard for you, Mitch and Indy, and hence this recording. Knowing you have restored the Constellation and have full control eases my mind." A smile flickers across his troubled face. "I can only hope I will embrace you soon. Come find me. You'll know where to look." He steps away from the camera, and I catch sight of an abundant world, lush greenery, rustic, nomadic-like accommodations and a fierce yellow sun. The image fades to black and we sit in stunned silence.

I look at Mitch. I expect my expression matches his.

Papa is alive.

I hope you enjoyed reading *"Constellation"*!

I'd like to gift you a free novella, which is not available anywhere else! It's called, ***"A Bar Room Brawl on Ganymede"*** and is the prequel story which unravels the mystery of how Indy came to leave Jordi on Ganymede (with a price on his head).

A gambling debt gone wrong, and a pirate captain on the trail of her father's killer.

Desperate to close a black-market helium three deal, India "Indy" Jackson arrives on Ganymede already in dispute with the Jovian mafia.

She needs money to track down who killed her father, but her ship's pilot disappears, and Indy is left to her own devices to deal with her shady contact.

Everything comes to a head in one of Ganymede's sleaziest districts, and she is faced with a choice: find her pilot and close the deal, or cut her losses and flee to safety.

Indy never was one to run away.

Discover one of Indy Jackson's early escapades on her journey to Galactic infamy!

Get your copy of "***A Bar Room Brawl on Ganymede,***" a free novella prequel to "Constellation" here:

http://robertscanlon.com/prequel

An author's lifeblood is his or her reviews. If you enjoyed "*Constellation*," I'd really appreciate your support with a review. It will help other Space Opera fans like you decide whether or not this story is for them!

If you're willing to do that for me (just use the link below), I'd be really grateful, thank you!

http://robertscanlon.com/constellation-review/

It's lonely work writing the first draft, but after that, it takes a full team of people to work it into the readable form you have here ... and then there's the cover. No author should be permitted to make their own cover—that's a very special talent.

So special thanks must first go to my wife, Gabrielle, who—besides writing her own nonfiction titles—is also a professional editor and is constantly besieged by me to put my work at the front of her queue (it doesn't always work, but then again, I'm not a paying client).

To Tom Edwards, at times possibly responsible for the entire Top 100 Space Opera book covers, many thanks for your artistic contribution.

Thanks also to my very good friends, alpha and beta readers, and general fabulous writing hosts of The Buderim Writer's Shed, who have provided endless encouragement, feedback and edits. Delicious food, and cake. Lots of cake. Jan, Leanne, Karin and Gabrielle: I thank you for your generosity of time and effort.

I'd highly recommend a "mastermind group" to anyone. Far from a secret clan of villains, it's a regular meetup of like-minded folks ("authorpreneurs," in our case). We encourage each other, and occasionally trigger a Simon tear-down or a Cohen-glower when we veer toward silly choices. Thanks to a wonderful two+ years of support from Simon Whistler, Bryan Cohen, Alida Winternheimer and Chris Fox, all of whom have pushed me in ways much needed, in a most supportive, yet insistent fashion.

And a very special thank you to Sherrie McCarthy, a fortuitous author friend, who took on the brave job of what I've come to call "pre-beta-reading" and managed to be extraordinarily encouraging at the same time as pointing out things that really didn't suit Indy's character (traits which, dear reader, shall forever remain unknown to you!). Sherrie, your excitement came at just the right time, thank you.

Finally to you. In the same sense as the Zen tree in the woods may be lonely without its philosopher audience, in my opinion, the point of publishing a story is for it to be read. So thank you for being a reader, may we meet again in some future pages!

I always welcome contact from any readers or authors.

You can always get me at **help@robertscanlon.com**;
at **http://robertscanlon.com/**
and on Facebook at
https://www.facebook.com/robertscanlonauthor

Thanks again, and ... happy reading!

Robert

PS. "*Nebula*" - Book Two in the Blood Empire series, is not far away! If you're keen to get your hands on an Advance Review Copy, please join my Space Pirates team here:

http://robertscanlon.com/space-pirates

ABOUT ROBERT SCANLON

Born in Australia, Robert was whisked back to England where he spent his childhood. After many years complaining about the weather, he did the only sensible thing, and moved back to Australia. Queensland actually. Where he enjoys walks along the beach with his wonderful family.

(Pssst. He still complains about the weather if it gets too cold!)

www.RobertScanlon.com

Printed in Great Britain
by Amazon